DATE DUE

V.C.B. 3/28/4	
SN	
Bd 2011	
RY	
R.E.	
Darrell	

WAR CRY

This Large Print Book carries the
Seal of Approval of N.A.V.H.

WAR CRY

CHARLES G. WEST

THORNDIKE PRESS
A part of Gale, Cengage Learning

Hm 4732
LTW
3-2011
$28.99

GALE
CENGAGE Learning·

Detroit • New York • San Francisco • New Haven, Conn • Waterville, Maine • London

GALE
CENGAGE Learning

LIBRARY OF CONGRESS CATALOGING-IN-PUBLICATION DATA

West, Charles.
   War cry / by Charles G. West.
      p. cm. — (Thorndike Press large print western)
     ISBN-13: 978-1-4104-3550-7 (hardcover)
     ISBN-10: 1-4104-3550-4 (hardcover)
     1. Large type books. I. Title.
  PS3623.E84W37 2011
  813'.6—dc22   2010048756

Published in 2011 by arrangement with NAL Signet, a member of Penguin Group (USA) Inc.

Printed in the United States of America
1 2 3 4 5 6 7 15 14 13 12 11

For Ronda

CHAPTER 1

Will Cason was not averse to a friendly drink at Mickey Bledsoe's saloon when he felt the need. Mickey's establishment was less than a hundred yards outside Camp Supply's perimeter. It was not the only saloon that had sprung up like a summer weed as soon as the fort was built. There were several more, but Will usually patronized Mickey's. It was the favorite of most of the civilian scouts as well as a good many enlisted men. It never ceased to amaze him how the building of a new outpost caused an immediate swarm of saloons, prostitutes, and gamblers to descend like flies around a cow pie. This post in the northwestern part of Indian Territory, in what was called the Cherokee Outlet, was built on the North Canadian River to supply troops scheduled to participate in the winter campaign of 1868–1869 against those bands of Indians still resisting efforts to move them to the reservation. Most of the saloons were actually tents. Some, such as Mickey's, had add-on shacks made of logs, with plans to build permanent structures that would be sufficient to house the *soiled doves* that followed the military.

On this hot, dry afternoon in July, Will was idly passing the time with one of those doves, a solidly built woman of indeterminate age named Lula, when Ben Clarke, chief scout at Camp Supply, walked in. Will had expected him to show up. He had enjoyed only two drinks — not enough for Lula to start looking desirable. Some of the soldiers at the post complained that by the time a man had downed enough whiskey to transform Lula into an attractive woman, they were too drunk to do anything about it. Will was of a mind that this was a bit too harsh on Lula. She was a hardworking girl with a good heart who was just trying to earn a living with the only tools God had given her. Over the years those tools may have become worn and dulled, but they were well padded enough to offer comfort to all in need — and in possession of three dollars.

As usual, Will had no thoughts beyond conversation with the hard-drinking damsel, although Lula may have had a more intimate agenda in mind. Always soliciting business, Lula was ready to shower her attention on any male who wandered into the saloon. But when it came to Will Cason, her interest in the free-spirited army scout was genuine. Maybe it was because, while he always enjoyed teasing her, he had never actually availed himself of her services. Possibly it was more than that. Tall and rangy, he moved in an easy manner that brought to mind the sleek motions of a mountain lion, with a ready smile for his friends that looked somehow out of place on his ruggedly handsome face — a face usually shaved clean, Indian style.

"I thought I might find you here," Ben Clarke said as he moved up beside Will and gestured to Mickey to pour him a drink. "I've got a little job for you." With only mild interest, Will acknowledged with a nod and a smile, and waited for Ben to elaborate. "The Seventh is gonna stay here at Supply for at least another week and the colonel's got some dispatches that gotta go to Fort Dodge — and I wanted to catch you before you drank so much of Mickey's rotgut you couldn't ride." Will responded with an amused grunt. It was not the topic he had expected to discuss with the chief scout. Clarke continued. "You need to ride out first thing in the mornin'."

"I was about ready to wind this up, anyway," Will said, giving Lula a wink, whereupon the buxom lady puckered her lips in a little pout to express her disappointment. "I was beginnin' to get a bit rusty, settin' around on my ass for so long."

The remark was delivered with a hint of sarcasm, which was not lost on Clarke. He was well aware that Will had just gotten in late the night before after leading a scouting party to Antelope Hills. But the colonel said the dispatches were important and requested Clarke to pick a good man to deliver them. And in Clarke's opinion, there was no man better than Will Cason, although that was not his primary motive for sending Will. "I know you've been rode hard for the last couple of days," he said, "but I need a man I can trust to get them dispatches to Fort Dodge."

"You're the boss," Will said, although he suspected Clarke had another reason for sending him off for a few days. "I'll be ready to ride at sunup." Turning to Lula then, he gave her a dismissive pat on her broad backside and teased, "You'll wait for me, won't you, darlin'?"

"Talk — just talk," Lula said with a snort, and turned to go to her wagon, which was

10

parked behind Mickey's shed. "Just like all men," they heard her say as she walked out the door. Will was not even vaguely aware of the special attraction the jaded prostitute had for him. He thought that she just enjoyed the good-natured banter between them.

The three men laughed. " 'Preciate it, Will," Ben Clarke said. "You'd best pick up the supplies you'll need this afternoon."

"Reckon so," Will replied. After settling up with Mickey for his whiskey, he followed Ben outside, figuring his boss had more to say.

Pausing with his hand on his saddle horn, Ben delivered the lecture Will expected. "You're the best damn scout I've got," he started. "But, dammit, sometimes you make it mighty damn hard to keep me from firin' your ass."

Will shrugged and replied, "I reckon Bridges didn't waste any time bellyachin' to the colonel."

"Hell, you shoulda known he wouldn't," Ben said.

"I just told him I wasn't hired on to be no orderly to no damn wet-behind-the-ears lieutenant," Will said.

"Yeah, well, I reckon you coulda told him in an easier way," Ben said. Then, unable to

11

suppress an amused smile, he went on. "Anyway, that ain't no way to talk to an officer, so I think it's best if you're out of his sight for a while — long enough for him to cool down."

Will appreciated the confidence that Ben had in him, but he had hoped to get a few days off before being sent out on another patrol — that is, providing he wasn't fired for insubordination. He never minded riding dispatch. It would afford him the opportunity for a couple of days away from greenhorn lieutenants. *And what the hell,* he thought, *I won't be herding a troop of soldiers.* The patrol he had just guided had been under the command of Lieutenant Lyman Bridges, an officer he wasn't partial to. The lieutenant was a brash young man, just recently assigned to the Seventh Cavalry and still primed with the sense of superiority instilled in him at the military academy at West Point. The major point of discord between Will and Bridges, other than the lieutenant's obsession with military protocol, was the young officer's assumption that Will answered to him just like any soldier in his command. Consequently, their relationship had started off on the wrong foot. Will had very few possessions, but among them his pride and sense of independence were foremost. He worked for the army on his terms, reserving the right to express his opinion if he was ordered to do something that didn't make sense to him — or something that he didn't feel was in his job description.

Such was the case on the recently completed patrol when, after going into camp on the Washita River, Bridges suggested that Will could help set up the lieutenant's tent. Will responded — courteously, he thought — that his job was as a guide and scout, and the lieutenant should assign that chore to one of his troopers. Somewhat taken aback, Bridges had then *ordered* Will to do as he was told — whereupon Will suggested a place he might stick his tent. Properly enraged, Bridges threatened to have Will court-martialed, causing Will to remind the young officer that he was a civilian. He might be able to get him fired, he told him, but that was about all. Bridges promised him that it was as good as done.

Ben Clarke could have sent any of a number of scouts to Fort Dodge with dispatches. Will could only imagine how hard he must have argued to save his job. He couldn't help but smile when he pictured the chief scout pleading his case to save his neck. *He must have convinced the colonel that he needed me,* Will thought. *Then I reckon he decided it best that Bridges doesn't have to look at me for a few days.* Lieutenant Bridges might turn into a good officer once he was seasoned a bit, but Will felt reasonably sure he wouldn't be requested to scout for him anytime soon. *I guess I owe Ben one for saving my job, though.*

The big bay on the far side of the corral lifted his head and whinnied softly as Will approached. "Morning, boy," Will called, and the gelding left the other horses grouped near the horse trough and plodded toward the gate. Named Spades for the spade straight that won Will the horse in a poker game, the six-year-old had become more like family than a working horse. Spades had delivered him out of more than one touchy situation when speed and stamina were called for to save his master's bacon.

After saddling his horse, Will swung by the headquarters building and picked up the dispatches. He wasted a few minutes' time talking to the company clerk before setting out for Fort Dodge, happy to be away from the army for a few days. The Sully Trail, named after Colonel Alfred

Sully, who laid it out, was the commonly used trail between Camp Supply and Fort Dodge. Nobody knew the country better than Will Cason, however, so he intended to save at least twenty miles by taking another route through Devil's Gap, across Buffalo Creek, and on to the Cimarron near the confluence with Bluff Creek, from there to Fort Dodge. It was the less-traveled route, and rugged, with no real trail established, but he had gone that way before and it shortened the trip by almost a full day.

There had been reports of raiding by Comanche as well as Cheyenne war parties earlier in the summer, but things had been pretty quiet for the past few weeks, so he didn't expect to run into any trouble. Of course, it was just good sense to be on the lookout for it anytime you rode anywhere in the Cherokee Strip. Recent treaties signed with peaceful chiefs of the Southern Cheyenne had caused a split within that nation when a number of the younger warriors refused to go to the reservation. Roman Nose, principal among these hostiles, had attracted great numbers of warriors to his band, and they raided ranches and farms in the territory and attacked a stagecoach now and then. The fabled Cheyenne war leader was never hesitant to attack military forces, as well, but his propensity for daring attacks had led to his death at Beecher Island on the Arickaree River in September a year before. His death was a major blow to the Cheyenne, but Will knew that with the rapid disappearance of the buffalo in what was once Cheyenne hunting grounds, these raids were bound to continue. There was little he could do about it, so he didn't spend a lot of thought on the subject. *Take care of my ass* was his creed, and all he needed to do that was a good horse, his repeating Henry rifle, and his .44 revolver.

This principle had stood him well since he had left his home in Missouri at the age of thirteen. His father, a man he worshiped, had fallen off a wild bronc and broken his neck when Will was eleven. His mother, a handsome woman, had remained a widow for only a year before marrying a prominent lawyer and moving to the bustling town of Independence. Will endured the strict regimen of Gordon B. Wallace's household for a year after that before hopping a ride west with a mule skinner named Seth Parker. He had been his own man ever since, doing whatever he had to in order to survive, occasionally on the wrong side of the law, but only when desperation drove him to it. At a young age, he wound up in Indian Territory, living with a Choctaw family until he signed on as a scout with Ben Clarke. Now at the ripe old age of twenty-seven, he was wondering whether he should try his hand at some other profession. He hadn't a clue what that might be. *Maybe,* he thought, *I'll think on it some when I get back from Fort Dodge.*

CHAPTER 2

Ned Spikes' upper lip curled up to form a sneer when he turned to see Edward Lawton approaching as he unsaddled his horse for the night. *I should have shot the son of a bitch as soon as we left the Arkansas,* he thought, but he managed to fashion a crooked smile for Lawton's benefit. "I hope your missus is about ready to cook us some supper," he said.

Ignoring Ned's attempt to steer him off his intended subject, Edward jumped right into his complaint. "Ned, I'm finding it hard to believe you really know where you're leading us. We've been traveling straight south for days now, when it seems we should be heading back to the west."

"Well, now, Mr. Lawton," Ned replied, affecting a look of injury, "I swear it grieves me to think you ain't got no faith in me no more." He pulled the saddle off his spotted gray gelding and dropped it to the ground.

"Like I told you before, we have to give Fort Dodge a wide berth. They're still actin' like the Injuns are raidin', so they won't let nobody pass on through Dodge unless they're with a wagon train. And you're the one that said you was in a hurry to get to Santa Fe."

"That may be true," Edward insisted, having heard that story too many times, "but we've been heading south for days. Fort Dodge must be fifty miles or more north of us now."

"Yeah, but they got them patrols, you see," Ned quickly responded. "They're always ridin' around lookin' for Injuns that ain't there, and ain't been there for over a year. And if we ran into 'em, why, they'd escort us right back to Dodge, and then where would you be?" He shrugged dismissively. "Besides, I'm takin' you on a shortcut."

Unsure what he could do about the situation, and absolutely lost in this country of rolling prairies, Edward knew he was at a distinct disadvantage. He was sure of only one thing — that he no longer trusted the man to do as he had been contracted to do. To make matters worse, Sarah had complained to him that she was uncomfortable with the way Ned had seemed to be leering at her the past few days. All Edward knew now was that he wished he had never listened to Ned Spikes back in Council Grove, and his only concern at this point was to get his wife and daughter back to some semblance of civilization. "Well, I hope you're right about this shortcut," he said, for lack of anything more forceful to say.

"Nothin' to worry about, Mr. Lawton," Ned replied, and stood grinning at Edward's back as he returned to the wagon. *Just go on back to your pretty little wife,* he thought. *Ol' Ned's had about as much of you as he's willing to put up with.* He *had* tolerated Lawton longer than he had planned, but he had just gotten too lazy to go ahead and finish the job. He figured that he might as well let Lawton drive the wagon for him and let his wife do the cooking. As far as the young'un was concerned, he looked forward to slitting the sassy little brat's throat. Her mother was a different story. Ned planned to keep her around for a while until his carnal needs were satisfied. Then she would get the same as her husband and daughter. Lawton was right about one thing, though — it was time to make his move, especially now that Lawton was openly questioning his ability to lead them. What he had told them about the lack of Indian war parties was an outright lie, and he was getting too deep into some dangerous country. Cheyenne raiding parties had been active along the Cimarron for the past six months, and he wasn't comfortable with the Indian sign he had noticed at their most recent campsite. "It's time to skin this possum," he muttered.

He was sure Edward Lawton had some money hidden away somewhere in that wagon. He just didn't seem like the type to start out across the country without a grubstake. Ned might have brought this little party to an end sooner except for the rifle Lawton always seemed to have at hand, and the shotgun that rode beside his wife in the wagon. And every time he moved around at night, the little girl appeared to be watching him over the side rails of the wagon. *I'll catch him when he ain't holding on to that rifle,* he thought, *and it better be soon.*

Morning broke warm and clear, another in a long line of days that never seemed to vary. Ned crawled out of his bed and stretched while he looked the camp over to see where everybody was. He knew after only a moment that there was never going to be a better chance to get things settled. Lawton was hitching up the horses, for once his rifle propped against the back of the wagon. His wife was making breakfast, the shotgun still propped by the wagon seat. It was made to order for what he intended. He started to head straight for Edward, but decided to risk the time to saddle his horse, just in case things went wrong.

He led his horse up to the back of the wagon and looped the reins over the tailgate. Glancing at Edward and Sarah to make sure their attention was not on him, he picked up Edward's rifle and laid it in the wagon bed. When he turned toward the front of the wagon, it was to meet the stare of six-year-old Emma, whose accusing gaze caused him to glare menacingly at the child. It was not enough to frighten the child into silence. "Papa," Emma called, but it was too late to warn her father. Ned whipped out his .44 pistol and leveled it at Edward, who was just finishing the harnessing of the horses.

At the sight of the revolver aimed at his stomach, Edward froze for a moment. "I was wondering when you were going to show your true colors," he said.

"You can make this easy on yourself," Ned replied. "Suppose you just get that money I know you got hid and I'll be on my way without no harm to nobody." He turned his head slightly to caution Sarah, who just then became aware of the danger. "You just sit right where you are, sweetheart, or this is gonna get ugly."

"So you are the scoundrel I suspected," Edward charged. "I have no money hidden away. I wouldn't give it to a scoundrel like you if I did. So get on your horse and be gone, and leave us in peace."

Ned sneered and cocked back the hammer on the .44. "Have it your way, you son of a bitch." Then he froze, startled by the sudden impact of a solid blow to Edward's chest, sending the man staggering backward. Ned heard the crack of the rifle as Edward's knees buckled and he dropped to the ground, mortally wounded. Still in shock, Ned stared at the pistol in his hand as if it had accidentally gone off. It was for only an instant, however, as the first rifle shot was followed immediately by several more, singing their deadly song as they ripped through the camp. He needed no further warning. With only a glance at the horrified woman as she rushed to her husband's side, he ran to his horse. Leaping into the saddle, he galloped away, leaving the woman and child to fend for themselves against the Cheyenne war party.

With absolute certainty that his life was flowing from his body, Edward tried to calm his hysterical wife and child. "Emma," he gasped, forcing every word, "fetch my rifle." When she hesitated, not wishing to leave his side, he urged, "Go, child, quickly now." When his daughter ran to the wagon, he said his farewell to his wife of seven years. "There isn't much time," he said, each word coming with more difficulty as he coughed feebly, trying to keep from choking on the blood now rising in his throat. "You must save our daughter. Take her and drive the wagon away as fast as you can." When she started to protest, he insisted. "There isn't time to argue. I'm dying. I don't know how much time I have left, but I'll hold them off as long as I can."

"No," Sarah cried. "I'll not leave you! I can't!"

Speaking now with the clarity of a man about to step through death's dark doorway, he admonished her. "Yes, you can. You have to — to save Emma. Know that I love you both and I am truly sorry for bringing you out to this wild country." He then took the rifle from Emma and commanded, "Now go, and don't look back."

Although he got started about an hour later than he had planned, Will had decided to push on into the evening and make camp where Bluff Creek joined the Cimarron. So it was past twilight when he had come to the river. He guided Spades down to the water's edge and dismounted while the horse drank from the brownish red water. The river was low, as it usually was this late in the summer, exposing more of its red clay banks where gooseberries and chokecherries grew along its winding course. The water didn't look fit to drink, but it had never done him any harm as far as he could tell.

When Spades had drunk his fill, he looked up at Will as if to signal he was through. Will had often commented that Spades acted more like a dog than a horse. "Come on," he said gently, and turned to walk up the bank to a stand of cottonwoods. The horse followed obediently without being led, stopping when Will stopped and standing patiently while he pulled off the saddle. After Spades was unsaddled, Will turned his attention toward building a fire and cooking his supper. He didn't bother to hobble Spades. He knew the horse would not stray far from him. There was plenty of grass there, so he decided to save the oats he had brought for the next night.

After his supper of coffee, bacon, and a couple of biscuits he had gotten from the enlisted men's mess that morning, he broke off a cottonwood branch about the size of his finger and sat down against the trunk of the tree to watch the darkness descend. Always at peace when he was alone on the prairie, he pulled out his pocketknife and went to work on the branch. Whittling the butt end of the branch to a sharp point, he fashioned a toothpick to dislodge the remnants of bacon that had found refuge between his teeth. When he was satisfied that his teeth were free of bacon, he used the toothpick to clean his fingernails. Content with himself and his place in the scheme of things, he had finished off the last drop of coffee with not a care about the Indians, Lieutenant Bridges, or anything else.

He was saddling his horse early the next morning when he heard the gunshots. Pausing immediately to listen, he counted seven or eight shots, maybe two or three miles to the west. *Indians,* he thought, since they sounded like the old single-shot rifles that many of the reservation Indians had. "Maybe a huntin' party ran up on some antelope," he suggested to Spades, whose ears were up and twitching to pick up the sound. "None of our business," he said, and finished packing up his camp.

As he stepped up into the saddle, there were more shots, though not as many as before and the source seemed to have moved a little from the first volley. *Like they are chasing something,* he thought. Trying to imagine what it might be, he told himself that buffalo had long since left this part of the country. Could be a herd of antelope, but they wouldn't be chasing after them unless they were riding antelopes themselves, because no horse could keep up with an antelope when it was frightened. Next he heard the distinct report of a shotgun. "I better go have a look," he decided then. The shooting seemed to have come from farther up the river. He hadn't planned to follow the river, heading north along Bluff Creek instead. "It's as good a way to go to Fort Dodge as any, I reckon," he decided and crossed over to follow the Cimarron west.

He had ridden approximately a mile and a half, following the serpentine river through the rolling hills of grass as the shooting became louder. He knew he couldn't be far away at that point, and although the firing continued, it was not as heavy as before, with only random shots now and then. Riding up the side of a shallow ravine, he almost rode right into the midst of the trouble, and was barely able to jerk Spades

27

to a halt just in time.

Backing the horse slowly until he was safely out of sight under the side of the ravine, he drew his rifle from the saddle sling and dismounted, dropped Spades' reins to the ground, and crawled back up to the rim of the slope to take a look. It was as he had already surmised. About fifty yards below him he counted nine warriors — Cheyenne, he decided — lying in a line behind a slight rise in the prairie. The rifle shots he had followed were coming from three of the Indians as they plunked away at a four-by-twelve farm wagon half in and half out of the water. It was obvious that the wagon, with two horses pulling it, had been in flight, but had gotten bogged down trying to climb up the opposite bank of the river. The attacking warriors were being held at bay by one person with a shotgun. Will strained to see whether there was anyone else behind the wagon, but could see no one. "Well, we'll see if we can even up this fight," he murmured.

Pulling his rifle up into position, he laid the sights on the warrior closest to him and squeezed off the first round. The Indian yelped in startled pain before rolling over holding his chest. Will didn't hesitate as he cranked out round after round in rapid succession, going down the line of warriors. At such short range there was little chance of missing, even firing as fast as he could cock his rifle and pull the trigger. With no protection against a rear attack, three lay dead before the remaining six realized from where the shots were coming, and had to scramble for cover. There was none behind them, so they had no choice but to run for their horses. Due to Will's rapid fire, the Indians weren't sure how many attackers there were, so they decided not to chance an encounter with a cavalry patrol. Thinking to add a little theatrics to the attack, Will stepped out in the open and made a distinct gesture as if signaling someone behind him. He hoped the hostiles looking back at him would take it as a sign there were soldiers following and would be discouraged from returning. He went for Spades and followed after the fleeing hostiles at a safe distance until he was satisfied they had no thoughts of mounting a counterattack. Reining Spades to a stop then, he went back to check on the three bodies lying on the grassy rise. All were dead and, as he had thought, they were Cheyenne. Only one of them had a rifle. The other two had bows.

Convinced that the danger was over for

the time being, he turned Spades toward the beleaguered wagon only to be startled by a blast from the shotgun. "Goddamn!" he roared as shotgun pellets rattled the leaves of the cottonwood tree above his head. "Hold your damn fire!" He backed Spades away a few paces. "I'm on your side, dammit," he yelled. "The Injuns are gone!"

"I'm sorry," a frightened feminine voice came back from behind the wagon. "I didn't mean to shoot at you. I accidentally pulled the trigger."

"Well, put the damn gun down. I'm comin' in." After a pause to make certain she did as he said, he again approached the river and splashed across to the wagon. As he dismounted, he looked right and left, trying to locate a husband, father, or brother, thinking surely there must be one. There was no one that he could see. "The Injuns have gone," he repeated. "You're all right now." He continued to stare at the face just partially visible above the side rails of the wagon. When she continued to hide behind the wagon, he asked, "Where are your menfolk?"

Finally deciding that she was, indeed, safe for the moment, Sarah Lawton came from behind her fortress to meet her rescuer. "My husband's dead," she replied, almost in a whisper. "They killed him."

Will thought about that for a moment before responding. "You're all alone?" He looked around him for a body. "Where is he?"

"Back yonder a'ways," she answered, and pointed toward the west.

He nodded his head, understanding, then surmised aloud, "And so you were drivin' the wagon and the Injuns were chasin' you." He looked at the team of horses, now standing quiet, then glanced back at the wagon. "Didn't pick a very good place to try to cross." He was merely stating an obvious fact; it was not intended as criticism. At once realizing that she took it as such, he quickly amended his statement. "Most likely too busy tryin' to save your neck. Don't worry — I'll get it outta there."

"I'm sorry," she offered sadly. "I should be thanking you for saving our lives."

"No thanks necessary," he replied. "I'm glad I happened along when I did." *Our* lives? he wondered. She had just said that her husband was dead.

"It's all right, Emma," she said then, "you can come out now." Will was startled to see a small child crawl out from a hole under the wagon that the front wheels had created in the soft bank. She was holding a Navy

31

Colt revolver that looked as big as she.

"Whoa, little lady," Will cautioned, after having been greeted with a shotgun blast from her mother. "Maybe you'd best give that to me."

With a fixed eye upon the stranger, six-year-old Emma Lawton was reluctant to hand over the weapon that her mother had given her in case things went bad for them. "It's all right," Sarah said. "He's come to help us." Emma dutifully offered it up to Will, muzzle first.

Will wasted little time in grasping the loaded revolver and placing it in the wagon bed. Getting to important things then, he said, "We need to get that wagon outta there and clear outta this place. I don't think that war party will be back soon, but they'll most likely come back sometime to pick up those three dead ones yonder. My guess is they'll lay low for a little while before comin' back. You never can tell about an Injun, though — especially a Cheyenne — and dependin' on if they figure out that it was just one man with a repeatin' rifle that run 'em off." He turned to take Spades' reins, then paused. "What in the world were you doin' down here? Where were you headin'?"

"Santa Fe," Sarah answered. "My husband knew some friends down there he was going to go into business with." Looking to be on the verge of tears, she nevertheless held on to her composure.

"How'd you get down here?" Will repeated. "You're way south of the Santa Fe Trail."

While Will tied Spades up to the tailgate of the wagon, Sarah told him of their misfortunes. She recounted how they had engaged the services of a guide at Council Grove named Ned Spikes, who claimed to have ridden the Santa Fe Trail a dozen times or more. They took the wet route to Fort Dodge instead of the dry one, but since they were not with a wagon train, Spikes said they would have to go around the fort. Spikes convinced them that there was no real threat — that the Indians had stopped raiding — and he guaranteed their safety. Her husband was skeptical, but eager to get to Santa Fe, so he agreed to bypass the fort.

When they had camped the night before, Sarah said she had noticed a change in Spikes' demeanor, almost belligerent, he seemed intent upon leering at her as she prepared their supper. But there had been no trouble from the sullen guide that night. This morning, however, after the horses were hitched, he had suddenly greeted them with a drawn pistol and demanded the money that Edward had packed in the wagon. It was at that moment, with the two men facing each other, that the Cheyenne war party struck. The first shot fired hit Edward in the chest.

Will listened without comment even though he had some knowledge of Ned Spikes. He had heard the name mentioned before, and always in connection with something vile and illegal. He had never had any personal dealings with Spikes, but he had seen the man hanging around the sutler's store in Camp Supply on several occasions. He was not surprised to hear that Spikes had persuaded the woman and her husband to bypass Fort Dodge. He was most likely wanted for some crime there.

Sarah could not hold back her tears as she went on to relate her late husband's efforts to save them. Lying wounded, his life's blood draining from his body, he had called for his rifle, then instructed her to put Emma in the wagon and try to save their child. Even though she understood that his life was draining as she knelt beside him, she could not forgive herself for lacking the strength to save him and her daughter.

Already exhausted, the telling of the story drained the last bit of strength from her. Emma went to stand beside her mother, trying to console her. It was an uncomfortable scene for Will. He didn't know how to deal with the situation. Feeling he should say something, he blurted, "Well, I reckon he held 'em off long enough to give you a head start."

She looked up at him with sorrowful eyes. "He only had five cartridges for that rifle, and I counted all five of them as I heard the shots while we ran, counting down his life."

Sensing her feeling of guilt for abandoning her husband, Will tried to ease her conscience. "Ma'am, you done the right thing. Your husband had the right of it, and he wanted you and the little one safe. Wouldn'ta made no sense to stay and try to fight them Injuns." Eager to change the subject, he said, "Now let's see if we can get this wagon outta here."

Following his instructions, Sarah climbed up onto the wagon seat and tried to back the horses. With a lead rope tied to the back of the wagon, Will urged Spades to pull it off the bank. With very little trouble, the wagon backed into the stream. As soon as it was free of the bank, Will examined the front wheels to see whether there had been any damage. "We were lucky," he reported to Sarah. "Now, gee 'em up and bring 'em around to head 'em toward that level spot," he instructed after untying Spades' lead rope. "They oughta be able to pull right out."

Once the wagon was on dry ground, he checked it over again, then told her to follow him to a better spot where they could hide it in the trees while he went back to look for her husband. It was in his better judgment to move out of that part of the valley as soon as possible, but he thought she might forever feel the guilt of leaving her husband behind. When he came to a suitable place, down a narrow ravine that allowed him to pull the wagon and team out of sight, he left them with the promise that he would be back.

As he followed an obvious trail left by the wagon wheels, he told himself that it might not have been the smartest thing to leave the woman and her daughter alone. But he felt that it was going to weigh heavily on Sarah's mind if there had not been some effort to recover Edward's body. Dead was dead, as far as Will was concerned. It made little difference where the bones ended up, but he guessed that women held it to be important.

He came upon the campsite soon enough, but there was no sign of a body. He found the spot where Edward had fallen and counted five empty shells on the ground next to a large stain where blood had seeped into the sand. His trained eye told him that there had been no struggle, indicating to him that Edward may have been dead by the time the Indians reached him. A trail in the sand told him that the body had been dragged into the water and up the bank on the other side. Following the trail for a few dozen yards in the tall grass, he discovered that it cut back on itself several times, giving him a clear picture of the grisly fun the warriors indulged in, dragging the body around in circles.

He found the body halfway up a ridge where they had left it before going after the woman in the wagon. *They must not have worried about catching up with her,* he thought. It was hard to tell what Edward Lawton looked like before his death. The body was badly mutilated, his bowels disgorged, and his bloodied face sagging sadly as a result of his missing scalp. "It ain't gonna do no good to let that poor woman see her husband like this," he murmured to Spades.

The only implement he carried on his saddle was a small hatchet to chop wood. He had no shovel to dig a grave, so he tried to chop a shallow pocket in the hillside with the hatchet and scoop out as much grass and dirt as he could. With considerable effort, he managed to lay a thin cover over the body. "Well, mister," he proclaimed when he had finished, "it ain't much of a grave. I expect it won't be long before you're invited to dinner with the buzzards, but that's about as good as I can do for you without a shovel. I'll try to see to it that your wife and young'un get to Fort Dodge all right."

Sarah walked out to meet him when she saw him returning, straining to see if Edward's body was behind the saddle. Seeing her frown of disappointment, he was quick to explain. "I found him where he died, and from the looks of it, he was dead before the Injuns got there, so I'm sure he didn't suffer no more." He watched her face closely to gauge how she was taking the news and decided to embellish the story a bit to set her mind at ease. "It was so peaceful there, I thought you wouldn't mind if I just buried him 'neath the trees where nothin' can disturb his grave."

With her lips pressed tightly together to keep from showing her grief, she nodded, then said, "I thank you, Mr. . . . ." She paused. "I don't even know your name."

"Cason, ma'am, Will Cason," he said.

"Mr. Cason," she repeated. "Maybe I could go see the grave."

He was afraid she'd want to do that. "Ah, I don't think that's a good idea, ma'am," he hastened to reply. "You see, I saw an awful lot of Injun sign all around there, fresh sign. I don't think we oughta risk yours and the little girl's life by goin' back there now — don't think your husband woulda wanted it."

Disappointed, she thought for a moment before replying. "Of course you're right. You've already risked your life by coming to our rescue. It wouldn't be fair to ask you to risk it again." She sighed sadly and looked toward her daughter. "I guess Edward would understand."

"I'm sure he would, ma'am. I expect he'd rather you get yourself somewhere safe."

With a deliberate show of determination, she affected a smile and offered her hand. "My name is Sarah Lawton," she said. "My husband was Edward, and this is Emma. Emma and I want you to know how grateful we are that God sent you our way. Thank you."

"Yes, ma'am," he replied, almost blushing in embarrassment. "You're welcome," he said, patently aware of the softness of her hand.

She stepped back then and sighed. Looking around her as if taking inventory, she confessed, "I don't know what to do now."

"The best thing for you and the little girl is to get back someplace where you'll be safe. I'll take you to Fort Dodge and you can decide what you're gonna do there."

She was grateful, but thought it her place to politely protest. "I'm afraid we've caused you an awful lot of trouble already. I hate to put you out further."

"Oh, it ain't no bother," he replied. "I'm on my way to Fort Dodge, anyway. I'm carryin' dispatches from Camp Supply."

She smiled. "In that case, I guess we won't be too much extra trouble."

He scratched his chin whiskers thoughtfully. "No, ma'am, no trouble a'tall," he said while thinking, *Did she think I was gonna leave her and the young'un out in the middle of the prairie?* "I expect we'd better get goin' while there's plenty of daylight left. Wouldn't hurt to put a little more distance between us and those dead Cheyennes back there. There'll most likely be some of their folks comin' to look for 'em." While he was genuinely pleased that he had come along when he did, he was somewhat perplexed over the prospect of escorting a grieving widow and her child all the way to Fort

40

Dodge. The peace he had anticipated in being alone on the prairie was now certainly lost to him for the next few days. He supposed, however, there was a reason why he had happened along at that particular time. It was a shame, though, that he could not have arrived in time to possibly save the woman's husband. Looking at it another way, however, he would have to say that Sarah Lawton and her child were first saved by the Cheyenne war party, because Ned Spikes would certainly have killed all three of them. A man of Spikes' character would hardly have left witnesses. It was kind of funny how things worked out sometimes. If he hadn't happened along when he did, she and her child would have been dead along with her husband.

CHAPTER 3

Bloody Hand bit his lower lip in anger as he looked down at the bodies of the three dead warriors. All three were young. One, Painted Arrow, was his sister's son, and it grieved Bloody Hand to see such a fine warrior lying dead. He made a silent promise to avenge his death. Tall Bull said that it was only one man who killed all three. He had one of the guns that shoot many times, and he fired so rapidly that they thought there were more soldiers behind the ridge. "Repeating rifles," Bloody Hand said, holding up his Spencer cavalry carbine. "The soldiers have them, and we must get more of them for our warriors."

They placed the bodies on the horses brought for the purpose, then rode back along the river toward their village. When they came to the place where the white people in the wagon had camped, one of the warriors pointed out what appeared to be a rather crude grave. They immediately set upon desecrating it. In only a matter of minutes, they uncovered the body of Edward Lawton. Already mutilated, it was left in the open for the scavengers to feed upon. "Let his spirit wander never to find his way," Bloody Hand decreed. "Let us take our dead back to their families now. Then I will lead a war party to kill more soldiers and take their repeating rifles."

Slowed considerably, moving at the pace of the wagon, Will estimated it was going to take the best part of four, maybe five days to reach Fort Dodge. By himself, he could have made it in two days if he had pushed Spades, but he could see no choice in the matter. Although more direct, it was not the easiest route for a wagon. Sometimes he would tie Spades' reins to the tailgate and drive the wagon over the rough spots to give Sarah some rest. Usually on those occasions, Emma would ask to sit in the wagon seat beside him. Although he always granted her request, he would have been more comfortable without the child beside him. He had never been particularly fond of children, regarding them in much the same category as varmints, like rabbits and squirrels, and maybe possum. But the precocious

43

little girl soon wormed her way into his heart before he was even aware that he was being captured. It was a new experience for Will, having spent very little time around children since leaving his mother's house in Missouri. The only time he could compare was the time he had spent with the Choctaws before signing on with Ben Clarke. There were children in the village, but he had very limited contact with them, by his own choice. Straightforward and sharp as a tack, Emma gave him no choice in the matter. Asking questions about everything her mind happened to light upon, she forced him into long discussions that would end only by his declaration that it was time to let her mother drive again. Aware of his awkwardness with children, Sarah would usually come to his rescue and move Emma out of the seat so she could sit beside Will. Emma didn't mind because on those occasions, Will would let her sit on Spades as the bay gelding plodded dutifully along behind the wagon.

When her daughter seemed to have put her grief for her father behind her rather rapidly, Sarah supposed it was due to the child's immediate attraction to the tall, broad-shouldered scout. She was not sure it was a healthy attachment for the child since it was temporary at best. But under the tragic circumstances, maybe there would be no lasting harm. As for herself, Sarah naturally found it difficult to let Edward's death go, but she was determined to accept it and move on — she had to think about Emma. On the second day of travel with the unassuming army scout, she seemed to have come to terms with the fate that had befallen her. Even though slight, the change in her demeanor was evident in the way she talked to Emma and Will. While he had spent very little time with children, he had never been exposed to a woman of quality with the exception of his mother, and never as an adult. Sarah Lawton was a lady, and that fact alone made it uncomfortable for him to be close to her. Awkward and bumbling in her presence, his tongue became thick with embarrassment, making it difficult to speak intelligently. If she noticed his discomfort, she gave no sign of it.

They struck Bluff Creek later that afternoon, and even though there was still plenty of daylight left, Will thought it best to stop there for the night. Sarah's horses looked in need of rest and he could see that it was going to take two more long days before they reached Fort Dodge. While Sarah gathered wood for a fire, Will unhitched the horses with Emma's help. The youngster insisted that her father had let her help him take care of the team, even though Will suggested that maybe she should help her mother. "You watch yourself around those horses," he cautioned. "You ain't much bigger'n a whisker, and they might step on you." The comment served to provide him with a pet name for the little girl, and *Whiskers* became her nickname.

Sarah smiled when Emma persisted in following Will, no longer concerned about the child's fascination for him. With rope he found on the wagon, he fashioned hobbles for Sarah's horses as Emma watched. "They won't go far with them hobbles on," he remarked when Emma said that her father had always tied them to the wagon. "Here, I'll show you how to do it." Then he demonstrated how to tie the knots to form the loops so they wouldn't hurt the horse. She tried a couple of times before she got it right. "You can hobble a horse any old way, I reckon, but that's the way I do it," he said. "That way you can get 'em off if you're in a hurry by just pullin' this end through." She giggled in delight at having learned something new.

"Why don't you hobble Spades?" she

asked when he had taken the saddle off his horse.

Will chuckled and answered, "He won't go far away from me. In fact, you couldn't run him off." The little girl found this interesting since her father's horses never seemed to want to come when called. "I expect most horses are like that," Will said, "but Spades don't know he's a horse."

Sarah paused in her preparation of the meal of pan bread, beans, and salt pork to look at her daughter chattering away at the elbow of the tall, rangy scout. A moment of sadness descended upon her as she thought that it should have been Edward patiently tolerating her daughter's questions. Just as quickly, she brought herself back from entering that shroud of melancholy that had devastated her during the two prior days. Telling herself that it was fortunate that Emma had found a distraction so soon after her father's death, she returned her attention to her supper. She could not, however, avoid a slight shudder when she was again reminded of what hers and Emma's fate might have been without the sudden appearance of Will Cason. He was a decent man, she decided, and one of conflicting personalities — a cool-hearted assassin as he executed those Cheyenne warriors, but a soft-spoken teddy bear in the presence of a child. He was not unattractive in a wild, untamed way, she thought, and then immediately scolded herself for noticing one way or the other. She wondered if he had a wife and children of his own somewhere, then at once told herself that a man like him had no room in his life for marriage. Those thoughts prompted others that had weighed heavily on her mind since Edward's death. Alone now to provide for Emma, what would she do? How would she survive on her own in a land so foreign to civilization as she had known it? She turned her head to look again at Will as he paused to stroke Spades' face, as much at home in the middle of this wild land as the deer and the antelope. She decided then that it was better for her not to entertain thoughts such as these.

The stone buildings of Fort Dodge rose on the horizon on the evening of the fourth day of their journey. Sitting on the north bank of the Arkansas River, the fort had been relocated from the original site and the old sod structures replaced by the present-day stone buildings the year before. Situated where the dry route and the wet route on the Santa Fe Trail came together, the fort was established to protect wagon trains heading to New Mexico. As was often the case this time of year, there was a wagon train encamped outside the fort, possibly one that had taken the dry route from Fort Larned. Folks that took that route usually chose to lay over in Fort Dodge to recover from the long trek with limited access to fresh water. Will suggested to Sarah that she should make camp near the wagons while he delivered his dispatches to the colonel. Aware of a look of concern on her face, he assured her that he would be back to make sure they were all right. "I ain't gonna leave you and Whiskers till I'm sure you know what you're gonna do."

Hoping he had not detected her worried look, she nodded and said that she and Emma would be all right. She had to admit to herself that she had experienced a moment of quiet panic over the possibility of being completely on her own for the first time. Although grieving over the loss of her husband of seven years, she admitted to herself that the past two days with Will Cason were the only days she had felt safe since leaving Council Grove. She did not wish to belittle her late husband's courage or ability. In fact, she would never forget his gallant effort to save her and Emma as he lay dying. But the rough-hewn army scout exuded a sense of quiet control that made her feel there was no situation for which he had no answer. She hoped that feeling cast no disrespect for Edward, for she honestly loved him every day of their marriage. She told herself that it was perfectly natural that she developed a strong sense of dependency on the strapping young man now leading the big bay horse around the end of her wagon — with her daughter sitting grandly in the saddle. While beaming at the pair of them brightly, she feared what might lie ahead when Will was gone. Where would she go — a woman alone with a small child? It was easy to say it had been a mistake to think she and Edward could make a new life in Santa Fe. Edward's death was blunt testimony to that fact. She was afraid now, afraid for herself and her child. She gazed intently at the broad back of her rough-hewn guardian angel as he rode away from the wagon.

On his way to the post headquarters, he thought about the past few days with Sarah and Emma. Ben Clarke was probably expecting him back at Camp Supply tonight or in the morning. "He'll probably think my topknot is flyin' on some Cheyenne warrior's lance," he remarked to Spades. "He oughta know better'n that." He certainly planned to return, but he wasn't in any particular hurry. Will had a feeling that Ben wanted him to ride with the Seventh. But Will didn't care much for Colonel George A. Custer's style of waging war, especially since that campaign on Black Kettle's village on the Washita. Custer had called it a battle. Most other folks called it a massacre. Will was glad he wasn't along on that one. He had ridden alone to Black Kettle's village a few weeks before that attack. *I never saw a more peaceful camp of Indians,* he thought. *There wasn't a handful of young men, and they were trying to surrender to the army even then.* He had no qualms about fighting the Cheyenne warriors who were intent upon raiding farms and towns and attacking stagecoaches. "But, damn," he exclaimed, "I can't see any satisfaction in killin' peaceful Injuns, especially women and children."

He turned his dispatches over to the duty sergeant. Will had seen the sergeant on prior trips to Fort Dodge, but he didn't know his name, only that he was one of a few ex-Confederate soldiers who had volunteered to fight Indians in the U.S. Army rather than loll around in a Union prison back east — *Galvanized Yankees,* they were called.

"There may be some dispatches to go back to Camp Supply with you," the sergeant said, "if you can wait around till tomorrow when the captain and first sergeant are here."

"I'll be hangin' around for a spell, anyway," Will replied. He was genuinely reluctant to leave Sarah and Emma until he was certain they would be all right.

"You've still got time to get somethin' to eat if you get on over to the enlisted men's mess," the sergeant said. "You can stable your horse and throw your gear in the cavalry barracks. There's extra cots there."

"Much obliged," Will replied, "but I reckon I'll make camp over near that wagon train." Then something else occurred to him as he headed out the door. He paused and asked, "That wagon train, they comin' or goin'?"

"Goin'," the sergeant replied. Both men assumed the question was whether the train was on its way to New Mexico, or coming back. "They's mostly freighters haulin' supplies for Santa Fe. There's a few settlers that have been camped here for a week that are goin' with 'em." He watched while Will thought that over, then started out the door. "Sure you don't wanna get some grub before the cooks throw it out?"

"I reckon not, but thanks just the same." He closed the door behind him.

The sergeant stepped over by the window and watched him as he rode across the parade ground, his body moving gracefully in rhythm with the motion of his horse. *As wild as any Indian out there on the plains,* he thought. *Probably couldn't eat if he had to sit down at a table to do it.*

To the contrary, Will was anticipating having supper with a proper lady and her daughter. Crossing the parade ground toward the circle of wagons, he could see some folks gathered around Sarah's. He wondered what she was going to decide — to go on to Santa Fe, or go back east? "It ain't none of our business," he said to Spades. "I reckon she'll decide what's best for her and the kid. Maybe there's grandparents or some other family back east." He told himself, although not really convincingly, that the sooner he could get rid of them, the better. Further thoughts on the matter were interrupted when Emma caught sight of the familiar figure on the horse.

"Will!" she shouted when he was still a hundred yards' distant, and immediately ran to meet him. Will could not hide the grin on his face at seeing the little girl running to greet him. He reached down, scooped her up as easily as lifting a sack of flour, and planted her on Spades' neck right in front of the saddle. "There's some folks talking to Mama about going to Santa Fe," she informed him. "Have you ever been to Santa Fe, Will?"

"Once," he answered. "I didn't care much for it. Too dry and dusty to suit me and Spades — nothin' but snakes and lizards. I never went back."

"I think those people talking to Mama want us to go with them to Santa Fe," she said, a hint of disapproval in her voice.

"I reckon your mama will decide what's best for you," Will said. "Whatever it is, I know you'll help her."

"I wish you'd go with us."

"Well, I don't know about that," he said. "I've got to go back to Camp Supply and scout for the army. Besides, you and your mama don't need me taggin' along." He had to admit that the child's open affection for him was a new experience, one he couldn't decide whether he liked. Most of his life had been wild and sometimes violent. There had been no time nor occasion for the tender moments common to a life with wife and family. He found the thoughts disturbing, and was glad to end the conversation as he pulled his horse up before Sarah's wagon.

Will lifted Emma from Spades' neck and lowered her gently to the ground while Sarah and the couple with her waited for him to dismount. "Will, this is Mr. and Mrs. Baldwin," Sarah said, and stepped aside to give the two men room to shake hands.

"Russell Baldwin," he said, and extended his hand to Will. "Sarah told us about her hard luck and how you stepped up to help her." Will responded with a self-conscience nod as he accepted Baldwin's hand. Russell continued. "We've just been tellin' Sarah that there's two more families headin' to New Mexico with these freighters. She'd be welcome to come along."

Sarah looked at Will as if beseeching his advice. "It is an opportunity to travel with friendly people, but I'm not sure what I'd do there without Edward," she said. "He was planning to open a law office with a man we knew back in Westport, Missouri. What on earth could I do to support Emma and myself?" She paused to shake her head in despair when considering her options. "There's not much more to look forward to if we go back to Westport — move in with my parents, I guess, but that would place a hardship on them. Edward's mother and

55

father have both passed on. I don't know what to do." She didn't voice the thought that lay heavy on her mind, that the only possible way she could take care of Emma and herself was to get married again.

Emma piped up at that point. "I don't wanna go to Santa Fe. It's too dry and dusty with nothing but snakes and lizards," she announced, causing her mother to cast a startled look in her direction.

"Baby, we've never been to Santa Fe," Sarah responded patiently. "We don't know what it's like there."

"I know it's dry and dusty," Emma retorted emphatically, which prompted Will's gaze to shift to avoid eye contact with Sarah, lest she suspect the source of her daughter's opinion.

When he glanced back at Sarah, it was to meet her direct gaze. "I'm sure it's like most places," he hastened to counsel Emma. "Got its good and bad things. Your mama will decide what's best."

Baldwin nodded his understanding. "Well, the train's pullin' out in the mornin', and like we said, we'd be glad to have you come with us. I'd be happy to give you a hand with any chores that are too much for you and the child." He glanced at Will then, wondering if the rangy scout had any notions of going with Sarah.

"That's so generous of you to offer," Sarah replied, "but I expect my prospects will be better back home in Westport."

It was settled, then. She said good-bye to the Baldwins and wished them a safe journey. Then she got back to the business of making camp. He helped her get her cook fire set up, and after he took care of the horses, he went in search of more wood for the fire. "When these folks move out in the mornin', we'll move your camp closer to the river. There's a better supply of wood there. I'll go over and tell the soldier boys that you're gonna camp here till a wagon train comes through headin' toward Council Grove."

She paused to look directly at him. "Will, you know how much I appreciate all you've done for Emma and me. I know you've got to go about your own business now. You probably feel like you got a lot more than you asked for when you came to our rescue, so you don't have to stay any longer and worry about us. We'll be fine. We'll stay right here near the post until a train heading east comes along."

"Well, you're right," he replied after some hesitation. A part of him was reluctant to say good-bye, for he realized that he really cared about their welfare. "I reckon I should get back to Camp Supply before I lose my job." He forced a smile and a pat on the head for Emma. "But I need to go over to headquarters anyway before I leave, and I'll tell 'em what happened to your husband, and what you're plannin' on doin'. I expect they'll keep an eye on you and Emma till you can get lined up to go back east."

Emma came at once to take Will's hand. "You don't have to go if you don't want to — do you, Will?"

He gave her hand a squeeze and smiled down at her. "I reckon I'd better go do what they're payin' me for," he said. "Looks like the army's gonna take care of you and your ma just fine. I'll stay tonight and get started first thing in the mornin', then you're gonna be responsible to take care of your ma in case the army don't do the job." He looked up at Sarah and grinned. She smiled back, while thinking that Emma had pretty much expressed the feelings for both of them. She might have expressed her reluctance to see him go, but felt that it would be improper to do so and might give him the wrong impression. She could not explain her feelings toward him. In the few short days she had known him she had come to regard him as a protector, and part of her wished that

58

he could stay with them. She paused to watch him as he pulled the saddle off his horse and carried it over to the base of a large cottonwood. She smiled as Emma and the horse followed along behind him. *Both children and animals love him,* she thought. *Emma's really going to miss him.*

As Will had anticipated, Sergeant-Major Michael Boyle was eager to help the newly widowed woman and promised to see that she was safe during her wait for an east-bound train. He personally accompanied Will back to the wagon to express his condolences for her loss, and said he would alert the colonel of her plight as soon as he was back from the field. "In the meantime," he said, "my wife will most likely want to come by to see that you've got everything you need." He fashioned a wide grin for Emma's benefit, then warned Sarah, "Edna's likely to wanna adopt this little one, and maybe you, too." When the visit was over, he informed Will that he had some routine dispatches for Camp Supply. "Nothin' that's so all-fired important that you have to wear your horse out to deliver, just whenever you're ready to ride."

Supper that night was a lighthearted affair. Sarah boiled a pot of beans spiked with a chunk of side meat, pan biscuits, and coffee. Sarah had to scold Emma a couple of times to let Will eat his food when the rambunctious six-year-old wanted to sit in his lap. "It's all right, Sarah," he joked. "If she don't behave herself, I'll tie her up to that tree yonder." The adults made a conscientious effort to keep the conversation light, although there were serious thoughts in the minds of both. Though their time together had been short and proper out of respect for her husband's recent passing, neither could deny a certain awkwardness over Will's intention to leave in the morning. He was not ready to admit it to himself, but he was going to miss the two of them. He tried to explain away his feelings as a natural respect for any kind and gentle woman, and nothing more than that. But he couldn't help admiring the way she sort of tilted her head to one side when she laughed, and the way she always managed to keep herself neat and clean, no matter what the chore. But, he told himself, he had never spent much time around proper women before. Maybe they were all like Sarah. *I better get the hell outta here,* he thought, *before I start thinking things I ought'n.* "Come on, Whiskers," he said, "let's go feed Spades some of the army's oats."

There was no need to repeat it, Emma was on her feet and running ahead of him. "Please, Will," she begged, "can I ride him?"

"I don't know," Will replied, frowning as if uncertain. "We'll have to ask him." He picked her up and held her beside the bay gelding's head. "Ask him if you can ride." Emma did as he said, asking in her most polite way. "Reach over and pet him on his face," Will said. When she did, the horse gently tossed his head up and down. "There you go," Will said. "He says yes."

Emma was delighted. "He said yes, Mama," she called back to Sarah. Will looked back to grin at Sarah before placing Emma on Spades' back. He never got around to telling either of them that Spades always tossed his head up and down when you tickled his face. With Emma perched on the horse's back, holding on to its black mane, he led Spades to the back of the wagon, where he had stowed a sack of oats. She watched while the horse ate the oats, silent for only a few moments before broaching a new subject. "I need a horse," she announced.

"What for?" Will replied. "You've got a horse, two of 'em."

"They're Mama's horses," she said. "They're just the horses that pull the wagon. I want a horse of my own, a riding horse, like Spades."

Will smiled at her and shook his head. "You ain't hardly big enough to take care of a horse yet."

"I will be," she insisted. "I'll be seven in November, and Mama says I'm growing like a weed. Can you get me a horse, Will? I could take care of it."

"Maybe when you grow a little more," he said, reluctant to tell her it was out of the question.

Her face lit up with a smile. "Promise?"

Afraid he had said the wrong thing, he nevertheless nodded and answered. "Promise, but it'll be a while yet." He didn't plan to say anything to Sarah about his promise, not sure she would approve, but he figured that he had been on a horse's back by the time he was Emma's age, and it hadn't done him any harm. "We'll just keep this a secret between you and me. All right?"

"Looks like I'm about to lose my daughter," Sarah teased when he rejoined her by the fire.

Will laughed. "She's a keeper all right, but I don't know if I could keep up with her." They finished up the pot of coffee before saying good night. Then Will retired to his blanket a few yards away from the wagon, and Sarah joined Emma, who was already in bed.

It was still early when the wagon train got under way, and as they were pulling out, Russell Baldwin called out as he drove by, "Good luck to you, Mrs. Lawton. Sure you don't wanna change your mind?"

"Thank you," Sarah replied. "Good luck to you as well. I guess I'll wait here." Smiling as she and Emma waved good-bye, she could not avoid a feeling of hopelessness as the wagons rolled out of the campground. Should she have gone with them? She wished she knew what was really best for her and Emma. Then she tried to reassure herself with the sensibility of returning to a place she knew, even though there was really no family there to welcome her. When the last wagon cleared the area, she turned to look at Will hitching up her team, with Emma's dubious help, in preparation to move her camp closer to the river and the fort. *I wish he wasn't going,* she told herself. The thought was confirmation of how alone she would be after this morning.

Once Sarah's wagon was relocated, Will looked around to see if there was anything else he could do to make them comfortable. When he decided that he had done all he could, he saddled Spades and prepared to leave. As he was saying good-bye, Edna Boyle, the sergeant-major's wife, walked up to greet Sarah. "Good morning," she called out cheerfully as she stepped carefully around fresh deposits left by the mules pulling the freighters' wagons. A pleasant-looking woman with graying hair and a comfortable plump figure, she stepped forward and gave Sarah a motherly hug. "Michael told me we had two attractive young ladies visiting for a spell," she gushed and cornered Emma for an embrace, causing the youngster to release Will's hand. "And just in time for the Fourth of July ball," Edna continued.

Sarah responded gratefully for her welcome and replied that it was still a bit soon after her husband's death to give any thought toward celebration. "I know, dear," Edna Boyle went on. "And we're all so sorry for the tragic loss of your husband. I guess you have to be an army wife to know that these senseless sorrows are going to befall many of us, and the best we can do is to accept what God gives us and go on from there. The Fourth of July dance isn't until next Saturday. Maybe by then you'll feel a little better." She turned her attention to Emma then. "And you're both invited. It'll do you both good. You can meet some of the other ladies on the post." Her nature was so infectious that Sarah could not help but smile. "In the meantime," Edna continued, "I've come to see what you might need and how I can help."

During the entire welcoming by the sergeant-major's wife, Will stood silently watching, seemingly unnoticed by the enthusiastic army wife. With Sarah's, and even Emma's, attention sufficiently captured by Edna Boyle, he realized that this might be the best time for him to take his leave. He could not deny a feeling of regret for having to go before knowing they were safely on their way back east. At least this was how he preferred to explain the feeling. He was not presumptive to the point of admitting that he was just going to miss them. *That's just plain nonsense,* he scolded himself. *That woman's on a level you can't even see from where you're standing.* He turned then and put a foot in the stirrup. Spades started walking before he had thrown his other leg over and settled in the saddle. He had gone no farther than fifty yards when he heard Emma calling after him. Turning in the saddle, he saw the youngster waving, standing on her tiptoes in an effort to make him see her. He smiled and returned her wave, then continued on to post headquarters to pick up the dispatches. Sarah and Edna. Boyle were still engrossed in conversation. Will did not notice the casual shift of Sarah's gaze toward him as he rode away.

Sergeant-Major Boyle walked out of the storeroom when he heard his company clerk giving the dispatches to Will. "You goin' back the way you came?" he asked. "Or are you takin' the wagon road back to Camp Supply?"

Will shrugged. "I figured to go pretty much the same way I came," he replied. "It's a little quicker than the wagon road."

"You'd best keep a sharp eye about you," Boyle said. "A fellow that's got a little place in the hills just this side of Bluff Creek came in this morning. He said his cow was run off last night along with some of his chickens and a full sack of oats. That doesn't sound like much more than a few thieving Indians, but it's mighty close to the fort. The captain's sending out a patrol to look into it. You wanna ride with 'em?"

"I reckon I could," Will replied. "Who's leadin' the patrol?"

"Lieutenant Bordeaux," Boyle answered. "He'd probably be glad to have a scout with him. They're saddling up right now. You can catch 'em at the stables."

"I'll be on my way, then," Will said, and took his leave of the sergeant-major. He had ridden with Harvey Bordeaux before, an officer everyone got along with. A lieutenant for over nine years, Bordeaux would probably never make captain. Good-natured and easygoing, almost frumpy in appearance, he looked out of place in his baggy officer's coat and sash. This fact may have partially accounted for his lack of promotion, in combination with his noncompetitive, nonaggressive attitude. Like most everybody else, Will was fond of the man and counted him as a friend.

"Will Cason," Lieutenant Bordeaux called out as a greeting when he turned to see the rangy scout approaching. "Somebody told me they thought they saw you come in with a wagon last night. I thought maybe you were taking up homesteading."

"Howdy, Lieutenant," Will responded. "Boyle sent me over here to see if I could help you find your way off the post."

Bordeaux laughed. "Is that a fact? Well, I have been known to get lost now and again." He extended his hand when Will pulled Spades up beside his horse. "Are you goin' with us sure enough?"

"Yeah, I was fixin' to go back to Camp Supply with some dispatches. Boyle thought you might want a little company as long as I was goin' that way, anyway. I reckon the dispatches aren't that important."

"Always glad to have your company," Bordeaux replied gallantly. "Don't see much of you since you've been ridin' out of Supply. How long has it been since you rode with me on patrol?" He paused to remember. "Last summer sometime," he said, answering his own question. Then he laughed when he recalled. "Over in that strip of no-man's-land beyond the Outlet. We were lookin' for a Comanche raidin' party — didn't find any Indians, but we found a herd of antelope. God, what a feast, I ain't ever ate that good on patrol before or since. I had to swear every man to secrecy before we reported back to post."

His comment caused Will to chuckle. He recalled the incident — five days out on a ten-day patrol. They were nowhere close to catching up with the Comanches, so Bordeaux gave the order to return to Fort Dodge. As was his custom, Will was a good mile ahead of the column when a herd of antelope crossed in front of the patrol. Jumping at an opportunity to have something to eat besides salt pork, Bordeaux gave permission for two of his troopers to chase after the swift-moving animals. They were unsuccessful in their efforts to overtake the herd, and wasted several rounds of desperation shots before giving up the hunt. Up ahead, however, Will heard the shooting and rode back to investigate. Although the troopers attempt to catch the antelope failed, it did serve a useful purpose, for the soldiers' gunfire drove the antelope straight toward Will. All he had to do was find himself a spot on the side of a ravine the frightened animals were heading for. With little effort, and no skill required, Will dropped two of the antelope as they passed below his perch.

By the time the advance scout caught up to him, he was already skinning the carcasses and preparing to quarter one of them. "Tell Lieutenant Bordeaux I decided the detail needed a little fresh meat," he had told the soldier.

Speechless at first, then delighted to see the two carcasses, and after hearing an embellished version of the skill with which Will had cornered the animals, the soldier took off at a gallop to take the news to the rest of the fifteen-man patrol. As pleased as the private who had delivered the message, Bordeaux called a halt to the march even though it was early morning, and declared a holiday. He ordered a feast in celebration of St. Antelope's Day, claiming that it was a regular holiday in the south of France, where he was born. Not a man in the patrol had spilled the beans about the holiday feast, although there were quite a few references to St. Antelope that the uninformed puzzled over for a week or two after. Bordeaux explained the extra day on patrol to the colonel as having been necessary to follow fresh Indian sign.

Will and the lieutenant had a good laugh recalling that day, and he couldn't help thinking of the contrast between his friend and Lieutenant Lyman Bridges. He could imagine Bridges pulling out a copy of army regulations and finding article and paragraph stating such a thing strictly forbidden. "Who's your point man?" Will asked. When told that it was Corporal Kincaid, he commented, "Well, you don't need me out front. Kincaid's about as good as they get."

"Yeah, you can ride with me," Bordeaux said. "We're goin' straight to this fellow's farm — Wilson's his name. There won't be nothin' to find there, but I figure we can start lookin' from that point north of Bluff Creek. That's when I can use you best. You and Kincaid can split up and scout out to

70

the flanks. Reports we've gotten lately say that Bloody Hand has been the one leading the raids against army patrols, but I doubt if this is any of his doing — stealing a cow and a couple of chickens."

"Don't sound like it," Will replied.

"Hey, Lieutenant, looks like you ain't gonna need me out front now."

Will turned to see Corporal Kincaid walking toward them, leading his horse. "I'll be damned," Will replied. "I'm just ridin' along so you soldier boys can protect me from the Injuns." He gave the corporal a wide grin. "How you doin', Kincaid? I thought you'da lost those two stripes by now." He reached over to shake Kincaid's outstretched hand.

"I thought maybe you were comin' along to help us hunt antelope," Kincaid said. They both chuckled over that.

It would have been fine with Will to be permanently assigned to scout for C Company. Lieutenant Bordeaux was easy to work for, and there wasn't a better man than Kincaid to ride scout with. Will's problem was Ben Clarke. Clarke knew Will was the best scout he had and he made sure the colonel blocked any requests from other regiments for Will's services. Will knew he was the best, too, but he never openly admitted it. Bordeaux had even suggested to him that

71

he should quit Ben, then come back to Dodge to look for a job. But Will was reluctant to quit a man who had hired him and treated him square, as Ben Clarke had. He had to laugh to himself when it occurred to him that another run-in with Lieutenant Bridges might solve the problem for him.

CHAPTER 4

After a ride of less than an hour, the patrol arrived at the farmhouse of Robert Wilson, his wife, and two young sons. Wilson, still dismayed over the brazen thievery so close to the fort, met the troopers with his shotgun in hand. "I didn't know they was even there," he confessed. "The dog didn't even bark, and he was sleepin' right there on the porch."

Will and Kincaid looked the ground over around the barn, but there were no clues that could serve to tell them much about the raiding party that ran off his cow and chickens. There were a few tracks showing where the thieves crossed the small stream that ran behind the barn, and removed three rails from the corral where the cow and two mules were kept. "I got my mules back," Wilson said. "I reckon they didn't want nothin' but the cow and two of my hens."

After a brief look around, Will said, "Don't

look like there was but two of 'em that done the stealin'. Course it didn't take no more'n that to lead a cow and grab a couple of chickens. They didn't go to much bother to cover their tracks. If I had to guess, I'd say there's a bigger party." He paused to point toward a line of hills to the south of the farm. "Maybe they waited for their supper in those hills yonder."

"You think they just sent two men to get the cow to eat?" Bordeaux asked. "Why didn't they take the mules, too?"

"I reckon since they had a choice, they preferred beef to mule," Will replied. "I can't blame 'em there. The thing that worries me is, if they were just out to steal livestock, they most likely *would have* taken the mules. On the other hand, if they were part of a war party on their way to raid somebody, they wouldn't wanna bother with two mules."

"I see what you're thinkin'," Bordeaux said, still puzzled. "But if they were out on the warpath, why didn't they attack Wilson and the house — burn it to the ground?"

"Damned if I know," Will replied. "Too close to the fort maybe — maybe we'll find somethin' in those hills." He turned to the corporal standing beside him. "What do you think, Kincaid?"

The corporal shook his head. "I ain't paid to think," he said, "but what you said makes sense to me. These tracks are plain enough. We might as well follow 'em and see if they lead to a bigger bunch of Injuns."

"Probably just a couple of hungry Indians lookin' for somethin' to eat," Bordeaux told the concerned farmer. "Most likely moved on — we'll see if we can pick up their trail, maybe run 'em to ground." Back in the saddle, the patrol left the family of four standing in the front yard, their confidence in the army to protect them somewhat shaken.

With close to a mile of open prairie between Wilson's farm and the hills, the patrol crossed the stream and headed south with Will and Kincaid about a hundred yards in the lead. They had ridden about one hundred and fifty yards across the prairie when they reached a spot where a dozen or more horses had waited. They paused for the patrol to catch up. "Here's where their friends waited, in case the first two ran into trouble, I reckon," Will reported. "Then it looks like the whole bunch moved on off toward the hills." He looked then at Bordeaux and paused. It didn't make sense to him and he expressed his doubts to the lieutenant. "What I'm wonderin' is what a bunch this size is up to. They ain't likely a huntin' party. If they were, they wouldn't be huntin' around here. If they're a war party, why didn't they strike Wilson's house and family? What do you think, Kincaid?"

"Me, I ain't paid to think," Kincaid answered, "but I've been studying on the same thing."

"Well, maybe we can find out. We'll keep followin' 'em," the lieutenant said. "That's what we're here for."

Upon reaching the base of the hills, the patrol turned and followed the tracks up through a steep ravine that led to a broad ridge. A few more yards along the ridge brought them to the remains of a campfire and the charred head and bones of Wilson's cow. Off to one side, near a thicket of scrubby laurels, a trio of buzzards fought over a scattering of chicken entrails. "Here's where they had their supper," Kincaid said.

"From the looks of things, they don't seem to be worryin' much about anybody followin' them," the lieutenant said. He was still thinking about how close they were to the fort, and the apparent boldness with which the Indians had raided. "It's almost as if they were darin' us to come after them."

"It does sorta look that way," Will agreed as he took note of the obvious trail leading away from the camp and down toward the valley on the other side of the ridge. He couldn't help but think of Bloody Hand even though the raiding party was smaller than the savage war chief usually led.

"Well, there're no more than a dozen warriors, accordin' to what you're tellin' me," Bordeaux said. "Let's get on the move and maybe we can catch up with them."

"Maybe me and Kincaid better move a little farther out front now," Will advised. "I don't like the look of this thing. They might be leadin' us into an ambush up in these hills. They're makin' it mighty damn easy to track 'em." Bordeaux agreed and sent the two scouts on ahead. They split up, Kincaid taking the ridge on the right side of the valley, and Will crossing over to take the left ridge.

Bloody Hand strode forward to meet his Cheyenne scout as he approached the stand of willows that formed a screen beside the creek where thirty-five warriors waited. "The soldiers are coming," Brave Elk sang out when he saw his war chief coming to meet him. "They found the place where we slaughtered the cow, and they are following our trail."

"Good," Bloody Hand said, nodding sternly. "How soon?"

"Before the sun is there," Brave Elk replied, pointing straight up over his head.

"It is time to get ready," Bloody Hand said, and returned to the creek to alert the rest of his warriors. Brave Elk, along with ten others, jumped on their ponies and rode back up the valley while those remaining with Bloody Hand found concealment on both sides at a point where it narrowed to form a pass to the neighboring range of hills. Bloody Hand positioned himself higher up the slope, where he had a clear view of the entire field of fire.

Will asked Spades for a little more speed as he loped across the valley floor to reach the left ridge before Kincaid got too far in front of him on the opposite side. Climbing the slope, he made as good a time as possible along the ridgeline, his eyes open and senses alert. Closing the distance now to parallel Kincaid, he caught occasional glimpses of the corporal between the trees as he followed the natural ridgeline. He stuck as close to the side of the slope as possible in order to see the valley below clearly. As the valley began to narrow, he started to sense a feeling of caution. Looking the situation over, he realized that it shaped up to be a perfect setup for an ambush. Thoughts of other ambushes where hostiles lured troopers into traps came to mind and he wondered if the dozen or so hostiles, leaving such an obvious trail, might in fact be leading Bordeaux's patrol into a hornet's nest. It made sense to him then — the theft of Robert Wilson's cow. The hostiles had to know a sizable troop would not be sent out to look for a few Indians that stole a cow — ten to fifteen normally. If they had killed Wilson's family and burned his house, the army would more than likely have sent out a detachment of company size. On the other hand, the smaller patrol would likely be outnumbered, allowing the larger party of warriors to annihilate them and gain firearms and ammunition in the process. This was a typical way for followers of the Cheyenne warrior, Bloody Hand, to acquire rifles, and Will was sure they'd like to get their hands on the carbines the cavalry patrol carried.

A decision had to be made in a hurry. Looking back the way he had come, he could see Bordeaux's troopers entering the mouth of the valley. Shifting his gaze back to search the opposite ridgeline, he tried to spot Kincaid again and somehow signal him. Seeing no sign of him, he decided to try to angle across the valley floor and hope to cut the corporal off. Down the steep slope he went, his back almost touching Spades' rump as the big bay slid through the shale and gravel of the hillside. Reaching the valley floor at a point where it took a sharp turn, he was about to relax when he was startled to find himself facing about a dozen Cheyenne warriors, their faces painted for war. Sitting calmly on their ponies, they were obviously waiting for the patrol to come into view. Brave Elk and his warriors were as surprised to discover Will suddenly appear from nowhere as he was to see them.

"Oh, shit!" Will exclaimed when he realized where he had landed. In the chaos that followed, there was a competition to see which party could react quickest. The decision went to the rangy army scout, who thankfully was naturally gifted with quick reflexes. While the hostiles struggled to get their horses in line, Will drew his Henry rifle and threw five quick shots into their midst. Not waiting to see if he hit anyone, he kicked Spades hard. The bay needed no further encouragement, and they were soon racing across the narrow valley to the tune of war cries and flying lead. From the ridge now on his left, he heard the welcome sound of Kincaid's carbine — at least he hoped it was Kincaid. It was, and the corporal was now lying low on his horse's neck as he sidled down the slope and galloped along the valley floor after Will. Brave Elk and his warriors raced after them.

The chase lasted only until the Indians saw Bordeaux and the patrol riding hard to meet them, whereupon they pulled up and let the two fleeing horses go. Angry at first that the ambush had been discovered, Brave Elk decided that the full plan had not been revealed. The soldiers could not know that Bloody Hand waited with more warriors beyond the turn of the valley. "Come," he said, "we will pretend to run away from them. Maybe they will still follow."

One of the warriors continued to stare after the two riders. Certain then, he turned to Brave Elk. "It is the same man," he said, "the white man with the gun that shoots many times. He is the one who killed Painted Arrow and the others when we attacked the woman in the wagon at the river." He turned again to follow the tall scout with his eyes before offering a cautious comment. "I think this man has strong medicine. Where did he come from just now? How did he know we were hiding here?"

"What Tall Bull says may be true," Brave Elk said. "We should be cautious, but he just shot five times into our midst and didn't hit anyone. Maybe his medicine is not as strong as it was by the river. I say we should lead the soldiers back to the others and see if his medicine is strong enough to save them." His statement was met with grunts of agreement from most of the warriors.

Back down the valley, Lieutenant Bordeaux halted his troop to receive his two scouts as they pulled their horses to a sliding stop before him. "Looks like they're runnin'," the lieutenant said. "Let's get after them before they disappear into the hills."

"You might wanna hold up a minute," Will said. "I can't say for sure, but I don't think they'll be scatterin' into the hills. I've got an itchy feelin' that there may be a whole lot more of their friends waitin' around that turn in the valley." He turned to the corporal. "What do you think, Kincaid?"

As before, Kincaid agreed in his usual style. "I ain't paid to think," he opined. "But what Will says struck me the same."

"You sayin' we oughta withdraw," Bordeaux asked, "instead of tryin' to engage them?"

"Well, I reckon that's up to you," Will replied. "What I'm sayin' is that you might wanna hold back until I can get up on the other side of those hills and get a look at what's around the bend. I'd keep movin' if I was you, but at a walk, like you were restin' your horses, so they'll think you're still chasin' 'em." He paused to look around at the lay of the land. "You might wanna keep your eye out for a good place to defend if you have to," he said, "like that hole by the creek over there."

Bordeaux looked ahead to where Will pointed. "All right, we'll stall until you have time to scout ahead. Maybe you'd better take Kincaid with you. What do you think, Corporal?"

"I ain't paid . . . ," Kincaid started.

"I know you ain't paid to think," Bordeaux interrupted. "I'm tellin' you to volunteer to go."

"Yes, sir," Kincaid replied.

"Let's go," Will said, and the two of them were off again, holding the already tiring horses to an easy lope.

Will waited for Brave Elk's party to disappear from view around the turn of the valley before retracing his original path up through the hills. They continued along the crest of the ridge past the point where Will

83

had descended before to land in the middle of the war party. "I wanna get on the other side of that bend in the canyon where the valley looks like it runs out," he told Kincaid. When they had gone far enough, they guided the horses behind a shallow swale. "I'll work my way down off this ridge on foot," he said, leaving Kincaid to take care of the horses. "If what I suspect is waitin' where that canyon takes a turn, I may need my horse in a hurry."

Satisfied to stay behind, Kincaid positioned himself at the top of the swale where he could look in both directions. Will disappeared between two large boulders that capped a rock field that covered half of the slope. Reaching a ledge that stood about fifteen feet above the canyon floor, he paused and dropped to one knee while he listened to the sound of the wind rattling the leaves of the few trees on either side of the narrow passage. After a few moments' time, he caught the sound of voices on the wind, and knew at once that his suspicions were verified. Intent upon gauging the strength of their numbers, he left the ledge and moved carefully down to take cover behind a clump of bushes. From there he was able to see both sides of the narrow passage where the canyon began. At first, he saw no one, but as he scanned the steep sides of the canyon, he saw a warrior rise from behind a hummock and move to another location closer to the canyon floor. Then, one by one, his sharp senses caught sight of a slight movement here, the sound of a low voice there, until he was confident that there was a force of hostiles sufficient to stage a deadly ambush.

I've seen all I need to see, he thought, and started to slowly withdraw from the bushes. He went back to the ledge and reached up to get a grip on the edge of a rock. In that instant, a bullet ricocheted off the rock just above his hand, sending a shower of granite bits to sting his face and arms. At almost the same time, he heard the report of the rifle. Within seconds, the canyon erupted into a fury of shouts and gunfire. With no decisions to make then, Will took off, running as fast as he could, skirting the ledge and scrambling up the steep slope. Luckily, the warriors had no real idea where he was and were shooting in the general direction pointed out by Bloody Hand.

From his position halfway up the slope, Bloody Hand had turned his attention away from the valley beyond the turn for a few moments and happened to catch sight of the soldiers' scout about to climb up on a ledge. Roaring out his rage, he had time for one shot before Will scrambled out of his view. Already concerned by the shooting he had heard from Brave Elk's warriors, he now knew that the ambush had been discovered. There was no choice but to attack in hopes of killing as many soldiers as possible before they could escape. His first concern, however, was to find the scout he had seen behind him, and any others who were with him. Signaling frantically to his warriors below, he motioned toward the ledge where he had last seen the white man. At once, Will had a dozen angry hostiles on his trail.

Behind him, he could hear the frenzied war cries as the Indians discovered the obvious marks left in the side of the slope by his moccasins, sliding and slipping as he had hurried to escape. It was a life-or-death footrace at this point, and he wasn't sure he could outrun the competition. Knowing that he was going to have to find a place to try to hold them off, he looked right and left as he gasped for breath. Feeling he was too winded to run much farther up the slope, he was about to drop behind a dead tree when Kincaid suddenly appeared leading Spades. Like a pony express rider, Will leaped to get a foot in the stirrup and swung the other leg over as Spades followed

Kincaid's sorrel over the top of the ridge and down the other side.

Up ahead, Kincaid's horse slid and almost stumbled as it reached the lower part of the ridge where a saddle joined it with the hill next to it. Behind and above, Will could hear the sound of mounted warriors already on their trail. "Easy, boy," he cautioned when he reached the patch of loose gravel that had almost tumbled Kincaid's horse. Spades took the area in smooth stride, never faltering. Across the saddle they raced to the next slope before Kincaid took a game trail down between the hills, heading back in a general direction toward the valley and the patrol.

Still riding at a measured pace down the middle of the valley, even after hearing gunfire, Lieutenant Bordeaux called his patrol to a halt when he saw his two scouts suddenly emerge from the sparse tree line at the base of the hill and race toward him. One look and he immediately formed a mounted skirmish line and gave the order to prepare to fire, for it figured that hostiles were not far behind. After a few moments, more than a half dozen warriors appeared at the base of the hill and pulled up short when they saw the line of soldiers with carbines raised. Bordeaux ordered his men to hold their fire since the Cheyenne were out of their effective range. The hostiles paused, apparently considering the odds, then turned and retreated toward the bend in the valley. Bordeaux waited for Will and Kincaid to report.

"They've got a right lively party planned for you," Will told him. "I couldn't spot every Injun hiding back there around the bend, but I would guess there's at least thirty-five or forty. If it hadn'ta been for Kincaid, I mighta been part of the entertainment." He paused a few moments while Bordeaux thought it over. "I expect they'll be comin' after you pretty soon now, since they know we discovered the ambush." When Bordeaux seemed slow in making a decision, Will nudged him a little. "There's way too many for you to fight head-on. I expect you'll be lookin' for a good spot to get ready for 'em." He paused again. "Back yonder way," he suggested, gesturing toward the hills behind them.

"I suppose you're right," the lieutenant conceded, and gave the order to fall back.

As Will had predicted, there wasn't a great deal of time available to find a suitable position to withstand an assault. By retreating, they were able to have some choice in the selection, picking a ravine with a trickle of a stream and a reasonable field of fire on three sides. The most vulnerable side was the hill above them where the ravine ended. Will volunteered to take that position, figuring he could move up the ravine and keep the Indians from getting in too close. Due to the need for every rifle possible, only two men were assigned to take care of the horses. That left fifteen to hold off a force of thirty-five or forty hostiles.

Again, as Will had advised, it was not a long wait before the attack began. Bloody Hand, seeing the defensive position the soldiers had taken, sent Brave Elk with six warriors to climb the hill above the ravine. The Cheyenne war chief then decided upon a frontal attack on the ravine, hoping to overpower the lesser force with his superiority in numbers. He soon realized the folly in that thinking. Though outnumbered, the soldiers laid down a devastating field of fire with their carbines. Brave Elk's probe at the rear of the troop was met with much the same reception, thanks to Will's Henry rifle and the two troopers with him. Reluctant to sacrifice his warriors' lives needlessly, Bloody Hand pulled his men back out of range of the carbines and surrounded the ravine, planning to wait the soldiers out until hunger and thirst forced them to make a run for it.

"Looks like some of them Injuns has got theirselves some army rifles," Kincaid observed when a rifle slug kicked up dirt at the rim of the ravine. "Sounds like a Springfield to me." It was soon followed by other shots from the front and sides. "They got a little more range than these Spencers we're using."

"I think they're plannin' to keep us pinned down in this gully until we run out of water or ammunition, or both," Bordeaux said. "I guess they don't know we got a stream here." He turned to give the trickle of water a long look. "I swear, it ain't much, is it?"

"As long as the horses can get enough to drink, it'll do," Will replied. "I expect you ain't figurin' on staying here long, anyway."

"Hell, no," Bordeaux responded. "As soon as it gets dark and these horses are rested up, I plan to break outta this damn hole."

"That's what I figured," Will said. "I hope they're satisfied to keep their distance, 'cause there ain't nothin' but open ground on three of our sides. The back door is the only way out and that's up a pretty steep hill."

"And if they put some of their warriors up on that hill," Kincaid opined, "they've pretty much got our back door shut tight."

Bordeaux took their comments under serious consideration. What he was hearing was not encouraging at all, and he realized that his intention to break out of the ravine might be too risky and he might take too many casualties. "Damn!" he suddenly swore. "Maybe we shouldn't have backed our asses into this hole."

"If you hadn't, those Indian ponies would have run us down and we'da had to fight 'em on open ground," Will said. "And there's too many of 'em for us to come out ahead."

"We'll see what happens after dark," Bordeaux said, still of a mind to try to slip out of the ravine.

As the afternoon wore on, there was nothing to do but watch and wait. At odd intervals, the Indians grew tired of waiting and sent a few random shots ricocheting off the rim of the ravine just, Will supposed, to let them know they were still there. The lieutenant expressed hope that the Cheyenne would become bored with the game and withdraw. Will figured there wasn't much chance of that. There was a common misconception among many of the officers that Indians were easily bored and prone to lose interest in a situation that showed no quick results. It was not a notion that Will shared, and he felt sure that these warriors were not about to turn away when the odds were so greatly in their favor. He expressed that opinion to Bordeaux, but the lieutenant was convinced that to stay until morning would surely see the ultimate destruction of his troop.

As darkness descended upon the prairie, Bordeaux pulled his pickets in a little closer and ordered his troopers to prepare to mount. As quietly as they could manage, the patrol started toward the mouth of the ravine, leading their horses. The back way out was already deemed too severe a climb to make without causing a lot of noise. Anticipating such a move, Bloody Hand had sent part of his force close in to within about fifty yards of the ravine on foot. Crawling under cover of darkness, some had advanced even closer to the mouth of the gully, where the soldiers would try to exit. Unfortunately, Will Cason's prediction was swiftly confirmed. The first of the cavalry horses to clear the mouth of the ravine were shot down by Cheyenne warriors who had crept to within a couple dozen yards with a blistering volley of rifle fire — some of it from repeating rifles. The night became ablaze, lighting the darkness around them with the constant flashes of muzzles, causing the soldiers to fall back to the natural breastworks of the gully and take up defensive positions again. Lucky to escape with two horses as the only casualties despite the fury of fire that Bloody Hand's warriors had unleashed, Bordeaux now fully realized the desperate position he was in. "At least we can hold them off," he confided to Will. "Maybe if we make it too costly for them to try to overrun us, they'll decide we ain't worth the casualties."

"Maybe," Will said, flinching slightly when a stray bullet kicked dirt up between them. "They know they got us outnumbered, and figure we'll eventually run outta ammunition." He stroked his chin thoughtfully. "What we need is to even the odds with a lot more soldiers."

"Well, now, why didn't I think of that?" Bordeaux replied with more than a hint of sarcasm. "We'll just call for reinforcements."

Ignoring the sarcasm, Will asked, "Any chance you've got a bugler on this detail?"

"Barnhart's a bugler," Bordeaux answered.

"Other than blowin' that bugle, is he a pretty good man?"

Bordeaux shrugged. "As good as any of them, I guess. Why?"

"Might not work worth a damn," Will said, "but at least it's somethin' to try." He went on to explain what he had in mind.

Bordeaux responded, somewhat skeptical, but with no plan of his own and his situation looking to worsen the longer they stayed pinned down in the ravine. He looked at Corporal Kincaid, who had stationed himself privy to the conversation. "You think it'll work?"

"I ain't paid to think," Kincaid responded, "but it's better'n settin' here waitin' for them to get up the nerve to rush us."

"Get Barnhart over here," Bordeaux ordered.

Barnhart came when summoned, hunkered over as he ran to keep from exposing himself over the rim of the ravine. Grim faced, like his comrades, he reported to the lieutenant. Bordeaux nodded toward Will, who did the talking. "You got your bugle with you?" Barnhart replied that he always had it with him, even though it wasn't usually called for on a patrol of this size. "Well, we've got a little proposition for you, if you're willin'. You might get your ass shot full of Injun lead, but, hell, ain't none of us gonna live forever." He went on to explain what he had in mind. Barnhart listened without apparent enthusiasm, but in the end he agreed to give it a try.

"Watch your ass," Bordeaux cautioned as

Will and Barnhart removed everything that might rattle or make any discernible noise from their saddles.

"I always do," Will replied. "Come on, Barnhart." He started up the back side of the ravine, leading Spades. Passing two troopers stationed there, he continued up through the scattering of trees on the steep hillside, his eyes constantly scanning the darkness before him, with Barnhart close behind. Suddenly a rifle fired. It was off to his left about twenty-five yards, and he froze for a few seconds until he determined that it was aimed at the ravine and not at him. Glancing back to make sure Barnhart was still with him, he then continued the cautious climb up the hill. Forced to pause twice more when shadowy figures moved across the slope before them, they finally crested the hill and hurried down the other side, confident that they were in the clear.

Feeling it safe to mount then, they rode up the neighboring hill to the top, where they dismounted again. That was as far as Will planned to go. There was nothing to do then but wait out the night. "Might as well make yourself comfortable," Will said. "We've got a couple hours before sunup. Sleep if you want to. I'll be awake."

"Sleep?" Barnhart replied, astounded by

the suggestion. "I'd be afraid to close my eyes long enough to sleep. I thought we were done for back on that slope when that rifle went off right beside us. Damned if I can sleep with these hills crawling with those devils."

"Hell," Will said, "they're all surroundin' that hole where the lieutenant is." He hadn't realized that the private was that afraid. He hadn't heard a peep from him when they were sneaking through the circle of Cheyenne warriors. "You gonna be able to blow that thing when I tell you to?"

"I'll blow it," Barnhart replied, "even though it ain't gonna do nothing but tell the damn Injuns right where we are."

"Maybe, maybe not," Will said. "You just blow it when the time comes."

The hours passed slowly, and judging by the sounds of random shots throughout the night, there was no all-out assault by the Indians. At a little before dawn, however, things became quiet, and Will suspected that the Indian war chief was moving his warriors in preparation for an attack. *I reckon now's the time,* he thought, and reached over to poke Barnhart with the toe of his boot. The bugler had drifted off to sleep in spite of his protests before. "All right, boy, let's hear that bugle."

Barnhart gave it his all, piercing the still morning air with the clear notes of the cavalry charge. Will prodded him to keep it up, and within seconds, they heard the sound of a rifle volley as Bordeaux ordered his men to fire into the air as Will had requested. As an added touch, Bordeaux had the men raise a cheer as well.

Kneeling on a grassy hummock beside the valley, Bloody Hand jumped to his feet, astonished by the reaction in the ravine. He could hear the continuous blare of the bugle, which he judged to be no farther away than the second hill beyond. And it sounded as if it was now moving even closer. Being an astute leader, he quickly assimilated the facts as he saw them. He could not be certain, but it was obvious that the soldiers had been waiting for reinforcements. They had fired into the air when they heard the bugle, which seemed proof that they had done so to guide the other soldiers to them. Suddenly circumstances had changed. He could wait to see if a superior force was about to descend into the valley before making a decision. His warriors, however, were spread out in the open valley with no cover but the darkness, which was rapidly fading away. The worried look in Brave Elk's eyes reminded him that his future success as a war chief depended upon his ability to protect his warriors. "We will fight another day," he suddenly decided and sent Brave Elk to recall his braves. Within a quarter of an hour, the Indians had vanished into the hills.

"Get 'em ready to ride!" Bordeaux ordered Kincaid. "I wanna get the hell outta here before they find out we fooled them." A second cheer rose from the ravine, this one legitimate, as the *cavalry* in the form of Will and Barnhart galloped up to the rescue. Wasting no time for further cheers, the patrol filed out of the ravine and hastened to retreat back up the valley with no one wounded and two horses carrying double.

On ponies fresh from an overnight rest, Bloody Hand's warriors fled to the safety of the hills beyond the valley. Only one warrior stayed behind. From the cover of a grassy draw on the far side of the valley, Brave Elk scowled in anger when he saw the two white men ride up to join the retreating soldiers. One of them, a soldier, continued to blow the bugle. The other was the tall scout that had been the cause of trouble before. "It is him," Brave Elk muttered, "the same white devil. There are no soldiers."

Bloody Hand was beside himself when he heard Brave Elk's report. He went into a rage worthy of his reputation upon learning that he had been tricked into letting the soldiers escape. It was too late to turn back to pursue the patrol. His warriors had already scattered. It would take too long to regroup. In addition to that, the soldiers had a good hour's start by the time Brave Elk had caught up with him. And it was especially galling to him that the same white scout always seemed to be the one constant thorn in his side. *"Okohome!"* he spat. "He is like a coyote! He turns up everywhere to cause his mischief. One day I will have this coyote under my knife." He remained there, fuming with frustration, this one white scout having become a symbol to him of all the hatred he possessed for the soldiers, and the desire to kill him in close combat was beginning to overshadow his sense of caution. "I am going to follow them," he suddenly blurted.

"Our warriors are scattered, on their way back to the village," Brave Elk replied. "By the time we gathered them again, we could never catch the soldiers before they reached the fort."

"I am going alone," Bloody Hand said. "Maybe I will catch the coyote away from the soldiers. He seems to ride out far from the others."

Having known Bloody Hand since they were both boys, Brave Elk knew there was no changing his friend's mind once it was set on something. He was concerned that Bloody Hand might do something foolish in his passion to kill the scout that might cost him his life. "I will go with you," he said.

Robert Wilson walked out of the barn and stood staring toward the section across the creek where his sons, James and John were working to clear a few acres of sage. *Might be a waste of time,* he thought. The soil was pretty dry and poor. At least he had recovered the mule after the Indians had made off with his cow. That was something else to think about. He had to have a cow, and there were not many places to get one. *I guess I'll have to go into Dodge and see if I can trade for one with some of the folks on their way west.* He shook his head at the thought. Dodge wasn't that far away, but he seldom left his farm to go anywhere. It wasn't often he saw strangers out his way as well.

Two hours earlier the cavalry patrol had stopped to water their horses in the creek on their way back to Fort Dodge — two of the soldiers were riding double. The lieutenant — Robert couldn't remember his name — told him of their encounter with the Cheyenne war party and told him he should be on the alert for any more signs of Indian activity. *Be on the alert,* Robert thought. *What the hell does that mean?* What could he do against a bunch of savages that were too much for a cavalry patrol to handle? The lieutenant suggested that he might consider taking his family to the fort for a while until the army could do something to stop the raiding. "Hell, I can't do that. Who's gonna take care of my farm?"

"Who are you talking to?" Ruth Wilson asked, coming from the house.

"Nobody," Robert snorted, "just talkin' to myself."

"You've been out in the sun too long," she teased. "Where's your hat?"

The smile on her face froze in the next instant when her husband staggered backward with the sudden impact of an arrow embedded in his chest. Paralyzed by the sight, she was unable to move as she witnessed a second arrow, this one in Robert's stomach. Still unable to move, she screamed as he sank to his knees, his eyes glazed, stunned by the two shafts protruding from his body. "Ruth, run!" he managed to gasp.

Finally shaken from the terrible image that had rendered her helpless, she thought of the shotgun inside the door of the house, and ran to get it, screaming for her sons as she fled. A blow from Brave Elk's war ax as he stepped from the corner of the house sent her crashing to the ground only a few steps before reaching the door.

Across the creek, James and his brother, hearing their mother's screams, grabbed their bush axes and came running. With his rifle still strapped to his back, Bloody Hand notched another arrow and drew it back, waiting for the two boys to reach the creek. James, in the lead, was struck by the first arrow as Bloody Hand notched a second. Still frustrated by his failure to catch up to the cavalry patrol before they were close to Fort Dodge, and the lack of opportunity to catch Coyote alone, he had a need to vent his fury on someone. John was the only one left to satisfy the warrior's blood lust. "Let him come!" he shouted to Brave Elk, who was in the process of drawing his bow. Then he stepped out of the shadow of the barn to meet the charging young boy head-on, his bow and rifle aside, his knife in hand. It was hardly a contest, more aptly resembling a slaughter. Brave Elk, aware of his friend's need to kill with his knife and hands, stood by, watching as Bloody Hand deftly dodged the bush ax John swung at him, then struck lightning fast with his knife in the boy's gut. Screaming in pain, John was helpless as the muscular warrior lifted him off the ground by the knife in his stomach. Holding him over his head with both hands, Bloody Knife roared out his war cry, then slammed the body to the ground, where he withdrew his knife and took the boy's scalp.

Feeling somewhat appeased, but by no means satisfied, Bloody Hand joined Brave Elk in the scalping of the woman and the other boy, putting them out of their misery only after they had been scalped. They didn't bother with the father since he was bald and apparently already dead. "Leave the arrows," Bloody Hand said, "so the soldiers will know who did this." Then they made a quick search of the house, looking for guns and ammunition before setting it ablaze. Not waiting to watch it burn, they jumped on their ponies and galloped away, unaware of the lone witness to the massacre.

Lying flat on his belly behind a scrub oak at the crest of a low ridge more than two hundred yards away, Ned Spikes watched the bloody scene being played out at the farm by the creek. Afraid at first that he had stumbled into a Cheyenne war party, he resisted the natural urge to run, and stayed to observe the raid. He was unwilling to believe there were only two Indians in the raiding party, but after lying there for the entire slaughter, he realized there were no more. So he remained where he was and waited while the family was murdered. When the warriors went into the house, he muttered, "Don't set it on fire. There might be somethin' in there I can use." In a few minutes, when he saw smoke curling up from the window, he uttered an oath. "Damn." He was gratified, however, to see the two hostiles immediately jump on their horses and leave.

Afraid to rush down to the farm immediately, in case the two decided to return, he procrastinated for several minutes, weighing the danger of it against the possibility of salvaging something before the fire destroyed everything. With greed the deciding factor, he got on his horse and rode down to the farmyard. He paused momentarily to survey the death scene, noting the bodies lying in the dust of the yard. Starting then to continue to the burning house, he stopped when he heard a moan from Robert Wilson. Dismounting, Ned went to the wounded man and knelt beside him.

"Help me," Robert murmured.

Ned took a look at the two arrows protruding from Robert's body and shook his head. "You're dyin', mister, sure as hell. The rest of your family is already dead." He lifted the doomed man's head so he could look directly into his eyes. "Now there ain't no reason to take any secrets to the grave with you. If you got some money hid in that house somewhere, you might as well tell me where it is."

"No money." Robert groaned. "For God's sake, help me."

"It ain't gonna buy you nothin' when you get to hell," Ned persisted. "Might as well tell me where it is." When Robert slowly shook his head without replying, Ned shrugged. "I'll help you on your way." With that, he pulled his knife from its sheath, and in one quick motion, cut Robert's throat from ear to ear. "Now let's see if there's anything in that damn house I can use."

Chapter 5

"I don't wanna go to any old dance," Emma Lawton complained as her mother tied the sash on the little girl's dress.

"It'll be fun," Sarah promised. "We'll meet some of the other families. They might have children your age."

"I wish Will would come back," Emma said.

"I'd like to see Will again, too," her mother said, "but I wouldn't count on it if I were you. He's busy scouting for the army and I'm sure he'd visit if he was anywhere near here. But I doubt that will happen. Now, let me look at you." She held Emma at arm's length and smiled proudly. "Just as pretty as a picture," she said. As much as her daughter, Sarah missed the soft-spoken rider of the wilderness. In the few short days they had spent together on the journey to Fort Dodge she had developed a dependence upon his strength as well as a trust in his character. She had told herself that it was a natural feeling toward anyone who had saved her life and that of her child, unwilling to admit to herself that it might go deeper than that.

Looking over her mother's shoulder as Sarah knelt before her, Emma announced, "Mama, there's a soldier coming."

Sarah turned to see a young officer striding confidently toward her wagon. Resplendent in his dress uniform, and walking as if on parade, the lieutenant hastened to offer his assistance when Sarah climbed down, wondering about the purpose of his call. "Lieutenant Braxton Bradley, ma'am, at your service. I've come to escort you and your daughter to the dance," he proclaimed as introduction.

Properly impressed, Sarah was surprised, unaware that an escort would be arranged for her and Emma. It was obviously more of Edna Boyles' arrangements. The sergeant-major's wife had been a frequent visitor the past few days, sometimes accompanied by one of the officers' wives, as they did their best to make Sarah feel that she was not alone. "How do you do?" Sarah politely replied. "I must say, this is quite a surprise, one I hadn't expected." She then introduced her daughter to the lieutenant, and for the child's benefit, he gallantly took Emma's hand, bowed and kissed it. His act had the desired effect upon the six-year-old, causing her to giggle with delight.

When Sarah ventured to speculate that the lieutenant must have been detailed to escort her by Edna Boyle, Braxton replied, "Not at all, ma'am. In fact, I requested the honor myself."

Not certain what she should make of that, Sarah hesitated to respond. "Well, Emma and I appreciate your kindness," she finally managed. "Don't we, honey?"

The evening proved to be a much-needed tonic for Sarah. She didn't realize how much until she found herself laughing happily and clapping her hands in the Virginia reel, and whirling merrily in Braxton's arms when they waltzed. Lieutenant Braxton Bradley was more than convincing in his role as the perfect escort, and as the evening matured, she learned a great deal about the bachelor officer from Philadelphia, his ambitions, and his hopes. Sarah could not help herself from admiring his jet-black hair that framed his perfectly proportioned face to form a classic profile as he guided Emma through the steps of a reel. It was not until the dance was over and she was saying her good-byes to the other ladies who had made her feel so welcome that she suddenly was visited by a wave of guilt. She had no right to be enjoying herself and should have been wearing black instead of the print dress she had on — with Edward so recently departed. But she didn't even have a black dress, she told herself. She immediately vowed to be more mindful of the respect she owed her late husband's memory. But then Braxton strode across the dance floor to walk her home, and his infectious smile made her forget her guilt.

During the walk back to her wagon, under a clear night sky filled with stars, he asked about her future plans. She confided that she had chosen to return to Westport simply because she didn't know what else to do. "I don't know anyone in Santa Fe, and at this point, I cannot say I have any definite plans once I return to Westport. Obviously, I can't stay here. Emma and I have a wagon and two horses, some household possessions, and that's all." She hesitated then, realizing she was baring her soul to the lieutenant. "I'm sorry. I didn't mean to burden you with my troubles."

He seemed genuinely interested. When he had seen her and Emma safely back to the wagon, she extended her hand and thanked him on behalf of her daughter and herself for sacrificing his evening to provide an escort for them. He took her hand, then asked if he could see her again. Later, when Emma was asleep, she would question her reason for saying yes in answer to Braxton's request. It seemed innocent enough when he asked, and she felt it impolite to tell him no. But now she had doubts. *Was it wrong?* She wasn't sure. *Oh, Edward,* she sighed inwardly, *please don't think harshly of me.* She lay awake for a long while, laboring with the guilt with which she now chose to burden herself — guilt for having enjoyed the evening immensely, and for a time, forgetting that she was recently widowed. *I'll worry about it some other time,* she decided, closed her eyes and tried to sleep. But sleep did not come easily, for she could not escape the sobering knowledge that she had no skills to sustain her daughter and herself beyond those that involved being a wife and mother. And without a husband, those skills were useless. With Edward so recently in the grave, she was not ready to entertain thoughts of someday marrying again. And yet she knew that she might have to ignore her feelings and do what was best for Emma.

"Well, I'll be damned . . . ," Ben Clarke

blurted when Will ambled into headquarters at Camp Supply. "I thought you were dead. What's it been since you left here? Ten days?"

"Nine," Will corrected. "I've got some dispatches here for the colonel."

"Nine, then," Clarke replied. "It ain't but ninety miles to Fort Dodge. What did you do, carry that horse on your back?"

"I ran into some trouble," Will said. "Then I rode a piece with Lieutenant Bordeaux — helped him with a little scoutin' on the way back — they've had some trouble with Cheyenne raidin' parties pretty close in to the fort. When I was done with that, I came on back here with dispatches from Fort Dodge." He didn't feel it necessary to go into greater detail about the skirmish with Bloody Hand's Cheyenne war party, or his encounter on the Cimarron and Sarah Lawton.

Clarke studied his best scout thoughtfully as Will explained his reason for delay. "Well," he said, after thinking it over for a moment, "there wasn't much goin' on here, anyway." In fact, the only troop action scheduled for the next couple of days was a routine patrol south of the post, and the officer in command was to be Lieutenant Lyman Bridges. Two scouts, Bill Bellmer and Cody Johnson, had already been assigned. He could send Will along as well, but the lieutenant was still a little chafed over his most recent confrontation with the independent scout. "All right," he said, "Lieutenant Bridges is leadin' a patrol out toward Wolf Creek. Bellmer and Johnson are goin' with him. You can go with them." He paused to watch Will's facial reaction, but there was none. He continued. "Or you can ride dispatch again back to Fort Dodge." This time he thought he detected a hint of relief in Will's face.

"I expect I'll ride dispatch," Will said without hesitation.

"I thought you might," Clarke said, suppressing a grin. "First thing in the mornin', then." Amused by the scout's anticipated response in order to avoid riding with Bridges, Clarke was not aware that Will's decision was weighted more toward riding to Fort Dodge for another opportunity to see Sarah. Will was reluctant to admit that to himself, and more inclined to credit his dislike for the lieutenant with his decision to ride dispatch.

"Howdy, stranger," Mickey Bledsoe sang out when Will walked into the saloon. "Where've you been? I thought the Injuns

112

mighta got hold of your scalp."

Will grinned and replied, "I've been up to Dodge for a spell, just waitin' till I could get back to drink some of your watered-down poison."

His remark was easily overheard in the compact saloon by the couple seated at one of the three tables in the tent. Her back to the bar, Lula turned to verify the voice she thought she recognized. Seeing that it was, indeed, the tall, rugged scout, she moved her chair around to get a better view, a move that seemed to irritate the soldier who had been plying her with Mickey's alcohol for the past half hour. "I knew you couldn't stay away for long," she called out.

"Hello, Lula," he replied, glancing her way for only a second. It would have been impossible to miss the couple at the table when he first walked in. And even though her back was to the door, Lula was easily identified by the expansive behind filling the chair. He also caught the deep scowl of irritation on her companion's face, and in view of that, decided it best to turn his focus back to Mickey. Lula, however, was not content to let it go with nothing more than a nod in her direction. She had long envisioned a conquest of the untamed young scout, and was willing to jeopardize a sure three-dollar transaction to pursue one that she might not even charge for.

The slighted corporal was not at all pleased with her attention to the civilian scout, and grabbing her arm, pulled her roughly back around in her chair. "By God," he swore, "I'm the one's been buyin' you drinks here. And I'm thinkin' you oughta have enough in you by now to get you primed. Let's go in the back and have a tussle while I've still got enough money left to pay for it."

Being a businesswoman, Lula decided she really couldn't afford to lose the corporal's money, so she tried to work the two parties to accomplish both goals. "Don't get cross with me, darlin'," she cooed. "I'm just sayin' hello to an old friend. You're gonna get your ride. Why don't you go on back in the room, and I'll be there in a little ol' minute."

"Hell, I will," the soldier spat. "We'll go back there together, and I mean right now!"

"All right, honey," Lula quickly replied, trying to control his agitation, "we'll go now. I'll just speak to my friend on the way. All right?"

"I'll be damned," the corporal responded, got to his feet, and pulled her up from her chair.

Aware of the altercation at the table, both

Mickey and Will chose not to notice as long as the situation did not get out of hand. Will had no interest in anything Lula had to offer, and at the moment, wished that he had not teased her before. He had to wonder whether he might have eventually succumbed to Lula's advances when the tensions below his belt became too severe if he had not met Sarah Lawton. He was reluctant to admit that she had been in his thoughts more than he felt healthy. One thing her acquaintance had done, however, was to make him realize the difference between the rough camp followers he had been exposed to and the Sarah Lawtons of the world. He was suddenly struck with a strong urge to see Sarah and Emma again and the thought of it prompted him to say to Mickey, "I'll just have a couple of short ones, and then I'll be on my way. I'm leavin' early in the mornin'."

On her way toward the back room after the corporal, Lula heard Will's remark and stopped. "Don't leave till I get done here, Will. I won't be long and we can have a drink."

"Damn you, bitch!" the soldier cursed, still smarting from her obvious disdain for him when Will walked in. "I told you to get your fat ass in that room!" He grabbed the back of her dress, ripping it as he jerked her toward the door and causing her to stumble over a chair.

"All right, soldier!" Mickey exclaimed. "I ain't gonna stand for that kinda rough-housin' in my place."

Will walked over and helped Lula to her feet. "You all right?" he asked.

"Hell, yes," she replied indignantly, her face flushed with the combination of anger and alcohol. Then she turned and spat at the corporal, "But you can get your sorry ass outta here. I wouldn't lay down for you for a hundred dollars."

"Why, you cheatin', double-dealin' bitch," the corporal yelled, and started toward her.

Stepping between them, Will confronted the infuriated soldier. "Just hold it right there, Corporal. This little misunderstandin' is over, so there ain't no need to go any further with it. The lady has changed her mind about takin' your money, so you'd best go on back to your barracks and sleep off some of that whiskey."

This had the effect of throwing kerosene on a red-hot stove. "Why, you son of a bitch!" he roared. "This ain't none of your business, and I'll break your damn back for you if you don't get outta my face." A husky man, he drew back his fist and launched a wild punch at Will.

Will quickly stepped back out of range, easily avoiding the punch. "I wish to hell you hadn't done that," he said calmly. "Now I reckon it is my business." Like a crazed bull, the corporal put his head down and charged, catching Will in the midsection and driving him up against the wall of the tent. It took Will a few minutes to figure the corporal out. His fighting style was to simply keep his head down and blindly throw lefts and rights, most of them landing on Will's stomach and chest. It was frustrating at first because the only targets for Will's retaliation was the soldier's back and the back of his head, which Will was not eager to break his knuckles on. And the soldier pressed so close upon him while swinging away with his fists that Will had no room to land any blows that might have effect. Finally he straightened him up with a firm knee to his chin. Then, before the corporal could get back in his turtle shell defense, Will staggered him with a series of punches to his jaw. Trying desperately to keep from losing his feet, the soldier fell against the bar, where Mickey ended the fight with a sharp blow to the back of his head with a three-foot piece of timber he had fashioned into a club. The corporal slumped to the floor, out cold.

"Damn!" Will exclaimed, breathless. "That boy's a handful."

Mickey came from behind the bar and together they dragged the corporal out of the saloon and left him on the ground where the hot summer sun could boil some of the alcohol out of him. Lula was waiting for them when they came back inside. "I guess I owe you a free ride," the dowdy prostitute said to Will, "for defending my honor with that bastard."

At a loss for a few seconds, Will tried to reply in some way that would not hurt her feelings. In truth, he would have reacted the same if the corporal had abused a stray dog. He settled for a lie. "That's mighty nice of you, Lula, darlin' — and hard for me to pass up — but I'm already late to report to the colonel and I'd best be on my way before he sends somebody to look for me." The look of disappointment on her face was unmistakable. "Workin' for the army sure takes up a man's free time," he added weakly. Wasting no more time, he said so long to Mickey and was immediately out the door, leaving a perplexed Lula to wonder if the conquest was hopeless.

"You don't know what you're missing," she murmured to herself woefully. Her despair lasted for no more than a few seconds, however, before her practical mind returned to business. Dismissing it with a sigh, she took a dipper of water from the bucket behind the bar and went outside to kneel down beside the corporal, who was just in the process of recovering his senses. "Here, darlin'," she cooed. "Take a drink of this cool water. Come on inside and let me clean some of the blood off your face. Then you can have your ride." *Three dollars is three dollars,* she thought. *No sense in letting him spend it on whiskey.*

It was almost dusk when Will rode into Fort Dodge. He guided Spades straight to headquarters to deliver his dispatches, but his mind was firmly concentrating on the lone wagon parked in the trees near the riverbank. Something new had been added, a tent the size of those used by officers in the field. Will was pleased to see that the army was making it as comfortable as possible for Sarah and Emma.

As quickly as he could, he gave the dispatches to the duty sergeant, who said he would give them to the officer of the day as soon as he returned from touring the guard posts. Will told him that he would check in later to see if there was anything going back to Camp Supply. "I ain't goin' anyplace before mornin', anyway."

His business for the army taken care of, he then headed straight for Sarah's wagon. On the way, he quickly tried to think about what he would say to her. Having finally given up on trying to convince himself that he had no serious thoughts toward Sarah, he spent almost the entire journey from Camp Supply deciding if he should tell her. Everything he had rehearsed on the ride had suddenly flown from his mind. But one thing he was sure of was his desire to marry Sarah Lawton. For a man who had wandered aimlessly all his life, there was now this one certainty. He had told himself that it was maybe a little too early in their relationship, but the more he thought about it, the more sensible arrangement it seemed to be for all three parties. He was ready to change his aimless free-roving lifestyle. She needed someone to take care of her. And he was certain Emma would heartily approve.

He was determined to express his feelings for her and her daughter, but he didn't want to be too bold since she had been a widow for such a short time. *I know it ain't been long since your husband died,* he rehearsed. *But you need someone to take care of you, and things just happen a lot quicker out here on the frontier. They have to. There's too much to take care of — Indians, drought, bad weather — you need a man, Emma needs a father.* He shook his head, dissatisfied. "I'll just tell her what's in my heart," he said to Spades. "It might be too soon to even think about it, but she needs to know what I'm thinkin', and I'm willin' to wait for her to decide."

Approaching the wagon, he could see the glow of a fire beyond it in the early twilight. *A cup of coffee wouldn't go bad right now,* he thought as his heart quickened in anticipation of seeing her again. Within a dozen yards now, he called out, "Hello, the wagon!"

A small head peered around the tailgate of the wagon. "Will!" Emma cried out in excitement. Within seconds, she was running to meet him, laughing delightedly. He leaned over in the saddle and reached down to scoop her up. With her arms locked tightly around his neck, she exclaimed, "I knew you'd come back."

"Nothin' coulda kept me away, Whiskers," he assured her, knowing now that the statement could not be any more sincere than it was with the little girl in his arms. "Where's your mama?" he asked.

"On the other side of the wagon," Emma

replied. "She'll be glad to see you!"

With a feeling that he was coming home, he guided Spades around the wagon and the tent next to it, where he found Sarah seated beside the fire on an army camp stool. The moment of joy he anticipated was drowned in a flash by the sight of a young officer sitting with her, drinking coffee.

Surprised and not quite certain what her feelings were at that moment, Sarah rose from the stool to greet her visitor. "Will," she said, speaking slowly in an effort to hide her embarrassment, although she could not justify any reason for embarrassment, "you came back. We were just having coffee." She turned to the officer briefly. "This is the man who rescued Emma and me," she said. "Will, this is Lieutenant Bradley."

Still in the saddle with Emma wrapped around his neck, Will was stunned and fighting hard not to show it. "Lieutenant," he heard himself say, "Will Cason."

The lieutenant rose and walked over to extend his hand. "Braxton Bradley," he stated confidently. Will shifted Emma around in order to shake Bradley's hand. "Would you care to step down and join us for coffee?" the lieutenant invited, then turned to give Sarah a questioning look.

"Yes, Will," she quickly responded. "Join

us for coffee." She could not rid her conscience of thoughts of guilt for no other reason than she had allowed herself to think about Will Cason many times since he had gone.

Impatient with the apparent lull in conversation, Emma gave Will's hand a squeeze. "We got a tent!" she exclaimed. "It's almost like living in a house."

Tearing his gaze away from Sarah, Will looked down into the precocious child's face. "I see you do," he replied. There was little doubt in his mind now as to where the tent and the camp stools had come from. Not only did Bradley look young and fit, he was handsome to boot, and Will had a sinking feeling that he was a fool to have entertained the slightest notion of wooing Sarah Lawton. At that moment, he had an urgent desire to run. "Uh, thank you just the same," he replied to the invitation, "but I expect I'll be gettin' along. I just wanted to see if you folks were all right."

"Ahh, Will," Emma whined in disappointment as he unlocked her arms from his neck and lowered her gently to the ground.

"I have to go, Whiskers. I've got things to do," he told her. "I'll come back to see you sometime when your ma ain't entertainin' company." He forced a smile for her. "You

123

make sure you take care of your ma, now."

Although he tried to disguise it, it was fairly obvious to Sarah how disappointed he was, and she was astute enough to know that his embarrassment was due to certain feelings for her that ran deeper than concern for her welfare. She owed Will Cason her life and the life of her daughter, and she could not deny having considered what it would be like to always have him. It pained her now to see him hurt. "Please, Will," she said, "won't you stay and have some coffee?"

"No, thank you, Sarah. I'm kinda short on time. I'll drop by next time I'm around."

"You're always welcome," she said. "Emma can't talk about you enough."

He smiled. "She's a special little lady. I'll try to come see her again." With nothing more to say, he politely touched a finger to the brim of his hat, nudged Spades with his heels, and rode off into the fading light.

Ain't that a helluva note, he thought. *You damn fool. Lula's more your speed.* He nudged Spades a little more firmly than usual, and misunderstanding, the bay gelding broke immediately into a gallop, causing Will to pull gently back on the reins. Knowing he could find a cot in the infantry barracks, he nevertheless guided Spades down

124

along the riverbank, preferring his own company. Intent upon putting some distance between his camp and the army post, he continued until he was sure he couldn't hear the noises of the fort. As he rode, he tried to recall the scene at Sarah's campfire in detail. Maybe it wasn't as it seemed to him at the time. The lieutenant may have been merely making a courtesy call, maybe even under orders from the colonel. *Maybe I'll stop by in the morning.*

It was difficult to sleep that night. He couldn't seem to turn his mind off, or prevent his thoughts from returning to Sarah. Could he have been so wrong? His instincts were usually reliable, but serious thoughts had never been spent on a woman before, and the possibility that he might one day marry had never occurred to him — until Sarah. It seemed a natural union with Sarah and Emma, and his senses had told him that she might be thinking the same way. It was a troubling time for him, and it was not until the wee hours of the morning that he finally fell asleep.

Riding back to the post the next morning, he was surprised to see an unusual amount of activity. The bugler sounded *assembly* and it appeared a company-sized detail was already in the process of shaping up and falling into formation on the parade ground. Something was going on and he decided he'd better see what it was. When he walked into the orderly room, Sergeant-Major Boyle greeted him with, "Where the hell have you been? I sent somebody lookin' for you an hour ago."

"Well, I reckon they didn't look in the right place," Will returned without emotion. "What's goin' on?"

Boyle explained that a rider had arrived at dawn carrying the news of an attack on a military scouting expedition near Pawnee Creek, not far from Fort Larned, another brazen raid close to an army post. The rider, a private, had made his way through the surrounding Cheyenne warriors, but was faced with a second band of warriors between him and Fort Larned. So he rode all night to get to Dodge. "C Company is saddlin' up to go hunt for the raiders. I told Captain Fischer that you knew that country between here and Pawnee Fork better'n anybody I knew, so get your ass ready to go," Boyle said.

"I'm as ready as I reckon I'll get," Will replied, "but Ben Clarke is probably gonna be lookin' for me to get back to Supply."

"Don't worry about that," Boyle said. "I'll take care of Ben Clarke. We'll most likely have somebody headin' over that way in the next day or two. You'd best get on out there and report to Captain Fischer."

"All right," Will said, and walked out the door. He found Fischer talking to his officers, one of whom was his friend, Lieutenant Bordeaux.

The lieutenant broke out a wide grin as soon as he saw Will approaching. "Relax, boys," he joked, "we're gonna be all right now."

Fischer, a serious man, and one not familiar with Will, turned to cast a scrutinizing gaze upon the easy-riding scout on the bay horse. Cason had been highly recommended by Sergeant-Major Boyle, but the captain had expected to see an older man. He frowned and continued to stare as Will pulled Spades to a halt before the circle of officers. With a grin and a nod, he gestured to Bordeaux. Following the gesture, Fischer glanced at Bordeaux, then returned his gaze to greet Will. "You're Cason?"

"Yes, sir," Will replied.

"I've got good scouts, but Sergeant-Major Boyle tells me you know the country better than most between here and Pawnee Creek," Fischer said. "I hope he's right." He nodded toward the lieutenant standing just to his right and said, "Lieutenant Gates is responsible for the scouts. You can report to him when we're finished here."

Will glanced at the officer indicated and nodded. Lieutenant Gates was a thin man with dark brown hair and a drooping mustache that just touched either side of his chin. "How soon are you gonna pull out?" Will asked.

"Inside thirty minutes," Fischer answered before Gates could respond. "So be ready to ride."

"Right," Will said, meeting the captain's unblinking gaze. Looking back at Gates, he said, "I've got just one little chore I've got to do and I'll be ready." Not waiting for any word of permission from Gates or the captain, he turned Spades and headed across the parade ground, toward the lone wagon by the river. The possibility of a fight with Indians was not enough to take his mind from the visit he had decided to make the night before. Lieutenant Braxton Bradley was apparently assigned to another company since he was not among the group of officers surrounding Captain Fischer. Will was not sure whether that was good or bad. He wasn't eager to campaign with the lieutenant, but he wondered if he'd rather have him in the field with him instead of here with Sarah.

"Howdy, Will." The voice came from a group of soldiers standing near the officers.

He turned to discover the smiling face of Corporal Kincaid. With a wide grin he replied, "Damn, Kincaid, is that you?" He paused then to shake the corporal's hand. "I'll talk to you a little later. I've got a chore I've gotta do before we move out."

Kincaid stood watching him as he rode across the parade ground, headed for the lone wagon by the river. It was not difficult to put two and two together, and a wry smile slowly spread across Kincaid's face.

She was standing before the fire with a coffee cup in her hand when he rounded the corner of the tent. Emma saw him first, however, and ran to meet him. He climbed down from the saddle and the little girl took his hand and led him to the fire, beaming at her mother as if to say *I told you so.* Sarah put her cup down and went to meet him. Smiling warmly, she extended her hand to him. He grasped it with his left hand since Emma had no intention of surrendering his right. "I was just having one more cup of coffee before I went down to the river to wash some of our things," Sarah said. "I'm sure there's a cup left in the pot."

"That would go mighty good right now,"

he said. "I haven't had any this mornin'."
He didn't tell her that it was due to his late
rising, the result of a near sleepless night. "I
don't have but a minute or two. I got
snagged by the sergeant-major to go out
with C Company and they're about ready
to leave now."

She got another cup while Emma was
busy complaining about his short visits.
Handing him the coffee, she said, "Will, I'm
so glad you stopped by this morning. I was
afraid I had seemed a little rude last night.
You know you'll always be welcome to visit
Emma and me."

"Think nothin' of it," Will replied. "I
didn't wanna just barge in on your party."

"Don't be silly," she said with a chuckle.
"It wasn't a party. Braxton had just brought
over these stools and I made some coffee
for him."

Feeling better about the situation already,
he gulped his coffee down. "I wish I had
more time to visit. I don't know how long
I'll be gone on this scout — might be a
while — but I'll come back to see you as
soon as I can — if that's all right."

"Of course it's all right," she quickly
replied, walking him to his horse.

He paused a long moment, hesitating. He
had been determined that he was going to

express what was in his heart, but with Emma clutching his hand, he was not comfortable talking of such things in front of the child. Besides, there was no time. He could see the troops already forming up, preparing to ride. "I'll see you when I see you," he finally said, handed her the cup, and stepped up in the saddle. Turning Spades around, he paused briefly and said, "I got some things I wanna tell you." He reached down and playfully ruffled Emma's hair, then nudged Spades and was off, relieved of the feeling from the night before.

CHAPTER 6

After talking it over with his scouts, Captain Fischer accepted the general opinion among them that the Cheyenne band that had attacked the patrol out of Fort Larned would probably head northwest toward Walnut Creek, possibly to join a larger village on the Smoky Hill. Will Cason confirmed the location of more than one village on that river — both Cheyenne and Arapaho. "But that was about a month ago when I scouted that part of the country," he said. "Don't mean they're still there, but that's a favorite campin' place for 'em, all along that river."

"All right," Fischer said, "we'll start out in that direction." He laid out a map to indicate the line of march to his scouts — Corporal Kincaid, one other soldier, and three civilians — then sent them forward about a quarter of a mile to each side. At Lieutenant Bordeaux's suggestion, the captain sent Will out alone to range about a mile ahead of the column. Will preferred to work that way, hoping to discover the presence of any hostiles before they spotted the cavalry column. There was no argument from the other scouts, civilian or army, for most of them felt more comfortable closer to the column. There was always the danger of being ambushed, but Will had complete confidence in his eyes and ears, and his horse. So when all was ready, he gave Spades the signal and loped off ahead of the company.

Like his idol, Woqini, whom the white men called Roman Nose, Bloody Hand was not a chief or medicine man, but a fierce leader in war. When little more than a boy in the Colorado Territory, Bloody Hand had gone into the mountains to fast and seek his medicine dream. After going without food for three days and nights, he had fallen into a deep sleep and dreamed of a monstrous bear killing a deer. The bear ate only the heart of the deer and left the rest of the carcass to the wolves and coyotes. When he had awakened and was on his way back to the village, he carelessly crossed a path between a mother bear and her cubs, inciting her fury. He barely escaped with his life when the bear slashed at him with a huge

133

paw, grazing his left hand. Though only a glancing blow, the bear's sharp claws opened a long cut on the boy's hand. Although weak from his fast, he summoned the strength to run. When he returned to his home, he told his father of his dream and the encounter with the enraged mother bear. His father gave him the name Bloody Hand as a result and told him that if his medicine was to be strong, he must never eat the flesh of a deer, only the heart.

Bloody Hand appeared to be in a state of anger ever since Roman Nose's death. He was in the war party that had trapped the soldiers on a small island in the Arickaree River almost a year before. The battle was theirs to win on that day until Roman Nose was struck by a soldier's bullet, effectively killing the will of the rest of the warriors, who became reluctant to continue the siege without their leader. But was it the soldier's bullet that really killed Roman Nose? Some said the real killer was a woman in his own village who inadvertently and innocently used an iron fork to tend the warrior's meat that morning. Consequently, his medicine, which shielded him from an enemy's bullet, was contaminated, since it was effective only if his food was prepared in the natural Cheyenne custom, using no white man's utensils. Bloody Hand and two others had carried Roman Nose away from the battle. He was with him later that night when the brave warrior died. He promised him then that he would never surrender to the white man as long as he could draw breath into his lungs.

Resting now beside Walnut Creek, Bloody Hand thought about his pledge to Roman Nose and knew that the noble warrior would be pleased with the success of the battle with the soldiers at Pawnee Fork. His medicine was strong. None of the soldiers' bullets could strike him, and he had killed two of them himself in close combat with his knife and ax — which gained him much more honor than if he had killed them at a distance with his rifle. It was a great victory for his warriors. They had killed eleven of the thirty soldiers. His only disappointment was that he had not seen the coyote there. The white scout had seemed to show up everywhere during the past few weeks, so Bloody Hand almost expected him to be with the soldiers. *Our paths will cross again,* he thought, *and I will add his scalp to my lance.*

"The others are ready to leave now," Brave Elk said as he led his pony up from the creek bank.

Bloody Hand nodded and got to his feet. "Good. The ponies are well rested now. We should reach the village before dark."

Even though the war party had stopped a while that morning to eat and rest the horses, they were still able to cover the distance from Walnut Creek to their village on the Smoky Hill before darkness fell. There was a great celebration in the village upon the war party's triumphant return. When told of the number of soldiers killed, the elders decided that a dance was in order to honor the warriors. Bloody Hand's kills and coups were the theme of more than one of the songs sung that night. His stature as a leader of men continued to climb, approaching that of Roman Nose. It was almost dawn before the people drifted off to their lodges to sleep.

It was close to noon on the second day out when one of the forward scouts called back to the column, "Rider comin' in." After a few seconds had passed, he yelled, "It's Will Cason."

Will, holding Spades to a comfortable lope, rode past the scouts and reported to Captain Fischer. "I think I found where they stopped to rest their horses after the attack," he said.

"You *think* you found it?" Fischer retorted, somewhat testily, his behind a bit sore after hours in the saddle.

Will, taken aback for a second by the officer's attitude, replied, "All right, I by-God found where the war party stopped."

Fischer couldn't suppress a grin at his scout's response. "How far ahead?"

"Two miles," Will replied, "no more'n that — on Walnut Creek."

"Good," the captain said. "We can rest and water our horses there."

Once they reached Walnut Creek, Fischer gave permission for the men to build small fires to make coffee while the horses were watered. Will let Spades drink, then drifted over to share coffee with Corporal Kincaid and Lieutenant Bordeaux while Captain Fischer searched the banks of the creek, looking at tracks and any other sign that might give him any information about the war party he was chasing — a waste of time, by Will's thinking. By this time there was a confusion of tracks with shod cavalry hooves mixed with those of unshod Indian ponies. When he had finished, having found nothing that would be of any use to him, Fischer walked over to stand before Will, who was stretched out beneath a tree, drinking his coffee. Hands on hips, striking an impatient pose, he asked, "Shouldn't you be scouting this area for information that might tell us where they went from here?"

"Don't need to," Will replied, taking another sip of coffee from his metal cup.

"Why not?" Fischer insisted.

"Already done it. I looked it over before I went back to get you, so you and your soldiers wouldn't trample all over what sign there was." He turned to point toward the cottonwoods behind him. "They rode outta here between those two big trees yonder, headed for the Smoky Hill. That's where we knew they were headin' all along."

Watching Fischer's face as the captain nodded solemnly, Harvey Bordeaux grinned to himself. Fischer was learning fast what the lieutenant already knew — you can put your trust in Will Cason. Just let him alone and he'll do the job for you. "All right," Fischer said, "we'll rest here long enough for the men to get some coffee and a little something to eat. How far are we from the Smoky Hill?"

"About thirty-five miles, I expect," Will replied. "I doubt you could make it before dark without runnin' the horses into the ground."

Fischer nodded thoughtfully. He was considering a night march to get into position to launch a dawn attack on the village as Custer had done on Black Kettle's village on the Washita. Somehow sensing what the captain might be speculating, Will offered a gentle reminder. "Course I don't know where this bunch's village is on the Smoky Hill, so I can't say how far it is to their village — only how far to the Smoky Hill."

Fischer didn't say anything for a moment while he silently rebuffed himself for forgetting that little detail. "We'll rely on you to find that village in the morning," he finally said. He glanced at Bordeaux, then raised an eyebrow and remarked, "I'm beginning to think you were right, Harvey." Then he turned to leave them. Bordeaux's grin returned to his face, for he knew what Fischer meant. The lieutenant had advised the captain earlier that Will was the best scout in the regiment.

A gentle mist lay upon the slowly moving water as the sun climbed up from the prairie behind him. Spades' ears flickered constantly, searching the quiet morning air for sounds of other life, but there were none, except for the scolding of a crow from its perch in the top of the tallest cottonwood on the opposite bank of the river. They had been there, but they were gone now. Will nudged Spades with his heels and the patient bay stepped slowly down into the water. Climbing the bank on the other side, he reined the gelding back for a few moments while he surveyed the empty circles where tipis had once stood. Then he prodded his horse again and slowly walked it through the pattern of circles. He counted forty-two lodges, and from the dead grass within the circles, he knew that the village had been there for some time. Tracks from horses and lodge poles following the river west also told him that the village had moved no more than one or two days ago, apparently almost as soon as the war party returned. All this told Will that the hostile Cheyenne expected a sizable detachment of soldiers to follow them, and they most likely were seeking to join another village farther along the river. The question facing Captain Fischer would now be the strength of the combined villages. It might be more than a company of cavalry could handle. *I'd best get on back and tell him his village has moved,* he thought.

"Okohome," Brave Elk spat in angry amazement to see the white man Bloody Hand had named Coyote. Watching him from a point some distance west on the op-

posite bank, Brave Elk seemed hypnotized by the actions of the white scout as he looked around the former camp site. Like the animal for which he had been named, he almost seemed to sniff around the ground where the lodges had stood. Brave Elk turned to one of his two companions. "It is the white coyote that the soldiers follow. I think his medicine is strong, but if we can catch this coyote and take his scalp back to Bloody Hand it will be a great loss for the soldiers." The appearance of the scout at the site of their village was verification to the Cheyenne warrior that the precaution of moving the people was a wise one, and Brave Elk felt that if they could kill the coyote, the soldiers would not know where to look for them. "Quick!" one of the other two said, "he is turning away."

Just as he turned Spades back toward the water, Will was startled by a sudden puff of sand in the riverbank a foot or so from the horse's front hooves. It was followed almost immediately by the sharp crack of a rifle. Spades reared up on his back legs, then leaped forward to plunge into the dark water when Will gave him a firm kick. Off to his right, Will saw three warriors riding along the bluffs in an effort to cut him off. "Get me outta here, boy," he implored and the big bay was quick to respond. Charging up from the water, he scaled the opposite bank and threaded his way through the willows at a full gallop with the sounds of wild shots stinging the air around him.

He was not inclined to call on Spades to race the swift Indian ponies for any length of time. On heart and pride alone, the big horse opened a sizable lead on the three warriors, but Will knew it was unlikely he could hold it. So he looked for the first reasonable cover he thought he could defend and hoped there were no more warriors behind the three shooting at him now. The problem facing him was the gentle rolling terrain of the prairie stretching out before him. Still Spades drove on at full gallop, his powerful stride pounding the prairie floor in a rhythmic beat, and Will knew he would continue the pace until he fell dead as a result. Determined not to let that happen, Will headed for a low mound with two lone trees standing on the crest. It didn't offer the best of cover, but it was the best he could see.

He jumped from the saddle as soon as he pulled Spades to a halt. Taking a quick assessment of the spot he had landed in, he led the bay behind the highest point of the mound, which was still not high enough to shield the entire horse. Snatching his rifle from the saddle, along with an ammunition belt, he scrambled up behind one of the two trees. The one he chose had a smaller trunk than its partner, but the decision was an easy one. The other tree was dying, having obviously been struck by lightning, which was enough to tell Will that it was an unlucky tree and he didn't like the idea of depending on an unlucky tree to protect him. He cocked the Henry and waited.

His wait wasn't long, since they were only seconds behind him, but he held his fire as long as they continued to race toward him. When they were well within the range of his rifle, he took careful aim and squeezed off a round, knocking one of the warriors off his pony. It was enough to cause the other two to veer away sharply and seek cover of their own. With little to choose from, they took refuge behind a low grassy hummock. A few shots were exchanged before both parties realized it was little more than a waste of cartridges. Neither side was willing to stick their heads up. It was apparent that there had been no more than the three, a fact that was encouraging to him. It eliminated the threat of being surrounded, especially key since he had no cover behind him. In addition, to get around behind him, one of the two would have to come out from behind that hummock. And at this short range, he would be dead the moment he showed.

With none of the combatants knowing how to gain an advantage, an extended standoff was the result and now it was a matter of who had the most patience. Either side could safely withdraw by backing away, but Will knew that would only result in another chase to another standoff. And Spades was already tired. *I reckon I'll just sit here and wait for the cavalry,* he thought. He wasn't sure about the two civilian scouts with the column — he'd never ridden with them before — but he was confident Corporal Kincaid could follow the same trail he had followed to find the village.

As the sun climbed higher in the sky, the morning began to heat up considerably and he began to think about the canteen hooked over his saddle horn. *Should have thought about that when I grabbed my rifle,* he told himself. Now he was reluctant to slide back away from the tree to fetch it, afraid he might draw fire toward his horse. So he shrugged off his thirst and continued to watch the hummock, hoping for a target. A full hour passed. A riderless pony slowly wandered over to stand before the hummock. It grazed on the grass atop the low mound until one of the warriors made a quick move to grab the horse's reins and pull it around to the other two. It was not quick enough, however, for Will had a brief glimpse of his shoulder. The Indian yelped in pain as the .44 slug found its mark.

Brave Elk pulled the injured warrior back down behind the hummock. "I think he has broken my shoulder," Wolf Kill groaned painfully. "I can't use my arm." There was a great deal of blood running down his arm, dripping from his fingers, and he tried to stem the flow, but the grass beneath him was soon shining scarlet. Brave Elk was afraid that Wolf Kill might bleed to death, forcing him to make a decision. His desire to kill this coyote man was second only to that of Bloody Hand's, but he knew he must take Wolf Kill back to the village as soon as possible. His decision was made for him in the next few minutes, for while he agonized over his dilemma, the forward cavalry scouts appeared on a rise in the prairie, no more than a quarter mile away — that meant a detachment of soldiers was close behind. "Hurry!" he urged, and helped Wolf Kill as best he could to slide back to their horses.

Fifty yards away, Will also spotted the forward scouts, one of whom was the familiar figure of Corporal Kincaid. A smile of relief appeared on his face and he thought, *saved by the cavalry.* Returning his attention to his immediate problem, he saw the two warriors sliding away from the brink of the hummock. Knowing he would probably get a chance for at least one clear shot, he inched up closer to the tree trunk and set his rifle in a position to fire. As he suspected, the two Indians could not retreat from their position without exposing themselves and their horses. Expecting them to jump on their ponies and bolt away as quickly as possible, he was surprised when they walked out from behind the hummock using the three horses as cover. "Huh," he grunted and hesitated. Then he raised his rifle again. First he aimed at their legs, which he could see under the horses' bellies, decided against it, then thought about shooting the horses. But he did not pull the trigger. He was kind of soft when it came to shooting horses. Then, curious to see how far they would walk before jumping on their ponies, he watched as they continued across his field of fire until he realized they were intent upon retrieving the body of the one he had killed. He would chastise himself later for being softhearted, but he decided to let them pick up the body and leave.

He got up from behind the tree and stood

watching as Brave Elk handed his reins to the wounded warrior and lifted the corpse up onto the pony's back. *Sure would be a clear shot,* Will thought, but he stuck by his decision. The warrior who did the lifting looked familiar — Will was sure he had seen him on the day he had inadvertently ridden down that hill and found himself staring at the war party waiting to ambush Bordeaux's patrol. Stepping clear of the tree when he realized Brave Elk was looking back at him, he felt that the Cheyenne warrior was silently expressing his thanks and understanding of the respect shown by his white enemy. Will was sure the warrior valued the gesture to hold fire so he could recover his dead companion — until the Indian suddenly raised his rifle and fired. Will jumped back behind the tree as Brave Elk's bullet ripped a piece of bark from the trunk. "Why, you son of a bitch!" Will shouted, feeling furious and very much the fool. He ran down from the mound as the Indians galloped away, throwing shot after shot after the retreating hostiles as he ran, none hitting the mark. Two hundred yards away, Corporal Kincaid pulled up to watch in astonishment when he saw the fleeing hostiles galloping away with Will chasing them on foot and firing wildly.

His thoughts occupied with his frustration over the Indian's actions, Will then remembered the troopers behind him. He turned around and started walking back toward the mound to get his horse. In a few seconds, Kincaid rode up to him and stopped. "Are you all right, Will?" he asked, genuinely concerned that the scout had gone loco. It would be a story that he would often repeat of seeing Will chasing the two Indians on foot, blazing away as fast as he could cock and pull the trigger. "Where's your horse?"

"Yeah, I'm all right," Will responded and answered the second question with a nod. Kincaid turned in the direction indicated to see Spades walking slowly toward them. "How far back are they?" he asked, referring to the company.

" 'Bout a quarter of a mile," Kincaid answered. "Oughta be showin' up directly." He waited for Will's explanation for his bizarre behavior.

Aware of the questioning look on the corporal's face, Will told him of the short standoff with the three hostiles. He left out the part where he had stood exposed while he had offered an implied truce. Eager to change the subject, he said, "That Cheyenne village was here, on the other side of the river, but looks like they cleared out about the time the war party got back." He paused then when the point rider of the detachment appeared in the distance. "I expect this bunch here decided to move on up the river to join forces with another village. Don't know how many warriors they can scrape up, but I expect it'll be considerable more than Fischer was expectin' to fight."

"I ain't paid to think," Kincaid said, "but if I was, I'd be damn careful 'bout marchin' on the next village." Both men knew that the column of cavalry could be seen for miles on the open prairie. So if the Cheyenne decided to fight, it would be because they were equal to, or greater in number than the soldiers.

Captain Fischer and his officers listened to Will's report and decided to rest and water the horses at the site of the former Cheyenne village. Since there had been no stop since starting out that morning, he ordered the men to prepare their noonday meal. After some consideration, he talked to Will. "Cason, I need to know how far that next village is, and their strength. Those two you say got away will report our strength."

"Yessir," Will replied, satisfied that Fischer was exercising some degree of caution, which wasn't always the rule with some of the younger officers. "But I doubt if those two know how many men we've got. All they saw was the forward scouts."

Fischer gave that some thought. "I hope you're right," he said. "Get yourself something to eat first."

"Yessir, I will," Will said. He wasn't really hungry, but he felt the need for a cup of strong coffee.

The column crossed over to the opposite bank of the river and soon a couple dozen small fires were glowing. Will joined Kincaid and several others to make coffee and cook some salt pork. When the pot started bubbling rapidly, he pulled it away from the heat and let it simmer down at the edge of the flame. Filling the battered old metal cup he had carried for years, he sat back and let his mind wander. Released to float unhampered, it drifted to thoughts of Sarah Lawton and that brought him a sense of contentment. He thought about his farewell a few days earlier. There were no overt statements from her, but her manner told him that he would be in her thoughts as well. In all his life, he could never remember ever having thought about being married and having a family. He had always blown with the wind with no responsibilities beyond himself and his horse, and no worries about the day following the one he was in. But that didn't mean that he couldn't change when the time was right, and that time was now. *I can take care of Sarah and Emma,* he thought. *It's time I settled down to be a more responsible man.* He liked the sound of it. The image of Sarah when she took his coffee cup and said good-bye made him smile.

"What?" he blurted. Suddenly shaken from his reverie, he realized that someone was speaking to him.

"Damn, Will," Kincaid said. "I thought you'd gone deaf for a minute. What the hell were you thinkin' about — grinnin' like a dog eatin' briars?"

"Nothin'," Will replied. "Just thinkin' how good this coffee was." With that he got to his feet and tossed out the dregs of his cup. Picking up his coffeepot, he swirled the contents around and said, "There's a swallow or two left. You want it?" Kincaid stuck his cup out to accept the last bit of the bitter black liquid. "Well," Will said, "I'd best get in the saddle and go see what kinda trouble I can find for you soldier boys."

"Watch you don't get an arrow up your ass," Kincaid called out after him. The corporal shook his head as he watched the scout walk down to the water to rinse out his cup and coffeepot. Will had acted kind of strange at the fort, as if he didn't have his mind on what he was doing; then he'd chased after those Indians on foot, and now, daydreaming with that simple smile on his face . . . In his line of work, he damn sure better be paying attention, or there was a good chance he could lose his scalp.

CHAPTER 7

An entire Indian village on the move leaves a wide trail, one easily followed by most anyone. Will was not concerned with actually scouting the trail. He knew the Cheyenne had followed the river west, staying close to water. It was just a matter of how far they had gone. The country the Smoky Hill wound through at this point was a vacant-looking prairie once you left the river, with barren bluffs of chalk in the distance, a land that looked incapable of supporting life, dotted with occasional formations of limestone and chalky towers. Yet he knew it sustained buffalo and antelope on its seemingly endless sea of grass and it had long been a favorite camping site for Cheyenne and Arapaho bands. Aware of the potential for ambush by the two hostiles who had just fled, he held close to the tree line along the river, cautious, although he thought the possibility unlikely.

Dusk came and then darkness. Still he pushed on, following the river under a starry sky, content to continue as long as Spades was showing no signs of fatigue. Finally he decided that he'd pushed his horse far enough and began looking for the best place to camp. It was then, after rounding a bend in the river, that he saw the rosy glow against the dark night sky, a glow caused by the many campfires of an Indian village. "Let's get a little closer and have a look, boy," he told the patient bay horse, and continued on. Closer now, he could tell that the village was on the same side of the river he was, so when he came to a place that looked to be a good spot to ford, he crossed over to the other side and continued to get closer still.

When within one hundred yards of the outermost lodges, he left Spades tied in the trees and made his way even closer on foot. It was a big camp. It looked to be larger than the band he had been following, and even though it was too difficult to count lodges from across the river, it stood to reason that it was the forty-two tipis he had counted downriver. And judging by the activity in the center of the village, it was easy to guess that they were getting ready for war. *Those two I shot at back there have told them that the soldiers are coming,* he thought. Determined to see how far along the river the camp extended, he moved farther along the bank until he came to an empty stretch of prairie some fifty yards wide that separated the two villages. Still the sky was aglow with more campfires for some distance beyond that. Knowing it important to give Captain Fischer as accurate a count as possible, he pushed on, aware now that his horse was several hundred yards behind him and darkness his only cover. *Helluva way to make a living,* he thought, but also confident that probably everyone was caught up in the dancing and preparation to go to war.

Still moving cautiously through a stand of willows, he worked his way along the bank paralleling the camp until finally deciding that he had a fair estimate of the number of warriors that C Company with its strength of seventy, counting officers and non-coms, would be facing. Making a conservative guess, he figured the soldiers were going to be outnumbered by more than two to one. Those odds might not be as critical if the Indians were armed with bows and a few muzzle loaders. But based on what had been the case with Lieutenant Bordeaux's patrol against some of these same Cheyenne, the soldiers would be facing well-armed hostiles, many carrying repeating rifles. Fischer might find himself dealing with a real hornet's nest. *Well, all I can do is tell him what I saw,* he thought. Then, thinking of Kincaid, he smiled and murmured, "I ain't paid to think."

When the dancing finally came to an end, he turned to reverse his course and head back to his horse. He couldn't tell Fischer what the Cheyenne had in mind, but they were preparing for something. They were no longer running, that much was apparent, so Will had to figure they somehow knew the strength of the cavalry troops looking for them and felt that their warriors were capable of defending the villages.

Making his way back the way he had come along the riverbank, he suddenly stopped short when he came to the stand of willows where he had left Spades. A Cheyenne warrior had untied Spades' reins and was trying to calm the reluctant horse, but Spades wanted no part of it. Snorting a warning, the horse backed away, almost dragging the Indian as it did. Realizing that the man was not aware that he was behind him, Will remained dead still while he quickly glanced around the darkened thicket to make sure the warrior was alone. Convinced that the

Indian had stumbled upon Spades by chance, he knew that he must act quickly before the warrior alerted the village, and he had to do it quietly.

He considered using his rifle as a club, but he decided against it because of the uncertainty of landing a solid enough blow on the back of the man's head, allowing him to cry out. So he carefully leaned the rifle against a bush and drew his skinning knife from his belt. *It's gonna have to be quick and lethal,* he thought, feeling the heft of the weapon in his hand, otherwise the man could still cry out. Carefully placing each foot, he moved silently toward the warrior, who was still trying to calm Spades, a task that was rapidly becoming more difficult because the horse now recognized Will approaching and looked for him to intercede. Unfortunately, the Cheyenne was astute enough to realize something had further excited the horse and just as Will was about to strike, he turned to discover the white scout.

Both men reacted instantly, rushing together with such force that the collision of their bodies caused them to go crashing to the ground. Rolling over and over, almost getting trampled under Spades' hooves, they struggled for advantage with neither able to overpower the other. The Indian managed to draw his knife, but Will caught his wrist in one hand while trying to free his other hand to strike a blow. The warrior was strong. Both men strained mightily to force the other to drop his knife, but to no avail, each knowing that the penalty for yielding was death. In a desperate attempt to end the stalemate, and fearing that it might be only a matter of time before someone else from the village would happen upon them, Will forced the warrior over on his back. Trying to pin his arm to the ground with his knee, he suddenly released his grip on his wrist and smashed his face with a punch thrown as hard as he could manage. The warrior was stunned, but Will paid a price for his action, grunting with pain when the Indian's knife slashed his arm. With no time to think about the wound, he hammered his face a second time, then grabbed the wrist again before the warrior could draw it back. The struggle continued, but this time, the Indian's arm was pinned across his chest where Will held it jammed against his body. Slowly he forced the arm up until the knife blade was touching the warrior's neck. For a full minute the life-or-death contest continued, until the warrior finally began to weaken, allowing the blade to penetrate his skin, drawing blood. In total panic, he released Will's knife hand in an attempt to grab his other hand. With his knife free, Will struck instantly, sinking his knife in the Indian's gut again and again until he finally lay still.

When he was sure the Cheyenne was dead, Will rolled away from the body and sat on the ground for a long time, gasping for breath, completely exhausted, knowing it could just as well have been him lying dead. Thankful that there had been no sound other than the grunting from the exertion of the struggle, he looked around him in the darkened willows just to be sure no one had heard them. Feeling sure that he was alone at the moment, he allowed his attention to focus on his wound, aware now of the stinging of the cut. It was just above his elbow and his forearm was dark with blood. *It'll have to wait till I can get to a place to tend it,* he thought. Knowing that the important thing right then was to get out of there, he forced himself to move, pausing only briefly to give Spades an accusing look for causing the warrior to turn to confront him. "Whose side are you on?" Indifferent to the question, the bay gelding followed him back to the bush to fetch his rifle, and with legs still weak from the terrible strain, he climbed up in the saddle. Intent now upon putting some distance between him and the combined Cheyenne villages, he retraced his path along the river.

The moon was sinking lower toward the hills on the dark horizon when he decided both he and Spades needed rest. He selected a spot where a miniature cove had been formed by the water's detour around a large tree extending from the bank. After unsaddling Spades, he pulled a piece of an old cotton shirt from his saddlebag and squatted on his heels by the water's edge, cleaning the blood from his arm. With the dry end of the rag, he fashioned as good a bandage as he could, using one hand to tie it. It was not an easy task and he tried a half dozen times before he secured it to the point where he thought it would stay on. Thoroughly tired then, he spread his blanket and settled down to catch a couple of hours' sleep, feeling secure in the knowledge that the ever-alert horse would warn him of any intruders. With no sound but the big bay's occasional snort and the forlorn song of a lonely bullfrog on the opposite bank, he was soon asleep. The last image he remembered before drifting off was Sarah's smiling face.

"Damn," Harvey Bordeaux exclaimed.

"Look what the cat drug in." He got up from the blanket he had been seated upon to greet the rangy scout as Will walked Spades through the camp toward him. He waited before Will got closer before commenting, "You look like hell." Eyeing the rude bandage and the bloodstained shirtsleeve, he asked, "What the hell happened to your arm?" He listened to Will's accounting of the fight with the Cheyenne warrior in open-eyed astonishment. "Damn, Will," he blurted when the scout finished with an indifferent shrug. "You want some coffee?"

"I sure do," Will replied, "about a barrel of it." He dismounted and got his tin coffee cup from his saddlebag. He helped himself to a cup from the pot resting in the coals. "I expect I'd better report to Captain Fischer right away, but I swear I need this first."

Bordeaux wasn't content to wait until Fischer heard the report. "Did you find them?"

"Oh, I found 'em, all right," Will replied between sips, "about two hundred warriors if I had to guess. And they looked like they were gettin' worked up to go to war."

"Ugh," Bordeaux grunted in concerned response. "That doesn't sound too good. They musta joined up with a bigger village

161

than this," he said, glancing around at the site where the cavalry company had camped.

"That's a fact," Will confirmed. He was stopped from elaborating by the appearance of Captain Fischer striding toward them.

"The customary protocol is for a scout to report to the commanding officer as soon as possible," Fischer proclaimed with a hint of irritation in his voice.

Bordeaux turned his face away for a moment as he tried to suppress a smile. Winking at Will, he turned back to address Fischer. "I'm afraid it's my fault for stopping him, Captain. He was on his way to find you."

"Indeed I was," Will commented at once. "But I got tripped up by the smell of that coffeepot. I didn't take time to make any breakfast this mornin' — figured you'd wanna find out what those Injuns were up to so I came straight on in."

"Well, let's have it, man," Fischer responded impatiently. He tried to maintain a proper air of discipline among his officers whenever possible. But gazing at the rumpled, almost bedraggled, appearance of Harvey Bordeaux, he knew he was wasting the effort on the most unconcerned officer in the entire army. As for Will Cason, the man was as wild and carefree as any of the

Crow scouts the army employed. But, he conceded, the man was fearless and as sharp as any of the Indian scouts in the regiment, and maybe a bit more dependable.

The captain listened as Will made his report, giving him a complete picture of the situation facing him. Like Will, Fischer would not have been concerned about the disadvantage in numbers if the hostiles were not armed as well as his troopers. There was no way Will could give him a report on exactly how many of the two hundred or so warriors were armed with rifles — and how many of those were seven-shot repeating carbines, like the weapons used against Bordeaux's patrol. To withdraw without engaging the enemy was not a palatable option for the conscientious officer, but he was also not eager to throw his men into a skirmish that would result in heavy losses. He could not lose sight of his orders to follow the band that ambushed the patrol out of Fort Larned and punish them. His decision was a difficult one, and he gave it a lot of thought before making it. "How far to that village?" he asked.

"About a day," Will answered, "unless they're thinkin' about comin' to meet you."

"You think that's what they've got in mind?"

"Don't know," Will replied. "They might, though, when they find that dead Injun by the river."

"Dead Indian?" Fischer responded.

"Yessir. I had to kill one. He caught me by surprise and I didn't have no choice."

"Is that how you got that wound on your arm?" Fischer asked, making note of it for the first time. When Will replied that it was, Fischer nodded, then got back to the business at hand. "You think they know how many men we have?"

"I can't say," Will replied. "All I can tell you is what I saw, and they were gettin' all fired up about somethin'. It sure looked to me like a war dance." He paused and glanced at Bordeaux as if seeking confirmation for what he was about to say. "Course, I reckon when they find that body on the riverbank, they'll know somebody was spyin' on 'em. I doubt they'll think he committed suicide."

Fischer frowned, unappreciative of Will's humor. He thought the situation over for a long moment. Finally, he submitted to pride and sense of duty. He gave the order to break camp and prepare to move out. After informing his officers of the line of march, he turned to Will. "I want you to go on back out front and keep your eyes open. I don't want to march this company into a damn ambush."

"Yessir." He turned to leave, but Fischer stopped him.

"Get that arm looked at first. Then you'd best take a man with you," the captain said. "You might have to send word back."

"Yessir," Will repeated. Then, glancing at Bordeaux, he said, "I wanna borrow Kincaid again." Bordeaux nodded and Will bellowed, "Corporal Kincaid!"

A couple dozen yards distant, in the process of saddling his horse, Kincaid looked back when he heard his name called. Seeing Will, he grinned and commented to the private standing next to him. "There's that feller that's always tryin' to get me scalped. I reckon you men will have to do without me to hold your hands."

Contrary to what Will and Captain Fischer suspected, Bloody Hand did not know how many the soldiers were, only that they were surely coming. A young girl had discovered the body of Little Crow while looking for blackberries that morning, causing a sense of alarm throughout the camp. His wife, brokenhearted, had said that he had been restless after the dancing and had complained that he could not sleep. So he told her he would walk a while to rest his mind and think about the battle to come. When she awoke that morning, he was not there.

The dancing had lasted late into the night as the Cheyenne camp prepared to defend their village against the hated army cavalry. Early that morning Bloody Hand and Chief Spotted Horse went to talk with Broken Knife, the chief of the village they had just joined, and the elders of the village. At first, the talk was primarily about the necessity to make plans to defend their villages against the coming attack and the need to send the women and children to a safe place. Then Bloody Hand rose to have his say. "We talk about protecting our villages, but I say that it may not be necessary to fight the soldiers here where they may kill our women and children and burn our lodges. I say we should send a scouting party to find the soldiers and see how many they are. We have many warriors in these two camps. Maybe we have more warriors than the soldiers bring. I say it would be better for us to send our warriors to attack the soldiers before they reach our village." He paused a moment to gauge the impact of his words on those assembled. "That is all I have to say."

"There is wisdom in what you say," Broken Knife said as the others in the circle nodded in agreement. "It is better to fight the soldiers away from our homes."

So it was decided to act on Bloody Hand's proposal immediately. Since it was his plan, Bloody Hand requested that he might be the leader of the scouting party. To go with him, he selected Brave Elk and two warriors from Broken Knife's village. He did not express his thoughts when told of Little Crow's death, but the first suspect who came to mind was Coyote, the white scout. There was no evidence to support his suspicions, but his instincts told him that none other would dare to come so near their camp to kill.

Broken Knife and Spotted Horse decided that it would be a wise thing for all the warriors to follow soon after the scouting party in case the soldiers were closer than they thought. So, leaving the rest of the Cheyenne camp to ready their weapons and paint their favorite ponies for war, the scouting party left as soon as the four scouts could be assembled.

They traveled less than a day before the forward scouts of the cavalry were spotted following the river. Taking care not to be seen, the Cheyenne warriors left the river and hid in the chalky bluffs some distance away. Bloody Hand gazed closely at the two forward army scouts in an effort to see whether one of them might be Coyote, but he was not to be seen. In a short time, the first troopers of the company came into view, riding in a column of twos. The Cheyenne scouts crouched in the bluffs, watching and counting until the last troops of the company came into view, and Bloody Hand grew more confident that his plan would work. They could defeat the cavalry detachment with their overpowering numbers. "There are no more," he said, pointing toward the empty trail behind the last of the column. "We must hurry back to meet the others and make ready to attack while we still have time to strike them before they reach our villages." They wasted no time in scrambling back down into the deep gully where they had left their horses. As he jumped upon his pony's back, Bloody Hand wondered why he had not seen the man he called Coyote — for he could almost feel his presence.

Fifty yards away in the same bluffs, the presence Bloody Hand felt rose from behind a limestone mound when he saw the four Indians ride out of the gully. "Damn!" Will exclaimed softly to Corporal Kincaid, who was crouching beside him. "There goes the element of surprise if that bunch gets back to the village." With no other choice, they both raised their rifles and fired as rapidly as possible, hoping to be lucky enough to stop all four, but knowing it unlikely. One of the fleeing warriors was hit, but did not fall from the saddle; the others escaped unharmed. "Better go tell Fischer the bad news," Will said.

Halting the column when he heard the rifle shots, Captain Fischer waited while Will and Kincaid rode down from the bluffs and loped across the prairie to join him. When told what the shooting was about, Fischer called his officers forward for conference with the scouts. "I know for sure they saw the whole troop," Will said in answer to his question.

"You don't think there's the possibility that they were unable to see the whole column?" Lieutenant Gates asked, directing his question at Kincaid. "They were way back up in those bluffs. Maybe there's a chance they took off as soon as they saw the forward scouts. What do you think, Corporal?"

"Well, sir," Kincaid replied, "I ain't paid to think. But I was back up in those bluffs and I saw the whole column."

Fischer looked at Will. "What do you think, Cason?"

"I think you're gonna have a helluva fight in a little while. There's a heap of warriors in those two villages, and I don't think they're gonna wait to fight you on their ground. If I was you, I'd pick me out a good place to make a stand, else you're gonna take a lot of casualties. Me and Kincaid can ride out ahead and give you as much warnin' as we can if the Injuns do decide to come after you."

The decision was as important as Fischer had ever been called upon to make, but he was in command and he intended to make it in the fashion he felt his superiors expected of him. He took his scouts' report under serious advisement, but he could not in good conscience yield the field to a bunch of wild hostiles. In spite of the difference in numbers, he felt he had a distinct advantage in terms of military discipline. He was not inexperienced in Indian warfare, having commanded successful campaigns against Cheyenne, Arapaho, and Comanche raiding parties. And it was his experience that the typical Indian war party was no more than a collection of warriors fighting as individuals with no real organization. Consequently, he gave the order to prepare to march, with the intention of meeting the enemy on the open field of battle, convinced that they would wilt under a cavalry skirmish line. Turning to Will and Kincaid, he said, "Find the enemy for me, and we'll see what they do when facing a company of seasoned troopers."

"Yessir," Will replied, turned without hesitation, and rode off toward the river. Kincaid rendered a casual salute, then turned to follow Will. When he caught up to the rangy scout, Will glanced at him and said, "This is liable to be a mistake. Somebody's been tellin' your captain some fairy tales about the Cheyenne warrior."

"Maybe," Kincaid responded. "I expect you're right, but I just take orders. I ain't paid to think."

"We'll see, I reckon," Will said just before giving Spades his heels. "But those Injuns got away from here, so they know we're comin' and they know how many men we've got. The way I see it is, if there's a big bunch of warriors already on the way from that village I saw last night, they might not be but a couple of hours ahead of us when those scouts meet up with 'em and tell 'em what they saw."

Holding their horses back to a spirited walk, they continued on along the river, carefully and constantly scanning the terrain before them and to each side. After approximately an hour with no sign to cause either of them to become concerned, they came to a narrow plain with a line of low-lying hills to the north. The fact that it formed a natural trough between the hills on one side and the river on the other caused Will to rein Spades to a stop.

"You see somethin'?" Kincaid asked, pulling up alongside.

"No," Will answered. "I *feel* somethin'." With raised eyebrows, he threw Kincaid a cautious glance. "If you were set on ambushin' a column of soldiers, this little valley through here would be a damn good place to do it."

"You think they'da had time to get this far?" Kincaid questioned.

"If they started out before their scouts got back, they coulda."

Both men scanned the treeless hills to their right, looking hard to catch any tiny telltale sign along the grassy hilltops, like a single feather that didn't belong, or the reflection of the sun off a rifle barrel. There was nothing, not even the sound of a bird. Figuring he had just spooked himself, Will nudged Spades again and the two scouts moved farther into the narrow valley.

Lying flat on his belly just beneath the crest of the hill, Bloody Hand watched the two scouts advancing along the floor of the valley, his muscles tense as he peered through the rifle trench he had fashioned with his war ax. He wanted to scream out his war cry; such was his agony in having to restrain the urge to kill racing through his muscular body. *It was him! The coyote — no more than a hundred feet below.*

Seeing the anguish of his war chief, Brave Elk whispered softly in an effort to calm him, "We must wait for the soldiers to follow them," he reminded. Bloody Hand only looked back at him with teeth clenched in angry frustration, but he knew he could not destroy the element of surprise.

Down on the valley floor, Will and Kincaid moved slowly now, the corporal watching the rangy scout even as closely as the hills to the north, alert for any signal of alarm. Suddenly a pair of quail burst from the tall grass near the top of the hill, their wings beating a sharp flutter as they fled toward the river. Will pulled Spades up again and listened to the silence left behind the quail's flight. He calmly turned to Kincaid then and asked, "Is that horse of yours ready to run?"

"I reckon," Kincaid answered.

"Well, ride like hell. We got to get our asses outta here!" That was all the warning he gave. Wheeling Spades sharply, he gave him a definitive kick and the big bay lunged into a full gallop. With no thought to question, Kincaid followed suit, and the two scouts raced toward the mouth of the valley.

As one, the line of Indians hidden in the hills leaped to their feet, knowing their ambush had been discovered. Screaming out his rage, Bloody Hand implored his warriors to get to their ponies. The coyote had once again destroyed his trap. "Cut them off!" he roared. "They must not escape!" He jumped on his war pony and galloped recklessly across the hilltop, angling toward the end of the valley.

Down on the flat, Will and Kincaid lay low on their horses' necks, urging each mount for more effort. Spades did not disappoint. He had been called upon to haul his master out of more than one scrape, and knew it was his role in the partnership. Kincaid was trailing, but not by far. Both men were well aware of the consequence of losing the race to the end of the valley. Behind them, like angry ants from a disturbed anthill, two hundred warriors streamed down the slopes in pursuit.

With the advantage gained by galloping along the flat floor of the trough, while the

Indian ponies were hampered by having to descend the steep slopes, the two white men were able to open a sizable lead on their pursuers. Riding as if the devil himself were chasing them, they flew back over the trail they had just traveled minutes earlier. With thoughts of the fabled endurance and speed of Indian ponies on his mind, Will was praying that Spades could stand up to this ultimate test. The courageous horse could maintain this pace for only so long. Then it was going to be a question of finding a hole to jump into and break out the rifles. He didn't care for the odds if that happened. The question was answered after a run of approximately three miles when Kincaid's horse started to stumble and the corporal was forced to pull up where the river took a sharp bend. Will reined Spades back and waited for Kincaid to come up beside him.

"She's spent," the corporal announced apologetically, then looked back to see if the warriors were in sight.

Walking the two exhausted horses, they both looked behind them, expecting to see the hostile hoard come into view around the bend in the river. "We've got a few minutes' lead on 'em at best," Will said. "I just hope their horses are as tired as ours." He would have considered crossing the river and finding a place to hide had it not been for the fact that C Company would have no warning of the war party about to descend upon them. "Damn," he uttered in response to the dilemma that faced them. Then, after a moment of thought, he said, "Maybe we can warn the captain, anyway." He pulled his rifle from the scabbard and fired three rapid shots in the air, hoping that the column was close enough to hear the warning. Following suit, Kincaid did likewise. Then, in an effort to complete their mission, they dismounted and set out on foot, jogging and leading their spent horses. Luck was with them, for it was not a long run. They met the forward cavalry scouts in less than a mile. Behind them, the Cheyenne war party had closed the distance to three quarters of a mile.

The company was already forming for battle when Will and Kincaid strode wearily up to the captain. "I brought you some Injuns," Will reported casually.

"I see you did," Fischer replied, shifting his gaze back and forth between the two obviously exhausted men. "Corporal," he said, "you can rejoin your troop." Fixing his gaze upon Will then, he said, "You can find you a spot to use that rifle of yours." He then returned to the business of preparing to meet the cloud of hostile warriors just descended on the plain before him.

With the enemy so close upon them, Fischer had little choice in tactics. Cason had not exaggerated the count, and after seeing the great number of warriors facing him, he was forced to assume a defensive posture. Still, he was confident that his soldiers would inflict far more damage upon the hostiles than they would have stomach for. Taking a stand with the river behind them, he ordered the company to assume standard procedures. A double skirmish line was formed with the men divided into squads of four, with one man behind to hold the horses and three to fall in the line, ready to fire. When all was ready, Fischer stood beside Will and peered across the open expanse of prairie that separated the two foes. "What are they waiting for?" Fischer asked.

"I reckon they're sizin' up the situation," Will replied, "tryin' to decide if they can overrun us or if they wanna surround us and gradually pinch in on us."

The Cheyenne strategy would be determined in most part by Bloody Hand's impatience to kill the soldiers, especially the coyote. "Come!" he shouted. "Follow me! We will crush those who come to take our hunting grounds." Caught up in his passion to kill, a large number of the war party followed him in a frontal assault on the two lines of soldiers.

"All right! Here they come, boys!" Fischer bellowed out orders for the first rank to kneel. "Hold your fire!" he yelled. "Wait for my order." The hostiles charged, numbering about forty or fifty by Will's estimate, screaming their fearsome war cries, shooting wildly. Fischer held off until the distance was about fifty yards before giving the order to fire. The first volley cut a sizable swath in the charging warriors. It was followed by a second volley that left even more riderless ponies to scatter from the field.

Realizing his folly too late, Bloody Hand called his warriors back while taking even more losses as the soldiers were firing at will. His assault had taken the lives of at least fifteen or twenty of his warriors while doing very little damage to the troopers. Trembling with rage, he retreated out of range of the cavalry carbines, humiliated by his foolish attack while Broken Knife, a cooler head, prepared to split his warriors to attack on three sides. Desperate to regain his pride, Bloody Hand advised Broken Knife that he would cross the river with his warriors to prevent the soldiers from escaping that way. Broken Knife nodded in approval. "We will hold the soldiers against the river until they run out of bullets and kill them if they try to escape."

And so the siege was set with hostiles on all sides of the company of cavalry, many with single-shot Springfield rifles that allowed them to snipe away at a greater range than that of the soldiers' carbines. Fischer was forced to huddle the horses together below the riverbanks and further divide his command in order to guard against hostile infiltration from the other side of the river.

After two dead and six wounded by the sniping of the hostiles, Captain Fischer drew his troopers back from the open prairie to take positions along the bank of the river. Digging in to form protected firing pits, the soldiers continued to exchange fire with the Indians, although neither side inflicted much damage. The company was effectively pinned down, however, and incapable of moving out without taking an unacceptable number of casualties. "The sons of bitches should be here with us in this damn hole," Fischer uttered to no one in particular, referring to all Indian Agents who had issued Spencer carbines to the Cheyenne, supposedly for the purpose of hunting for food. There was a definite feeling of anger, knowing the government was furnishing the Indians with weapons to use against them.

Several times during the long afternoon the hostiles attempted to move in closer to the riverbank. Each time they were forced back by the soldiers. Looking for any helpful ideas from his officers, Fischer had to reject all suggestions to try to forcefully break out of their trap and make a run for it. The probability of casualties was too high to gamble on luck. And even if he was successful in escaping from the riverbank breastworks, he would then find himself on the open prairie, trying to outrun the faster Indian horses. It was painfully obvious that his command would be chewed to pieces. The only hope he had was to send for help, and that brought another concern — the odds were not very good that a messenger could safely get through the ring of hostiles surrounding his company. To add to his dilemma, Fort Dodge was ninety miles away. It would take the better part of a week before a relief column could possibly reach him. By that time, they would be without food for men or horses. He summoned all his scouts to confront the problem, but his concern was directed fully at Will Cason. Huddled under the riverbank to avoid presenting tempting targets for the Cheyenne sharpshooters, the scouts listened to the captain's account of their impasse.

Having already assessed the situation before being consulted, Will expected the captain's call for a volunteer. "Dodge is ninety miles away," he said, "but Fort Hays ain't but about forty or maybe a little bit more. How many troops are billeted there now?"

Fischer at once felt chagrined for not having thought of that himself. "I don't know if the Nineteenth Kansas is still there, but the Tenth Cavalry should be billeted there. In fact, I'm sure they are."

"I can make Fort Hays before daybreak," Will said, "and should get back here by tomorrow night with some help. I'll leave as soon as it gets dark." He was not especially eager to stick his neck out, but in his honest opinion, he wasn't ready to trust the job to anyone else.

It was a dangerous undertaking, and Fischer knew he couldn't order the civilian scout to take such risks, so he was pleased and relieved that Will had volunteered — and in such a manner that implied he intended to go with or without approval. "I appreciate it, Cason," he said. "You can take your pick of any of the horses."

"I reckon I'll take my own," Will replied. "Spades would get homesick if I left him here. Besides, he's rested up enough now." To lighten his horse's load as much as possible, however, he removed everything he didn't need, keeping only his weapons and extra ammunition.

As the shadows lengthened, the besieged company continued to receive random shots from all sides, including some from the other bank of the river. Two of Bloody Hand's warriors were killed when they attempted to swim across in the growing gloom of twilight. It was enough to discourage further attempts. Will readied himself to leave as Fischer ordered fires to be built in several places on either side to cast some light on the perimeter and lessen any attempts by the Indians to creep in closer.

Corporal Kincaid walked over to talk to Will as he finished checking Spades' saddle. "Dammit, Will," he started, "there's a helluva lot of Injuns surroundin' this hole we got ourselves in. How are you gonna slip by all of 'em? I mean, even in the dark — hell, it ain't *that* dark."

Will replied matter-of-factly. "I'm not gonna try to slip through 'em. I'm hopin' I can swim by 'em."

Kincaid slowly shook his head. "I don't

know about that," he said, his tone reflecting his doubts. "Maybe I oughta go with you."

Will smiled. "Probably got a better chance if there's only one splashin' around in the water," he said, appreciating the fact that Kincaid was sincere in his offer to go with him. "I'll be all right. Hell, Spades ain't gonna let nothin' happen to me."

When he was satisfied that a hard dark had settled over the river, Will led Spades down to the water. Captain Fischer walked with him and extended his hand as Will prepared to go. "It's a dangerous thing you're about to undertake, Cason, but if you make it, you may save a lot of lives." He stepped back then and said, "Godspeed."

"I'll see you tomorrow evenin', Captain," Will said. "Just tell your boys to keep their heads down till I get back." He turned then and led Spades into the dark current. The water was warm, warmer than the late-summer night air, and he felt his clothes suddenly become heavy as they clung to his body. With his rifle held above his head in one hand, he held on to the saddle horn with the other and let the big bay pull him gently down the dark river. Confused, the gelding at first started toward the opposite bank, and each time Will gave him a gentle tug on the reins until Spades finally realized what his master wanted and drifted quietly downstream. In no more than a couple dozen yards, he could hear the sounds of soft voices on both sides of him as he floated slowly past, holding his breath for fear a gunshot or an arrow might suddenly come his way. After a hundred yards or so, Spades' natural instinct to gain the other side was enough to cause him to ignore Will's insistence on a long swim, and he made for dry land. Will had no choice but to climb in the saddle as the horse clamored up the bank much to the surprise of a startled Cheyenne warrior in the process of loading his seven-shot Spencer rifle. Not sure whether he was seeing friend or foe as Will rode directly up to him, the warrior hesitated a second too long. It was the defining second of the young Cheyenne's life as Will fired at point-blank range and galloped away into the darkness of the prairie. With the sound of scattered shots behind him, as the hostiles continued to harass the soldiers, he hoped that his shot would not be noticed. At least there was no sound of alarm that would indicate his passing had been discovered, and after a few minutes and no sign of pursuit, he pulled Spades back to a pace the horse could maintain.

CHAPTER 8

With a large full moon rising above the hills before him, he followed the river east, still shivering from his wet clothes as the chill evening air pressed the garments against his skin. On into the night he rode, holding Spades to a ground-eating pace, dismounting every couple of hours to walk and let the horse rest a bit. Fixing the run of the river in his mind, he had to rely on his memory and his instincts to decide where to leave it and take a more northerly line to strike Fort Hays. When he reached a point where the river seemed to bend gently in a more southerly direction, he stopped for a short while to let his horse drink and rest before leaving the Smoky Hill and heading north. If his instincts were right, he figured he was no more than twenty miles from the fort, but he had never approached it from this direction in the dark when all the landmarks looked decidedly different.

The moon had already passed beyond its highest point in the sky when he came to a lone chalk pillar that he recognized, and realized that he was two miles west of where he had figured to be. Had he continued on that line, he may have missed the fort, but now he at least knew where he was, and corrected his course. Sure of himself then, he pressed Spades for a little faster pace.

His clothes were almost dry when he spotted the buildings of Fort Hays in the predawn light. A few minutes later, he was challenged by a guard as he approached the outer compound. Taking a quick minute to identify himself and why he was there, he proceeded to the post headquarters building just as the urgent call of the bugle sounded reveille. After hearing Will's purpose for being there, the lieutenant on duty immediately sent a runner to alert the colonel. In short order, two companies of the Tenth Cavalry were ordered to the field. While they prepared for the march, Will got himself and Spades something to eat. The one hundred and sixty man column under the command of Captain Daniel Forrest, with Will beside him, left the compound before mess call was sounded for the rest of the post.

■ ■ ■ ■

Captain John Fischer knelt behind a low hummock covered with bushes and peered out through the branches at the enemy surrounding him. Although he knew there were fully two hundred warriors holding his company hostage, he could spot no real targets within range of his men's carbines. It was amazing, but equally frustrating to know that there were so many hostiles almost invisible to the eye in the open prairie right before him. And the only ones he could see clearly were about ten or twelve sitting their horses on the top of a hill comfortably out of rifle range. They were no doubt the chiefs, like generals overlooking the siege.

The responsibility for the lives of his men weighed heavily on his conscience as he contemplated the possibility of a desperate attempt to break through the ring of hostiles encircling his command. Up to this point, his casualties were light, only because they were able to keep the Indians at bay. But he knew a point would come beyond which he would have to make an offensive move. A few more days would see the depletion of rations for men, horses, and ammunition.

Will Cason had said he would be back by this evening, but what if he didn't show? Fischer had no way of knowing if Cason was able to slip through the hostiles even though his scouts assured him that the hostiles would most likely have let him know. "They'da paraded his body back and forth so you could see it," Kincaid commented to Lieutenant Bordeaux.

Fischer's thoughts were interrupted by a sudden volley of gunfire behind him and he turned to investigate. In a few moments his first sergeant moved up beside him. "Another try by that bunch on the other side of the river," the first sergeant said. "Maybe we oughta let 'em get some of 'em across so we could kill 'em. At least we'd have something we could see to shoot at."

"Make sure the men aren't wasting ammunition shooting at something they can't see," Fischer said. He knew that some of his men would shoot solely out of frustration, and like the food rations, ammunition would also run out if they remained there too long. The night just passed proved to be long and tiring. Although his men had tried to sleep in shifts, no one really got much rest — the Indians saw to that with stray shots and flaming arrowheads throughout the night.

The day bore on through the noon meal, which was greatly reduced in order to save food, and into the afternoon. As evening approached, Fischer crawled back to the hummock and trained his field glasses on the chiefs on top of the hill. While he watched, a warrior rode up to them and, with excited gestures, delivered a message of some apparent importance — Fischer could only guess. Much to the captain's surprise, the Indians disappeared from the hilltop. A few minutes later, a shout went up from his men. When he looked to see what had caused the outburst, he was astonished to see warriors pop up from every bit of concealment and retreat to the hills. It appeared they had evacuated the field entirely. After a few minutes passed, the mystery was solved as a long column of cavalry troops appeared near the bend of the river with Will Cason in the lead.

Surely as dumbfounded as Captain Fischer to see Broken Knife's warriors retreat from the field, Bloody Hand moved quickly to the riverbank to see what had caused the unexpected turn of events. Thinking of the time he had been tricked by Coyote and the bugle, he paused to listen, but he could hear no bugle. He remained confused over the untimely exodus until moments later when Brave Elk pointed toward the hills where Broken Knife had watched the siege. "Many soldiers!" Brave Elk exclaimed. "No trick!"

"Augh!" Bloody Hand cried out in frustration. "We can fight the soldiers!" He looked around him at his warriors, all of whom were watching the dark column cresting the hill and descending into the valley. "We must stay and fight."

"There are too many," Brave Elk said, aware of his friend's passion for eradicating the white man from the Cheyenne's traditional hunting grounds, a passion that often blinded Bloody Hand's practical sense.

Brave Elk's calm reminder served to restore Bloody Hand's rational mind, and after a long moment's thought, he nodded his understanding and called for all to withdraw. Still, he remained, reluctant to leave the siege, while the others quickly stole back to their horses. As usual, the faithful Brave Elk stayed with him, even as the soldiers approached within one hundred yards of the cheering troopers trapped in the bluffs of the river. "They are the Buffalo Soldiers," Brave Elk said upon recognizing the black troopers of the Tenth Cavalry, so named by the Indians for their dark curly hair, like that of the buffalo.

Bloody Hand did not respond, transfixed as he was on the scout leading the soldiers. "Coyote," he uttered in a soft, angry voice. Enraged by the helplessness of his position on this side of the river, too far away to take revenge, he could only glare at the tall figure riding beside the officer. With his own eyes, he had seen the coyote retreat to the river with the other soldiers, yet there he was now, leading more soldiers to fight him. It infuriated him to think that he had slipped by the ring of warriors surrounding the trapped soldiers.

Feeling the siege had been lifted, many of the encircled soldiers left the cover of the river bluffs to welcome their relief column. Seeing the careless disregard of the soldiers, Bloody Hand grasped the opportunity for a clear target and immediately started firing. Two troopers were cut down before the entire company rose up to return fire. Forced to retreat in the face of the blistering rain of bullets, Bloody Hand and Brave Elk hurried to get to their ponies and chase after their friends. The taking of the two troopers' lives afforded Bloody Hand some measure of consolation, but his burning hatred for the white coyote continued to spread through his veins like wildfire.

When it was apparent the last of the Indians had fled, Captain Fischer walked out of the bluffs to greet his relief. He stood there, appraising the two full companies of cavalry as they pulled up before him, and Captain Forrest stepped down to shake hands. "Daniel Forrest," he said. "Looks like you were in a bit of a tight spot."

"John Fischer," the captain replied. "Indeed I was and I'm damn glad to see you." He paused then to nod at Will, still seated aboard Spades. "Well done, Cason. We're all in your debt."

"Not at all," Will replied politely. Then, figuring his job was done, he turned Spades' head toward the river and left the officers to confer.

"By God, we can go after those devils and punish them now," Fischer said, returning his focus back to Captain Forrest. "With three full companies, we can match their numbers."

Forrest shook his head apologetically. "Afraid I can't do that, Captain. My orders are to relieve your company and ensure your safety in returning to your post. Due to the need for these troops to guard wagon trains on the Smoky Hill Trail, I was specifically ordered not to pursue these Cheyenne, and to return immediately to Fort Hays as soon as you were safely on your way back to Fort Dodge."

Totally perplexed by Forrest's answer, Fischer complained. "Jesus, man, this is an opportunity to destroy this band of renegades, burn their village, kill their livestock. It would be pure folly to simply let them go."

"I understand what you're saying," Forrest replied. "And I totally agree with you. But I've got my orders and I can't turn a blind eye to the need for these troops back at Fort Hays. I'm sorry." Signaling an end to the discussion then, he said, "Now, if you'll get your men ready to move out, we'll ride with you until we're satisfied there's no threat from that band again."

Bitterly disappointed, but understanding the captain's position, Fischer again thanked Forrest for pulling him out of a desperate situation and ordered his lieutenants to get the men ready to depart. Sympathetic to Fischer's point of view, Will shook his head when told that the Indians would not be followed. In his opinion, there would never be a better opportunity to defeat a sizeable band of hostile Indians. They were on the run, and would have little time to evacuate their village with the soldiers right on their heels. *But hell,* he thought, *me and Kincaid ain't paid to think.*

With time to consider other things now while the company assembled to move out, Will decided it suited him just fine that they were not going after the Cheyenne hostiles. Once again his mind was free to think about Sarah and Emma, and what changes in his life would have to be made if she saw fit to accept a proposal of marriage. *Proposal of marriage!* The thought sent a cold feeling racing through his veins. This was not the first time he had allowed his mind to even form the words, but each time he did, it caused the same feeling of blood rushing though his veins. It occurred to him that he might not be bold enough to even broach the subject — she had not been a widow very long. She might think him insensitive and crass for suggesting a marriage of convenience, hoping she would learn to love him as time went by. His mind seemed to go loco just to be in her presence, but he was sure he perceived an interest on her part. *I'll damn sure get up the nerve somehow,* he thought. Then he smiled and thought, *I'll tell Emma what's on my mind. She'll make sure her mama comes up with the right an-*

swer. He was suddenly aware that his mind had drifted far from the riverbank beside him when he realized someone had spoken to him. "What?" he replied, and turned to see Corporal Kincaid pulling up beside him.

"I said, 'What's that silly smile about?' "

"Nothin'," Will said. "I guess I was just thinkin' how much better my life will be if I give up this job with the army. Maybe it's about time."

Kincaid's head cocked back and displayed a questioning face. "And do what?"

"I don't know," Will answered honestly. "Farm, run some cattle, raise horses." He shrugged, unconcerned.

"Shit," the corporal uttered, "that'll be the day. You'd last about a month. Then you'd more likely be runnin' around in the woods, eatin' bark and briars."

Will chuckled at the thought. "Maybe," he said. "We'll see." Possibly Kincaid's prediction was an accurate one. He had always been a restless soul who could not tolerate any ropes that threatened to tie him down. But there came a time when a man, even one as carefree and footloose as he, became ready to give up chasing the wild hawk and think about things like family, home, and hearth. With Sarah, he could see himself as that man.

"Gotta go," Kincaid said when the call came to form up and prepare to march.

The column marched due south for about ten miles before approaching darkness called for a halt. Breaking camp the next morning, they continued south until reaching the north fork of Walnut Creek, where Captain Forrest left them and turned back to the north. With scouts trailing behind and forward scouts ahead of the column, there had been no sign of hostiles. A day and a half's march found them approaching Fort Dodge just at suppertime.

With one thing foremost in his mind, Will was reluctant to accompany Fischer to report to regimental commander, Colonel Alfred Arnold, but the captain insisted, thinking that the scout was the only one in his command who had actually seen the Cheyenne camp. Fischer's speculation was accurate in assuming that a punitive campaign would be in the immediate offing. After hearing the reports, and the number of warriors encountered, the colonel decided to punish the renegade Cheyenne village with the force of a full regimental assault. "We'll give your men one full day's rest," he said, "and march day after tomorrow."

Upon arriving at the fort, the first thing Will had checked on was to make sure the lone wagon was still parked by the river. He did his best to keep it off his mind during the debriefing with the colonel, but as soon as it was over, he took his leave of the captain. He wondered if he shouldn't take the time to clean up from the trail, but the evening was already getting thin, and he couldn't abide the thought of waiting until tomorrow to see her. Rubbing his face with his hand, however, he decided that he should at least scrape the stubble off his face before calling on the two ladies in his life, so he took a quick detour down by the river. *I wish I had some of that sweet-smelling soap,* he thought as he razored the whiskers from under his chin. Running his fingers through his long hair in an attempt to at least smooth out the snarls, he also wished he owned a brush. *I reckon this'll have to do,* he thought. "What are you lookin' at?" he exclaimed to Spades when he turned to find the horse watching him with bored curiosity. Thinking again of the lateness of the hour, he stepped up in the saddle and turned Spades toward the wagon.

As usual, Emma was the first to spot him when he rounded the tent next to the wagon. "Mama!" she screamed delightedly,

"It's Will!" She sprang up so suddenly that she knocked the camp stool over when she ran to meet him.

"Hello, Whiskers," he said, and dismounted to receive the child's greeting.

"I thought you were never coming back," Emma complained. "Mama said you were off leading the soldiers somewhere."

He chuckled. "That's right, I was," he replied, "but you oughta known I'd be back to see you." He started to ask where her mother was, but Sarah had heard and came out of the tent to meet him. He was stopped cold by the vision of loveliness that almost caused his heart to stop beating. She was more beautiful than the image of her face he had carried with him during the long march just completed, and he knew at that moment that he was making the right decision. A moment later, he was stunned when she was followed out of the tent by Lieutenant Braxton Bradley.

"Will," Sarah greeted him cordially, a warm smile upon her face. "We're so happy to see you back safe and sound." She offered her hand then and glanced at Lieutenant Bradley. "Braxton said that C Company had just gotten back and Emma's been about to drive me crazy asking about you."

The lieutenant, who had stood silently by

while the greetings were exchanged, spoke for the first time. "Cason," he acknowledged stiffly.

"Lieutenant," Will replied, equally formal. He had not counted on Bradley hanging around. He had things to say to Sarah, things he was literally bursting to tell her, and he couldn't very well say them with him standing there like a poster from the military academy.

Noticing the bandage on his arm, Sarah expressed concern and asked if it was serious, but quickly flew to another subject when he assured her it wasn't. "You'll be one of the first to know," she said, affecting a smile. "Braxton has asked me to marry him, and I've said yes." She rushed on. "I know it's a little soon, but we both feel it's the right thing." Her smile widened as she added, "Like Edna Boyle said, things have to happen faster out here." She looked at her daughter, still holding Will's other hand, and exclaimed, "And Emma's going to have a father again." For Braxton's sake, she tried to appear excited over her announcement. She could not, however, avoid a feeling of apology, approaching embarrassment, when telling Will.

He had been stunned before, even shot, but nothing in his entire life had ever struck his whole body with the impact of Sarah's words. His veins seemed suddenly filled with a numbing cold that drained his brain of oxygen and rendered him incapable of feeling the child's hand that he still held in his. He would remember later the arrogant expression on Bradley's face. It was questionable if Sarah knew of his feelings for her, but the lieutenant knew. A man was quick to identify a rival for a woman's affection.

He wanted to run and hide someplace where his anguish could burst forth from him like an enraged mountain lion, but he fought to keep his hurt from his face. Finally trusting himself to speak, he said, "Well, I reckon congratulations are in order." He nodded to Braxton and tried to form a smile for Sarah.

"Where are my manners?" Sarah gushed then. "You must be hungry, Will. Can I get you some coffee? I know how much you like coffee."

"Ah, no, ma'am," he forced a reply. "I've got to be goin' along now. I just wanted to stop by to see if everythin' was all right, but I can see that the lieutenant has everythin' taken care of." He gave Emma's hand a little squeeze and released it. "I gotta go, Whiskers."

"Ah, Will," the child complained. "Can't you stay for a little while?"

He just smiled down at her, then looked back at Sarah and said, "Like I said, congratulations. I'll be goin' now." Before Sarah or Emma could protest further, he turned abruptly and was gone.

He needed space, and he needed to be alone. Settling Spades into a gentle lope, he rode northeast along the Arkansas River as the first shades of night fell. *How could I have been such a damn fool?* he asked himself, still smarting from the humiliation he feared he had been unsuccessful in hiding. *How could I have led myself to believe she cared for me — a damned wild-ass saddle tramp like me?* It was difficult to determine which could be the most painful, the rejection, or the humiliation of the rejection. *That slick son of a bitch,* he thought, then conceded, *Hell, I reckon compared to me, there really wasn't much of a choice.* At the age of twenty-seven, Will Cason was experiencing his first broken heart. It was not an easy thing for him.

After riding far enough to put all signs of the army post behind him, he reined Spades back to a walk and entered the second stage of his heartbreak — consolation. "Well, I don't have to worry no more about bein' tied down to a damn farm," he announced to his horse. "And I don't have to worry about feedin' a wife and child. I can ride where I please when I please." They were all strong points that had held considerably more weight before he met Sarah Lawton. *Soon to be Sarah Bradley,* he thought, gritting his teeth as a result. "Damn!" he swore.

Finally, he decided there was nothing he could do about it, so he might as well get on with the rest of his life. That settled, he realized that he needed some coffee, so he guided Spades over closer to the water and dismounted. Breaking out his old coffeepot, he emptied out the last of the beans he had ground and soon had the pot boiling over a fire. *Might as well make camp here tonight,* he thought, so he unsaddled Spades and let him graze free. There was nothing left to eat in his saddlebags but a few pieces of dried jerky, but he wasn't really hungry, anyway. So he made himself as comfortable as possible and began the first night of trying to forget Sarah Lawton, a process that would never be completely accomplished. *I guess I'll keep on working for the army,* he thought. *Hell, I don't know anything else.*

CHAPTER 9

When Will rode back into Fort Dodge he witnessed a bustle of activity that told him the troops were preparing for the campaign to the Smoky Hill. It came as somewhat of a surprise for him that the regiment could be ready to move this quickly. In reality, however, it was not a full-strength regiment on the move. Fort Dodge was normally a four-company post, while a full regiment was composed of ten to twelve companies. For the past four weeks, two additional companies had been assigned to the post, one of which was the regimental band, so it was more like a half regiment that was preparing to take the field.

Riding by the stables with thoughts of getting some grain for Spades, he saw Corporal Kincaid directing a detail that appeared to be inspecting the hooves of some of the horses. Will steered Spades over to speak to his friend. "I thought you boys were goin' to get a day's rest before you got ready to go," he said.

"Huh," Kincaid grunted. "So did I, but it didn't surprise me none. I been in the army long enough to know better'n to count on somethin' an officer says when it comes to benefitin' the enlisted men."

"Sounds like treasonous talk to me. Maybe I'd better detail a firing squad." They both turned to see where the voice had come from and found Lieutenant Bordeaux rounding the corner of the stable, a wide smile across his pudgy face.

"Well, hell," Kincaid replied, knowing the lieutenant was joking, "he did say we was to get a day's rest."

Bordeaux shrugged. "It takes a little longer to get a whole regiment on the road, and I reckon he's eager to get moving before the Cheyenne decide to leave the Smoky Hill." He glanced at Will then. "Did you see the colonel yet? He's been lookin' for you."

"What for?" Will replied. He didn't as a rule have much direct contact with the regimental commander.

"I guess he wants to make sure you're gonna be ready to go with us," Bordeaux said. "I think Captain Fischer sang your praises so loud that he's got the colonel thinkin' you're the only man who can find the Indians."

"Is that a fact?" Will responded without emotion. He might have been pleased by the praise had his mind not been dwelling upon more sober subjects.

Kincaid glanced at Will, remembering all his talk about quitting the business of scouting. "You plannin' on goin' on this little tea party?" he asked.

"Well, I don't have no other plans right now," Will said, "so I reckon I am."

"You might wanna go see the colonel," Bordeaux reminded.

"I reckon," Will replied. "I planned on stealin' some of the army's grain for my horse first. He ain't had much but grass for a while." He left his two friends then, and after securing a sack of oats to his saddle, he turned Spades toward the headquarters building.

Passing the barracks that housed F Company, Will was hailed by a mounted officer who had been overseeing a work detail. He turned to recognize Lieutenant Braxton Bradley coming toward him. "Cason," Bradley called out again, "a moment."

Will reined Spades to a halt and waited for the lieutenant to catch up to him. The very sight of him caused the blood in his veins to simmer, even though he tried to tell himself that Bradley could not be blamed for courting Sarah. He had to admit to himself that it amounted to a simple case of jealousy on his part. Determined to be as civil as he could, however, he said, "What can I do for you, Lieutenant?"

"I just wanted a word with you," Bradley replied. "Sarah is extremely grateful for your part in saving her and Emma from that Cheyenne war party. It's certainly natural that she feels kindly toward you. Any woman in like circumstance would. And, of course, I am grateful, too, for saving the woman I am going to marry. I'm sure Sarah has told you we plan to marry as soon as the regiment returns from this action against the Cheyenne." Will was puzzled by the lieutenant's comments, not sure why Bradley was telling him this. There had been no occasion for Sarah to tell him when her wedding was planned. The lieutenant continued. "In view of this, I think it would be a good idea if you did not call on the lady and her daughter. I'm sure you can appreciate the awkward position it places Sarah in, and she is too kindhearted to tell you this herself. It's confusing to the child as well, and I want Emma to know that I will be her father. It's important that she sees that right away, and I don't think it a good idea for

207

you to assume an uncle's role either. It's just best that you stay away from Sarah and Emma. I'm sure you can see the harm that could be done."

Will was taken aback by the lieutenant's request. In fact, it went beyond a request. He was being told to stay in his place, scolded like a servant or a schoolboy. He immediately felt his blood come to a boil and his fists tightened on the reins as he stared into Bradley's face, a face expressionless except for bored indifference. Astonished by the lieutenant's frank notice to him, Will hesitated a moment before responding. "Well, Lieutenant, I gotta admit, you've got all the gall an officer's supposed to have, and there ain't no mistakin' where you stand." He paused a moment before continuing very slowly so the lieutenant clearly heard his response. "As far as I'm concerned, you can kiss my ass." Bradley's head jerked back as if he had been slapped, unaccustomed as he was to being spoken to in that tone. Will went on. "I'll let Sarah and Emma decide whether or not they wanna see me. And if they do, I'll come a'runnin'. Hell, I've known both of 'em longer'n you have."

Bradley backed his horse away, aghast that a lowly scout dared talk to him that way.

Unable to think of a proper retort, his face flushed red, he blurted, "You've been warned, sir!" With that, he wheeled his dark Morgan gelding and returned to his company.

Will sat there, watching the arrogant young officer as he galloped away. *What in hell does Sarah want a pompous ass like that for?* he asked himself. "I've been warned," he repeated. "Wonder what he meant by that." *If it's satisfaction he wants, I hope it's with fists. I'd enjoy bradding that aristocratic nose of his to his upper lip.* He remained sitting there for a few seconds while he calmed down, then said to himself, *I guess I'll get my lower-class ass over to see what the colonel wants.*

There was little doubt what the regimental commander wanted from Will, and as was customary with officers of that rank, it didn't come as a request. "Cason, are you always this hard to track down?" he asked when Will was shown into his office.

"Sometimes," Will answered indifferently. "I reckon it depends on who's lookin' for me."

"The regiment will be moving out of here in the morning and I want to make sure you're ready to go. I want to find that Cheyenne village as soon as possible before

209

they scatter to the winds, so I need you in advance of the column."

Will shrugged. "I planned on goin' with you, but, hell, anybody can find that village. Just follow the Smoky Hill west and you can hardly miss it."

The colonel fixed his unblinking gaze directly on Will's eyes when he replied. "I want you there." He understood Will's comment, but he was not willing to chance any failure of this opportunity to crush a sizable band of hostiles who refused to go to the reservation. If, as he had been told, Cason was the best, then he wanted to make sure he went with the column.

"I'll be there," Will replied, with no hint of enthusiasm. In his present mental state, he really didn't give a damn where he found himself in the next few days. After leaving the orderly room, however, he had a change in attitude, deciding that he would rather be by himself out on the prairie, so maybe this scouting trip might be the best thing for him.

Satisfied that he had everything he needed for the campaign after he drew extra cartridges for his rifle, Will went to the sutler's store for the purpose of buying needle and thread to repair the tear in his shirtsleeve left there by the warrior's knife. He had washed the shirt thoroughly, but the blood-stains never came completely out. However, since it was his best shirt, he couldn't afford to throw it away. While standing at the counter, he heard the door open behind him and the sound of lighthearted conversation. He turned to see Sarah, Emma, and Braxton Bradley entering the store. "Will!" Emma exclaimed and immediately ran to him.

"Hello, Whiskers," he said, patting the little girl on the head as she locked her arms around his leg.

"Will," Sarah greeted him, "I'm glad we got to see you before you all go off to find the Indians tomorrow." Will made no reply, smiling at her and nodding. He glanced at Bradley and almost laughed when he saw the expression of resentment on the lieutenant's face. "Looks like you're planning to do some sewing," Sarah continued.

He looked down at the pack of needles and the spool of thread he had forgotten he had been holding. "Yeah, I'm gonna see if I can sew up this tear in my shirt," he replied.

"I can sew," Emma immediately piped up. "Can't I, Mama?" Not waiting for her mother to answer, she said, "I'll sew it up for you."

"I bet you can," Will said, "but I wouldn't

wanna trouble you with such a small job."
He couldn't help but be amused by Bradley's painful expression as if he had just
eaten meat that had turned bad. Will could
imagine how steamed up the lieutenant was
becoming while hesitating to say anything
in Sarah's presence. To make matters worse
for him, Sarah took control of the situation.

"Here, I'll sew it up for you," she insisted.
"I can do it right now." She held out her
hand for the needles and thread, ignoring
Will's insistence that he would take care of
it himself. Emma protested, but Sarah told
her that the job needed to be done quickly.
"I have some things back in the wagon that
you can practice on," she said.

"I wanna sew Will's shirt," the child protested.

"Emma," Sarah stated sternly, "I don't
have time for this now." She immediately
stepped closer to Will, threaded the needle,
and set to work on the rip.

While the child puckered her lips in
protest, Will glanced up at Bradley, enjoying
the lieutenant's irritation. His attention was
quickly captured, however, by the clean
smell of soap that he always associated with
Sarah. And suddenly it became painful for
him to be near her and he was relieved when
she tied the knot and broke the thread off

with her teeth. "There, that oughta hold it," she announced.

"I'm much obliged," he replied gratefully.

"No trouble," she said. "I'm glad that you're going to be along on this mission tomorrow. I hope you will keep an eye on my fiancé, and see that he gets back for his wedding day."

Her remark stung like fire, reminding him once again that the only woman he had ever loved had chosen the lieutenant instead of him. *I could have taken care of you,* he heard a voice deep within him crying. He could not take consolation even in the expression of humiliation on the lieutenant's face, but he strived to keep his own face expressionless. "I'll keep an eye on him," he said. Then, longing to be somewhere else, he quickly said good-bye, reached down, and gave Emma a hug. "Take care of your mama, Whiskers." Careful not to glance in Sarah's direction, lest she read the hurt in his face, he offered a quick expression of appreciation for the mending job and headed for the door. Outside, he breathed in deeply, feeling he needed to sweep the hurt from his body.

Inside, Braxton spoke for the first time since the encounter. "A most confounding man," he stated, "just as wild and uncivilized as any red savage on the plains."

Sarah smiled, having already realized Braxton's tendency toward jealousy. "We owe him a lot," is all she said, but she could not help wondering if things might have taken another path had not Braxton proposed. She would always wonder about Will and how strong her attraction was to him. She reminded herself then that she had made a decision based on what she thought best for her welfare and her daughter's. Marrying Braxton was a solid future for both of them and a sensible decision when all was considered. Braxton, as an officer in the army, would provide a comfortable life for her, with no worry about food or housing. She owed Emma that. Will was as fine a man as she had ever known, but who could say what their future would be? A solid marriage could not be based on physical attraction alone. She sighed sadly, hoping that Braxton did not notice, and vowed to think no more on the wisdom of her choice.

Threatened by an attack of melancholy, Will decided he could use a drink before supper. He couldn't honestly say that whiskey ever helped his moods one way or another, but on occasion it seemed the right thing to do.

So he guided Spades off the post and headed for a popular saloon much like Mickey Bledsoe's back at Camp Supply. It was named the Soldier's Friend, run by an amiable man named Johnny Tate, and most folks simply called it Johnny's Place.

It was a busy evening at Johnny's Place, although it was still early. Will wasn't surprised, what with the entire regiment taking the field in the morning. Johnny's tent was not really big enough to accommodate the number of soldiers and scouts who had chosen his establishment to patronize. On this evening, it was lit up like a giant Halloween lantern. Hardly in a mood to rub elbows with a mob of drunks, semidrunks, and unruly drinkers, he almost turned Spades around, hesitating for a moment before thinking, *What the hell? I want a drink.*

Stepping inside the tent, he paused to look the crowd over before weaving his way to the bar. A harried bartender looked up and forced a smile for Will when he found a small place to belly up to the bar. "Looks like you're doin' a helluva business," Will said.

"I reckon," Johnny replied, wiping the sweat from his face with the bar towel. "But it's about to work my ass off. What'll you have?"

"I just want a shot of whiskey," Will replied. "Some of that sour mash you had last time I was here."

"If you don't mind waitin' a minute or two," Johnny came back. "I'm outta glasses right now, but there'll be one come along any minute."

Will forced a chuckle. "Hell, Johnny, you're gonna make enough money tonight to retire."

"You think so? Wait till tomorrow. The whole damn regiment will be gone who knows how long and I'll be lucky to see a soul for the next few days."

"Hell, you get most of the regiment's pay, anyway, you're just takin' it all in one night this month." Will turned to see who made the remark, then made room as Kincaid elbowed his way in beside him. The corporal was well on his way to a rendezvous with a miserable morning hangover. His speech was already slurring as he grinned at Johnny. He shoved his empty glass toward the bartender and signaled for a refill. "I wanna buy my partner, here, a drink," he said, and fished around in his pocket for some money. When he found none, he complained, "What the hell happened to my money?"

Then, favoring Will with another foolish grin, he said, "I spent it. You're gonna have to buy me a drink." Then he took on a serious face for a moment when he said, "I was gonna save enough for a go-round with Pauline back yonder." He shrugged, the smile returned, and he mumbled to himself, "She's gonna be disappointed."

Will exchanged glances with Johnny and they both shook their heads. "I'll buy you one more," he said to Kincaid. "Then I think you've had enough. Your head's gonna be so big in the mornin' you might have to carry it on a packhorse."

"Aw, Will, I ain't even drunk yet," he complained, although already holding on to the bar to steady himself.

"You're broke, though," Will said, "and Johnny don't give no credit, so you're done." Nodding toward Johnny, he said, "Pour it." Johnny did as he was told, filling the empty shot glass, and Will put his money on the bar just as Kincaid slid down on the floor, passed out. Will glanced down at the unconscious man for a moment, then picked up the glass of whiskey and tossed it down. Looking back at Johnny, he said, "One's all I wanted, anyway. I expect I'd better get him up before somebody steps on him."

Asking some of the patrons to step back and give him some room, Will hefted Kincaid up onto his feet. Kincaid was not a big man, but even a small man is heavy when he's out cold and nothing but deadweight, so Will shifted him around until he got him settled squarely on his shoulder. Then, telling the crowd to make way, he carried the corporal outside and draped him across his saddle. There was no sound from Kincaid except one grunt when he met the saddle with his belly. Reasonably certain that the body would not slide off the saddle, Will led his horse back to the C Company barracks. Kincaid was cooperative enough to keep from falling off the horse until Will stopped in front of the barracks, where the corporal slid off the saddle and crumpled onto the ground. Will left him there while he went inside to find the soldier unfortunate enough to have gotten barracks orderly duty on the last night in camp. With his help, he carried Kincaid in and dropped him on his cot. He pulled his boots off and set them at the foot of the cot, then stood watching his drunken friend for a moment. "That's as far as I go," Will said. "If he wants his clothes off, he's gonna have to do that himself.

Kincaid's eyelids fluttered for a moment

and he murmured softly, "Thanks, Will." Then he was out again.

Will didn't reply, but just stood there for a moment looking at the sleeping man. The picture was enough to cause him to be thankful he had decided not to drown his sorrows that night. *I wouldn't wanna be inside that head in the morning,* he thought.

The departure on the following morning was not as early as it could have been. At least that was Will's opinion. But then it was always that way when an entire regiment took to the field. With plenty of time to spare, Will dropped by C Company to have breakfast. While he was sitting at the end of a long table, Kincaid came in and headed straight for the coffee urn. With shaking hands, he grasped the cup and tried to steady it long enough to get some of the hot black liquid inside. After a few quick gulps that burned the inside of his mouth, he looked around the room and spotted Will with a wide grin on his face, watching him. He made straight for him and plopped down heavily on the bench opposite his friend.

"Good mornin', Corporal Kincaid," Will greeted him in as cheery a voice as he could effect. "My, but you look like you're rarin' to go this mornin'."

"Damn," Kincaid responded. "I ain't ever gonna get that drunk again. I've already chucked up three times this mornin'. I hope to hell I can keep this coffee down. I swear, I can feel the skin on my stomach rubbin' up against my backbone."

"You need the hair of the dog that bit you," Will said.

"The hell I do," Kincaid blurted. "I'm done with drinkin' — tired of throwin' my money away on it. I woke up this mornin' flat on my back with a puddle of puke on my chest — don't even know how I got there. Bradshaw said you brought me home. Did you?"

Will nodded. "You gonna be able to make it this mornin'?"

"Hell, yeah," Kincaid exclaimed. "This ain't the first time I've been drunk. I'll be there when it's time to go. I'll just wish to hell I wasn't."

"Well, I reckon it's gettin' pretty near that time. I guess I'll go saddle up my horse," Will said. "I'll see you on the trail." He left Kincaid to wrestle with his demons.

Apart from all the routine formations and protocol that had to be performed before the troops could actually mount and start moving, the column would be accompanied for a mile or so by the regimental band with a stirring sendoff to the spirited strains of "Garry Owen," George Custer's favorite marching tune. Will sat patiently through the procedure as the bugle sounded *Boots and Saddles,* and the troopers stood ready with horses saddled. Next came the command "To horse!" Each man stood by his horse, ready to mount, waiting for "Prepare to mount!" followed by "Mount!" It always seemed like an awful lot of fuss to Will, when they could have simply told everybody, "Climb on your horses and let's go."

Finally on the move, the regiment paraded by the cavalry barracks and the hospital, where many of the wives stood watching their gallant men march off to war. Will tried to pretend he didn't notice Sarah and Emma waving as he loped off in front of the column, but Emma's wave was so frantic, he didn't have the heart to ignore it. He touched the brim of his hat with his forefinger as he passed them. The column was a mile outside the post and the sun was already high in the morning sky before the band dropped off and returned to the fort, leaving only the monotonous sounds of the padding of horses' hooves, creaking leather, and the jingle of bit chains. Added to these, the small bits of casual comments between the men that normally occurred at the start of a long march would soon die out as the sun rose higher in the summer sky.

Among the spectators that had come out of the sutler's store as the regiment marched out of the post, a half-breed Comanche named French and a one-eyed man named Boley stood watching with considerable interest. "Now, that oughta be somethin' to make ol' Ned smile," Boley commented as he flipped his black eye patch up on his forehead while he dabbed at the empty socket with the point of his bandana. "That there's damn nigh ever' soldier in the place."

The sullen half-breed grunted in response. The deployment of the entire regiment would indeed be of particular interest to the man who had recently taken the two of them as partners. Opportunities had been scarce of late with the added army patrols out to stop the bloody attacks on the smaller ranchers in the territory. With the regiment on a campaign, there would be fewer patrols to worry Ned Spikes. He was well known by the garrison at Fort Dodge, but they had been unsuccessful in catching him in the act. Unknown to the army, Ned had picked up two men to help him in his bloody crimes. Free from suspicion, French and

Boley were able to come and go unhampered when the three outlaws needed supplies or wanted to see what the soldiers were up to — as on this occasion.

There was little expected of Will and the other scouts during the first couple of days of the march. The column knew where it was heading, and there was no concern on the officers' part for the possibility of ambush or open attacks upon a column of regimental strength. Consequently, he was free to do pretty much what he wanted. So he ranged wide of the flanks, just looking around, coming back to join the others at mealtime, usually with Lieutenant Bordeaux's company. The colonel wanted to make it to the Smoky Hill in two days, but due to the lateness of their departure, they went into camp the first night at Pawnee Creek, leaving a long day's ride before striking the banks of the Smoky Hill approximately fifteen miles below the last reported location of the Cheyenne village. It was now time for Will to perform the duties he was hired for. The colonel's plan was to make a night march the following night in hopes of a surprise attack at dawn. *Just like the one Colonel Custer led against Black Kettle's village on the Washita,* Will thought when told of it. Captain Fischer had the same thought when they went after the war party that ambushed the patrol out of Fort Larned. *It ain't none of my concern, but it seems like every officer wants to follow Custer's example.* Before the colonel could plan his attack, however, he had to know exactly where the village was now located. That was Will's job, and he had until dark the following day to do it.

Gone before sunup, he followed the river, just as he had before when he had scouted for Captain Fischer. This time, however, he was reasonably sure the Cheyenne were not expecting him. Even so, he kept a keen eye for any sign of Cheyenne hunting parties that might warn the village to make ready to fight or run. Early in the morning he passed the place where C Company had made their stand against the Indians, and proceeded across the narrow valley where he and Kincaid had to run for their lives. All was peaceful now as he rode close to the trees that lined the river. On he rode until the sun was high overhead and he decided it time to rest Spades.

He guided his horse into the trees on the riverbank and dismounted where a series of gullies led down to the water. From the multitude of old tracks, he could see that it was a popular watering spot. Looking around him, he saw an abundance of dead limbs for a fire, so he decided he'd take enough time for some coffee and the biscuit he had carried in his pocket. Feeling confident that there was no one to see his fire, he nevertheless built it in a pocket created by a gully in the side of the bank. It was more or less a habit. In a short time, he was sipping his coffee and eating his biscuit while watching the big bay grazing on some shoots growing out of the water. It was peaceful until an image of Sarah strayed into his thoughts. He shook his head, trying to cast such thoughts out of his mind forever. It was hard to do, maybe impossible, he admitted, and the realization of it almost caused him to cry out in frustration. He might have done so had he not just then noticed Spades' ears, almost always twitching, were now pricked up and motionless. Will realized at once that the horse heard something — maybe another horse. A moment later the bay whinnied inquisitively, which told Will that Spades had detected a strange horse or horses approaching. Not waiting to find out, he quickly kicked dirt over his fire and scrambled up to the head of the gully to scan the prairie beyond the river.

There were four of them, hunters as far as he could tell, and they appeared to be heading directly toward the spot that he had picked to rest his horse. *The whole damn river to choose a spot and they have to pick this one,* he thought. He knew he didn't have a lot of time to decide what to do, but he waited a few seconds longer in case they suddenly changed their minds and moved farther up the river to water their ponies. *Damn,* he said to himself when they were within fifty yards and continued on a straight line directly toward him. *Next time I'll be more careful where I decide to make coffee.* There was no thought toward ambushing the hunters. Since there were four of them, he had no guarantee that he could kill them all. The odds were too great that one or more of them would escape and alert the village. Even if he got all four of them, the sound of the gunshots might reach the village, especially if the village had not moved, because he estimated that he was no more than two or three miles from where he had last seen it.

He quickly looked behind him at Spades, the horse watching him with interest now. Then he looked up and down the river to decide which way to run. From where he crouched in the gully, the trees were closer

226

downriver, but the foliage was thicker in the trees upriver with thickets of berry and plum bushes. He decided upriver was best. The other was closer, and he could hide behind a tree, but it wasn't so easy to hide a horse. He wasted no more time. Scrambling back down the gully, he picked up the hot coffeepot, grabbed Spades' reins, and ran along the water's edge, leading the horse. Once he reached the thicket, he led his horse behind the thickest part and dropped the reins to the ground so Spades would know not to stray. Only then could he empty his coffeepot in the bushes and put it away. Then, with his rifle out, he crawled back to a point closer to the edge of the thicket where he could watch the hunters. He thought about his fire that he had covered with dirt and hoped that, if they found it, they would not be overly interested in it, perhaps thinking that it had been made by one of the many Indian visitors to the water hole.

Close enough to catch a word or two of the conversation, and with a fair knowledge of the Cheyenne tongue, he was able to determine that their hunt had not been very successful. One of them, a taller than average man with a muscular body, seemed to be the leader, for the others were inclined to go along with whatever he said. Will couldn't help but speculate that the man would be a formidable foe. There was no indication that the hunters suspected anything out of the ordinary, and appeared content to water their ponies and move on. From what he could hear of their comments, they were returning to their village with plans to hunt again the next day. The muscular one determined that tomorrow would be a better day, and they would find the game that had eluded them today. *Sounds like a good idea to me,* Will thought, lying there in the brambles, *get on your ponies and go.*

Their horses watered, they prepared to leave, pausing to wait while one of them walked over toward the thicket where Will lay. Will tightened his finger on the trigger guard of his rifle and held his breath while the hunter relieved himself, knowing that if the man had chosen to aim his stream upwind, there would have been a fifty-fifty chance he would have seen the barrel of a Henry rifle partially covered with dead leaves. Finished, the man returned to jump on his pony and lope after his friends. Will released a sigh of relief and got to his feet. Knowing the hunters were going back to their village, he would simply follow them.

As he retreated to fetch his horse, he couldn't help but smile when he thought of a discussion he once had with Kincaid. The corporal maintained that Cheyenne men squatted to pee, like women, while Will had argued that it was not always the case. It depended upon the situation and whether they were wearing a simple breechcloth or leggings. When he got back, he would tell Kincaid that he knew one Cheyenne who did his business standing up.

He waited in the trees until the four hunters were almost out of sight before he fell in behind them. It didn't take much time to reach the Cheyenne village, no more than an hour. Much to his surprise, they had not decided to move from the camp he had scouted before. Although locating the camp was all he had been sent to do, he decided to take a closer look if possible, intent upon seeing any signs that would tell him they were preparing to move the camp. He had heard the muscular hunter say they would hunt tomorrow, which would indicate no plans to move the village. Still, he decided to confirm it. Moving along the river bluffs as he had done the last time, with Spades tied in the willows, he approached as close as he dared in the bright daylight. From where he stopped, he could not see a great deal of the village, but the drying racks for skins still staked in the ground near the tipis he could see told him that they weren't planning to move anytime soon. Their chiefs and elders must have decided the village was not in danger of sudden attack, since the soldiers had shown no interest in pursuing them, turning for home instead. This was a poor assumption on the part of the Cheyenne, Will thought, in mind of the full regiment of troops already marching upon them. *I better get back and tell the colonel,* he thought, after moving up as close as he dared to the camp.

He met the forward scouts of the column after a ride of two hours, approximately twenty-five miles from the Cheyenne village. When Colonel Arnold learned how close he was, he ordered the column to go into camp to rest the men and horses in preparation for an early march in the predawn hours of the morning, timed to hit the Cheyenne while they were sleeping. Will was present when the colonel gave his company officers their orders, and he was pleased to see that the man had some compassion for his enemy. His officers were told that it was inevitable that women and children would be killed, but he made it clear that his intention was not wholesale slaughter of the band. Their targets were the warriors, the pony herd, the food stores, and the lodges. "The purpose of our mission is to punish the renegade warriors who defy the government's order to return to the reservation," he said. "We must destroy their means to survive, as well as their will to fight."

Being a free spirit of sorts himself, Will was not entirely apathetic about the Indians' resistance to giving up their ancient way of life. He was certain that he wouldn't like living on a reservation if he were in their shoes, especially the area selected for them — an area between the Kansas line and the Cimarron River. The land there was in a gypsum belt. The streams were bitter and there was little game to hunt. The only thing that made the planned attack tolerable for him was the fact that this particular band of Cheyenne had been killing settlers, attacking towns and army patrols. They needed to be stopped.

The column moved out approximately four hours before dawn on a chilly late-summer morning with the moon still above the distant hills. All loose equipment, coffee cups, and mess kits were muffled, and only the creaking leather of the saddles and occasional clinking of the bit chains disturbed the silence, along with an occasional snort from the horses. Under instructions to select a suitable staging point for the attack, Will was in his usual place far in advance of the column. His choice was a long open expanse of prairie running up to the bluffs of the river, about two miles shy of the village. That settled, he continued on to the edge of the sleeping camp, just to have a final look. All seemed peaceful, so he returned to the staging point and waited for the column.

When Colonel Arnold and his officers arrived to look over the area, he gave his approval and immediately laid out his plans for the assault. He decided to split the column into three attack forces, one on each side of the river, and the third to march beyond the village before crossing the river to be in a position to cut off escape in that direction. F Company was assigned that responsibility. Having fulfilled his part of the attack, Will was free to join any group in the battle. As usual, he chose to ride with Lieutenant Bordeaux's troop in C Company. When all was ready, F Company was given a head start of forty-five minutes to get into position beyond the camp. The colonel figured this would make the time of the attack right at sunrise.

CHAPTER 10

Bloody Hand awoke with a start. At first confused, he paused to listen. There was some cause for trouble in the huge pony herd grazing by the river. He leaped from his blanket, waking his wife, Lark, in the process. "What is it?" she exclaimed.

"I don't know," Bloody Hand replied as he grabbed his rifle and slipped through the flap of the tipi. In that moment, the first shots were fired, and within minutes, he saw a wave of cavalry descending upon the village from the eastern end of the camp. "Get up!" he yelled to Lark. "Hurry!" he commanded as warriors, women, and children were now pouring out of the lodges. "Run to the river," he directed and pointed toward the west. Ducking back inside the tipi, he quickly snatched up all the ammunition he could carry and followed his wife, who was running away from the line of soldiers already burning lodges on the lower end of the camp.

Soon the air was filled with the sound of rifles, bullets zipping in all directions amid the screams of the women and the crying of the children trying to gain protection in the streambed. Before he got very far, he was forced to steer away from the river, for another line of soldiers crossed over from the other side to close off that line of escape. Filled with anger at having been caught so unaware, he dropped to his knee and emptied his Spencer carbine at the charging soldiers. Then, with no choice but to seek cover, he sprang up and ran to the west, only to find another line of soldiers in position to stop any escape in that direction. There were many others who had sought the same escape route as he, and in the flood of terrified people, he lost sight of his wife.

He turned to find Brave Elk running toward him. "Come!" his friend called out. "We must break through or they will kill us all!" With no hesitation, Bloody Hand followed him. With bullets snapping all around them, they made it safely into the trees by the river, where they found a dozen or more warriors already hiding under the five-foot-high banks. Some were armed, but about half the number had run out of their lodges without their weapons and now it was too late to retrieve them, for the soldiers were already moving among the tipis in the lower part of the village. Those with rifles were frantically digging rifle pits, preparing to fight the soldiers.

"This is no good," Bloody Hand told them. "Our warriors are scattered, running for their lives. There are too many soldiers. They have come to destroy us. They will soon search the riverbanks, and we are too few to fight them. We must find a way to break through the line of soldiers at the upper end of the village." He got to his feet and paused a moment to say, "Come with me if you want to live to have your revenge." Accustomed to following him in war, there was no hesitation on the part of the other warriors. Running in a crouch to avoid being spotted above the bank, they successfully made their way to a point just short of the advancing line of soldiers from F Company. Bloody Hand halted his warriors there while he searched for a possible escape route. The converging cavalry troops formed a solid line of fire as they closed in on the upper end of the village. "We cannot pass without being seen," he said. "We must let them pass us instead." Spotting two good-sized gullies behind him, he pointed to them and said, "There! They are big enough to hide all of us. Cover yourselves with brush."

The warriors split up and took cover in the two gullies, with barely enough time to pull brush and dead branches over them before the line of cavalry moved even with them. Luck was with them due to the many gullies that reached down from the bluffs. It caused the terrain to be too rough for the soldiers to maintain a tight line, resulting in only two troopers able to urge their mounts along that stretch of the riverbank. As the two exhorted their horses to hurry over the gullies and cracks, they began to fall behind their comrades, resulting in carelessness on their part. Consequently, when the first trooper noticed the Indians hiding in one of the gullies, he was not quick enough to avoid the bullet from Bloody Hand's rifle. With no time to react, the other soldier was pulled from his saddle by the Cheyenne warriors in the other gully and stabbed repeatedly.

The way clear before them now, the warriors broke from the gullies and entered the dark water. With no soldiers close to them, they were safely across before they were discovered. In possession of the two cavalry mounts, they left the burning village behind them and headed for the nearby hills —

Bloody Hand and Brave Elk on one of the horses, two of the other warriors on the second. The rest ran after them on foot.

Across the river, Captain Richard Evans, company commander, F Company, turned in time to see what had happened behind his line of cavalry. "Damn!" he cursed, cognizant of his orders to let no warriors escape. "Bradley," he ordered, "take a squad and run those men down."

Lieutenant Bradley was quick with a snappy, "Yes, sir" and picked a detail of fifteen men to immediately give chase. "Hurry, men, let's overtake the devils before they reach those hills and scatter."

"Ride with caution, Braxton," Evans warned, "and don't pursue them beyond those hills."

"Yes, sir," Bradley replied, thinking to himself that he was capable of estimating the risk as to how far to follow a frightened bunch of hostiles.

Looking back and seeing the detachment of soldiers break away to come after him, Bloody Hand kicked the army mount hard, heading the horse toward a narrow ravine that separated two hills. He signaled the warriors on the other horse, and they followed his lead. Behind them, the other Indians had no choice but to run as best they could. Eager to seize upon the chase as an opportunity to exact revenge, he told Brave Elk what he intended to do. As usual, his friend was ready to follow him. As soon as they entered the ravine, and were far enough in to be out of sight of the charging cavalry detail, Bloody Hand pulled his horse to a stop and he and Brave Elk leaped to the ground. One of the other two warriors was instructed to lead the horses over the ridge of the ravine and hide them. "Get back as quickly as you can," Bloody Hand said. With the horses out of sight, the four warriors hid themselves in the rocky sides of the ravine, two on each side, and waited for the soldiers.

With his saber drawn and extended toward the fleeing Indians, Braxton Bradley led his troops as they bore down on the desperate hostiles. The four on horseback had apparently escaped into the hills, but there were nine on foot, running like rabbits before the hounds. Hoping to overtake them before they reached the ravine, he urged his men on. Only twenty yards or so behind them, he galloped into the ravine. With carbines blazing, his men shot at the hostiles as they tried to zigzag into the rocks to seek cover, when suddenly the sides of the ravine opened up with gunfire and his horse collapsed under him. In a matter of seconds, the ravine turned into a valley of death as his troopers were cut down before they knew where the shots were coming from. Dazed by his fall, Braxton lay still beside his dying horse. Around him lay the bodies of his men, most of them dead. The hostiles he had been chasing were now going among the dying to finish them off with their knives. Knowing it would be his turn any second, he drew his pistol and aimed it at one of the bushwhackers coming down from the side of the hill. Before he could pull the trigger, a bullet from a rifle slammed into his shoulder, causing him to misfire and drop his pistol. As he fumbled to pick it up again, a warrior kicked it out of his reach and grabbed him by his hair. Yanking his hair back, the warrior shrieked a war cry of vengeance and started to scalp him.

"Wait!" Bloody Hand shouted. "He is an officer, a chief. He is one who tells the soldiers to kill us and our families. I say we should take him with us and let him know how it is to die slowly."

The warrior paused, his knife still threatening to split the skin on Bradley's forehead. It was obvious that he wanted the scalp, but he respected Bloody Hand's standing as a war chief. In a state of terrified shock, the lieutenant was helpless to resist and made no effort to defend himself. Finally the warrior released Bradley's hair, and delivered a consolation blow across his cheek with the butt of his knife. Bradley sank to the ground with a raw cut across his face; the blood from his shoulder wound had now soaked his tunic. While he slumped there, several of the other warriors descended upon him to rain blows across his back and head until he lay almost unconscious in the long grass of the prairie.

"We cannot linger here," Bloody Hand cautioned. "We must find the others who have escaped." They were all thinking about their families, unsure if their wives and children had managed to hide from the soldiers. "Those who escaped will try to run to the village of Lame Fox." The others agreed, but it would mean a trek of about thirty-five miles to the Arapaho camp on the Saline River, a difficult journey with no food or water. With horses and weapons now from the slain soldiers, the Cheyenne warriors rode off to the north, hoping to find some of their people making their way through the hills to their Arapaho friends. A leash was fashioned with the reins of Bradley's horse — the loop tied around the lieutenant's neck and the other end around the saddle horn of Bloody Hand's horse. There were extra horses, but Bloody Hand did not see fit to let the soldier ride. Barely able to stand, Braxton struggled to keep from falling, knowing he would be dragged to death.

Back in the village, Colonel Arnold surveyed the scene of destruction his soldiers had wrought, with every lodge burning and the clearing strewn with bodies, most of them warriors, but also many women, children, and old men. He felt gratified, and pronounced the attack a success. The village was destroyed. Most of the large pony herd were captured and there appeared to be only a small number of military casualties. His intention now was to leave the area right away, armed with the knowledge that there were other Cheyenne villages farther along the river. He was mindful of George Custer's quick retreat after the battle on the Washita after finding himself in like circumstances. Arnold's objective had been accomplished. This band of hostile Indians had been severely punished, and at no great loss of his men. In the next few minutes, however, he was to learn of the loss of an entire squad of men and their lieutenant when Captain Evans reported that Lieutenant Bradley and fifteen men had chased a group of Cheyenne warriors and had not returned. "Dammit, man!" the colonel swore, having already congratulated himself on the success of the raid. "Find them!" Again thinking of Custer at the Washita, who left Major Joel Elliott and his detachment behind to be slaughtered, he did not want the same stigma on his victory. "Send a detachment to look for them," Arnold ordered. "And do it fast. I don't intend to remain here long." Eager to get it done quickly, he added, "Take Cason with you."

Sitting on Spades off to one side of the burning village, Will reloaded his rifle. He had not fired very many times during the attack — only when he had to in order to keep from being shot himself. He couldn't bring himself to shoot at the backs of women and children, in spite of a general feeling among many army officers that, "Any Indian is a worthy target." In fact, he had not fired the rifle enough to heat the barrel up, a negative point with the Henry. In a sustained gun battle, the barrel would get too hot to hold in your bare hand. He had considered trying to buy one of the new Winchesters that featured a wooden forearm and a loading port beside the breech. But his Henry had been so reliable as to become almost a part of him, and he couldn't bring himself to trade.

His loading complete — fifteen .44 cartridges in the magazine, and one more in the chamber — he glanced up to see Lieutenant Collins from F Company riding toward him. "Colonel Arnold says you're to come with me," Collins declared upon pulling up beside Will.

"Is that so?" Will replied. "Where we goin'?"

Collins explained that a detachment of troopers had chased after a group of Indians and had not returned. "We know where they were last seen, and Colonel Arnold wanted you to track them. He wants to pull outta here." Will nodded and turned Spades to fall in beside the lieutenant's horse, and they rode to the upper end of the camp, where a detachment of twenty men waited. It was not until the detail moved out and crossed the river that Will learned the identity of the officer leading the missing squad. Like the jolt from a gunshot, he was stunned into silence for a few moments — *Braxton Bradley, Sarah's betrothed!* A multitude of thoughts ran swiftly through his brain. Among them, one that had to be said, *Good riddance.* He couldn't help but think it, although he knew it was a terrible reaction to the news.

The trail was easy enough to follow, tracks of sixteen shod horses galloping toward a ravine in the hills a few hundred yards away. According to Collins, his company commander had spotted the hostiles, and said they were no more than a dozen. Looking ahead toward the hills, Will thought to himself that, if they were armed, it would not have taken many to ambush a hard-riding cavalry detachment intent upon running them to ground. He was not surprised to find his speculations were right, for they came upon the mutilated bodies of fifteen soldiers just inside the ravine. The one dead horse was identified as Lieutenant Bradley's, but the lieutenant's body was not among those of the other soldiers.

"They took him captive," Collins said as he stepped up beside Will.

"Looks that way," Will replied while still staring down at Bradley's horse.

"Why would they kill these men, but take Bradley captive?"

"Hard to say," Will responded, still sorting out his feelings on the matter. "Who knows why they sometimes take hostages and other times they just kill 'em?" He gave the lieutenant a sideways glance and added, "Probably because he was an officer."

It was a tough decision for the lieutenant to make, having been ordered to find the detail and return as quickly as possible. He stood gazing toward the upper end of the ravine, where the tracks led away from the ambush, weighing the odds of whether Lieutenant Bradley was still alive. He knew it was only a matter of time before Bradley was dead, and it might have already happened. Thinking of the men he was now responsible for, he was not eager to lead them into the hills after the Cheyenne hostiles for fear of another ambush. He took one more look at the foreboding hills before giving the order to load the bodies on their horses and return at once to the regiment, leaving Will still searching his conscience for his personal decision.

His mind was churning with thoughts of Sarah, trying to imagine how she might react to news that Braxton was presumed dead. Had she known the lieutenant long enough to be devastated by his death? Possibly, he allowed, she might come to him for consolation. He could live with the knowledge he was second choice, he told himself. Maybe over time she would come to genuinely love him. He was almost certain that he was Emma's choice, if that was a factor in her decision. He was still sitting there, deep in his thoughts, when the bodies of the slain were draped behind the saddles of fifteen of Collins' detail, and they prepared to ride.

"Well, I guess that's about all we can do for them," the lieutenant said, and waited for Will to turn his horse toward the village.

Will remained motionless for another few moments. "I ain't goin' back," he announced quietly. "I'm goin' after Lieutenant Bradley." In spite of all the thinking he had done to the contrary, he knew what he had to do — for Sarah. Bradley was her choice and he owed it to her to find out what happened to her fiancé. Dead or alive, she deserved to know for sure.

"Hell, man," Collins exclaimed, "there's more than a few hostiles that got away from that village, and this bunch that took Bradley are armed with army carbines. Going after them alone isn't the smartest thing a man could do. They're bound to join up with the others." He continued to search the stoic scout's face for a moment, thinking the man was judging his courage. "Listen, I'm not saying I'm a special friend of Braxton Bradley's. We didn't have much in common, but, dammit, he's a fellow officer and I'd lead this patrol after him if I thought there was a reasonable chance he's still alive

247

— and I was halfway confident I wasn't endangering more lives."

Will dismissed the lieutenant's concern with a casual shake of his head. "It would be a mistake for you to trot these soldiers after them," he said. "You're most likely right about what you'd run into. Ambushin' is how those Cheyennes make a livin'. I'll do better by myself. I don't plan on lettin' 'em see me."

Somewhat mollified, Collins nodded vigorously. "You're sure you wanna do this?" When Will assured him that he did, the lieutenant said, "All right, then. I'll tell the colonel what you're planning to do. I don't know what he'll say about it."

"I don't reckon it's up to him to say one way or the other," Will replied as he turned Spades' head toward the upper end of the ravine. "I'll be seein' you, Lieutenant."

One of the men who had been listening to the exchange between the lieutenant and the scout turned in his saddle to watch Will ride off up the head of the ravine. "That'll be the last we see of him," he commented to anyone interested as Will disappeared over the top of the ridge.

Braxton stumbled, almost falling as he fought to stay on his feet when Bloody

Hand yanked the reins around his neck. Staggering along doggedly, his right arm hanging limp at his side, the blood from his shoulder drying now to form a sticky red film down his arm and over his fingers, he knew to fall would be his end. The muscular Indian would drag him to death. His boots, made for riding, were rubbing his heels raw, but the blisters went unnoticed as he struggled to keep from falling. In a few brief moments, his world had been turned inside out. He could not have imagined that he would ever find himself in such desperate circumstances. These savages held no respect for him as an officer, and he was terrified by the feeling that his death could come at any instant, depending on the whim of the fearsome warrior leading him by a leash. Could he possibly hope that Evans would send the entire company to rescue him? Even if the troops suddenly appeared, it would be a sentence of death for him, for he was sure he would be immediately killed. Still, he held on to the hope that he would somehow live, although it made no sense to think it. Foremost in his mind was the thought that it would have been more merciful had they killed him with his men. His fearsome captor seemed to promise as much with his insolent gaze.

Well into the afternoon the party of hostiles continued until finally they stopped to rest the horses at a small stream that seemed to come from nowhere to bubble up in the midst of a stand of willows. He was certain he could not have walked another step had they not stopped where they did. As soon as Bloody Hand dismounted, Braxton slumped to the ground exhausted. He was immediately rewarded with a kick in the back and told to get to his feet. Struggling to all fours, he grabbed the slender trunk of a small willow and painfully pulled himself to a standing position. His performance was met with laughter and derision. "The old women in our village could walk farther than that and not be tired," Brave Elk said. "When are you going to kill him?" Braxton did not know the language, so he didn't know what was said, but he had a strong feeling that they were discussing his execution.

"I don't know," Bloody Hand replied. "He amuses me. I don't have a dog, so maybe now I do. I will keep him a while longer." Then to Braxton, he spoke in English. "You will be my dog. If you are a good dog, I will beat you only a little."

"I am an officer of the U.S. Army," Braxton started, but that was as far as he got before Bloody Hand cuffed him hard across his face with the back of his hand.

"Dogs do not talk!" Bloody Hand raged. "If this dog talks again, I'll cut out his tongue." Braxton sank back against the willow, longing to drop to the ground, but afraid to.

They had nothing to eat except what little they found in the saddlebags, which consisted of some moldy hardtack and a small quantity of bacon. After consuming that, they rested only a little longer before setting out to the north again in search of other refugees from their village. Exhausted beyond rational thought, Braxton somehow managed to take one step after another, knowing to drop was to die. Later in the afternoon, they found a group of women and children, and a few old men, who had also started out for the Arapaho village — about twenty people in all. Their immediate reaction upon seeing Bloody Hand's captive was to hurl anything that could be thrown at him, attacking him with sticks and dirt clods. Bloody Hand made no effort to stop it, letting it continue until the women grew tired from the effort. Not seriously injured, but sore and bloodied anew, Braxton protected himself as best he could by curling up in as tight a ball as he could manage. Over the next couple of days he was to learn how much of this treatment he could stand and how long he could go without food.

The combined group of refugees, with Bloody Hand as their leader, set out again for the Saline River, but upon reaching the site of the Arapaho village, they discovered that the village had gone. Perhaps word of the cavalry attack on the Cheyenne village had prompted the Arapahos to move farther north to prevent the same fate overtaking them. It was decided that they should continue north to strike the south fork of the Solomon, since tracks of the Arapaho village led that way.

In need of food and rest for their people, the men decided to camp there for a day and a night to hunt for game. While they were there, a few more stragglers from the raid found their way to the camp. Bloody Hand and the dozen warriors in his party had arms and horses, so he sent out three groups of hunters to search for game. Brave Elk and one other backtracked on their trail to see if the soldiers had found the bodies of their comrades in the ravine and might now be following them. The prisoner was tied to a cottonwood and left with two small boys to watch him and give the alarm if he tried to escape. Braxton did not possess the strength or the will at that time to attempt anything. He was just grateful to be allowed to sit on the ground.

It was a slow process trailing the Cheyenne. The trail was plain enough, but after leaving the hills, the terrain was open, undulating prairie where a man on a horse could be spotted from a great distance. Often he was forced to zigzag to make his way to a rise or ravine where he could take cover. He felt that for every mile he hung back, the Indians were gaining two. Just beyond a small plateau, he came upon a point where another group joined the one he was following. This group, however, was not on horseback. It stood to reason that this second group was most likely women and children who had escaped Colonel Arnold's purge. It also figured that the combined group would slow down to accommodate the walkers. He took a good long look at the prairie before him to pick out the next possible point to take cover. He was about to nudge Spades to continue when he spotted two Indians on horseback at the top of a small hill. They were looking back over the way they had come. He held Spades back, fairly certain they had not seen him. When they turned and disappeared, he gave Spades his heels and headed for the hill. He continued trailing the hostiles in this fashion, from one vantage point to the next as the afternoon wore on. He would be happy to see the evening, for he intended to catch up to the Indians by riding at night.

On into the night he rode, thinking that the Saline couldn't be much farther away. In less than a quarter of an hour after thinking it, he saw the rosy glow on the horizon that told him he was nearing the river and the hostile camp. From the size of the glow, he figured that it came from one large fire. Eager to see whether Bradley was with them, he pushed onward, even more cautious now that he was so close. Approaching the river, he was glad to see that the party had crossed over to the other side to make their camp. It would make it easier for him to get closer since he would have the cover of the cottonwoods on the banks of the river. When within about fifty yards from the river, he paused for a long minute, carefully scanning the dark bluffs, looking for anyone acting as a sentinel. He saw no one, so he continued on to the bank. Evidently, the two scouts he had seen before had reported that the army was not following them. Once inside the tree line, he dismounted and dropped Spades' reins to the ground.

As he expected this late in the summer, the river was low, with tiny islands rising above the water line, covered with brush, and the current divided into separate streams. It would almost be possible to walk across except for the main channel. Making his way to a sand spit near the middle of the river, he paused for a while to listen to the sounds from the Cheyenne camp. So far, there were no shouts of alarm indicating that he had been spotted, so he waded across the waist-deep channel, holding his rifle and cartridge belt over his head. Although close to the camp, he could not really see it from the riverbed, so he crawled up the bank until he could clearly see the circle around the big fire they had built.

At first there was no sign of a hostage, and he was about to decide that he had missed Bradley's body somewhere along the trail he had followed. He was almost relieved to think he could now report to Sarah that her groom was dead, and he could remove himself from the potential danger he now faced from a dozen or more heavily armed hostiles. As he had figured, there were at least twenty or so men, women, and children who had joined with the warriors in this refugee camp. Most of them were gathered close to the fire, and it appeared that they had been fortunate to find game to kill, for the picked remains of two carcasses could be plainly seen from his vantage point. *Well, I'd better get my ass outta here,* he thought, and turned to slide back down the bank. At that moment, a group of small children just outside the fire's glow caught his eye. They appeared to be involved in some sort of game. When one of them suddenly ran toward the fire, there was a space created, big enough to reveal someone lying on the ground. Pausing to take another look, he realized it was Braxton Bradley. Lying on his side with his hands and feet tied behind his back, the lieutenant was the focus of the children's game.

He is alive! The thought caused Will to hesitate for a long moment. He had fully expected to find Bradley's corpse somewhere along the way, and he had persevered in following the hostiles so he could confirm the fact to Sarah. Then she could get on with her life without the nagging worry that he might be held captive somewhere. Now he had the responsibility of having to try to rescue Sarah's fiancé. *A helluva note,* he thought, *but I reckon I'll have to try — sure as hell not for that snobbish son of a bitch. I'll do it for Sarah and Whiskers.*

Although it was settled that he was going

to do it, the question now was how was he going to do it? Bradley was just going to have to hold on until he saw an opportunity to get to him. He sure as hell couldn't walk into an armed camp and shoot his way out. There were other things to consider. He didn't know what kind of shape Bradley was in — if he was physically able to run if he was given the opportunity. Another matter was the acquisition of a horse. He didn't like the notion of Spades carrying double with a gang of angry warriors chasing him. *It'd be a helluva lot easier to tell Sarah her sweetheart was dead,* he thought, without seriously thinking of that possibility.

There was nothing to do now but wait until the camp turned in for the night, then see what his options were. It might be that there would be no chance to get to Bradley that night and he would be forced to withdraw and continue trailing them to the next camp. Will didn't care much for that possibility, because he had a notion that this bunch was on their way to another village, maybe on the Solomon or farther still to the Republican — leading him deeper and deeper into hostile territory. "Damn!" he swore, just under his breath. A few moments later, he whirled around, ready to defend himself, when he heard a noise behind him.

He was at once relieved to see Spades casually crossing the river to join him, evidently having heard him swear. "Dammit, horse, I wasn't callin' you," he whispered. "You're gettin' more like a dog every day." *Maybe you're just coming over to tell me to get a horse,* he thought.

With that thought in mind, he looked below the camp where he could see the cavalry horses bunched, their saddles still on. *Helluva way to treat a horse,* he thought, at the same time appreciating the fact that it would save him valuable minutes. There was no evidence of concern on the part of the Indians, for there was no one guarding the horses. Impatient to act, yet knowing that there was nothing he could do until the camp settled down to sleep, he walked Spades back across the river, found a place to secure the horse, and waited.

It was not long before the camp grew quiet. The people who had walked were tired, and combined with their full stomachs, were ready to sleep. Some of the warriors remained around the fire for a time after that, then they too laid down to sleep. Apparently unconcerned about their prisoner, they left Bradley trussed up on the ground where he had been before. Feeling it a mistake to act too soon, Will waited until he was reasonably sure all were asleep. "All right, boy," he whispered to Spades, "it's time to go to work." Leading his horse down the river to a point opposite the cavalry horses, he crossed over and walked Spades toward them. Counting on the notion that the army mounts would not shy away from the smell of him or Spades, he led the bay into their midst. Had they been Indian ponies, they would most likely have scattered as he approached, fearful of the strange smell. As he suspected, they paid him no more than a mild curious concern. He took the reins of a sturdy-looking roan and quietly walked it and Spades back to the riverbank.

He had stolen horses before. That was the easy part. Now came the part that could cost him his life. All it would take was for one awake person to bring the whole camp down on him — or one awake dog. While he had watched the camp before, he had not seen any dogs. That didn't mean there weren't any, but there was a pretty good chance that none had come with the people when they escaped. Leaving the horses below the bank, he crawled up to the top and paused there, watching to see whether anyone might have noticed. All was quiet, so he carefully rose to his feet. Still there was no outcry and no dogs. He looked at the still form of Braxton Bradley and thought to himself, *If you're dead, I'm gonna shoot you for my trouble.* Walking as quietly and as casually as he could under the circumstances, he went directly to the trussed-up body lying only a dozen paces from a sleeping form. Coming up behind him, he knelt down and clamped a hand over Braxton's mouth to keep him from making a startled sound. There was no attempt to call out. The lieutenant had become so accustomed to constant beatings and abuse that he no longer had the will to protest.

"Can you walk?" Will whispered as he hurriedly sawed away at Bradley's binds.

Braxton, in a state of shock, and not sure he was not dreaming, nodded, although he was not sure whether he could. His eyes grew big as saucers as his mind began to function and he recognized the angel who had come to rescue him. "Don't make a sound," Will warned. With Will's help, he managed to get to his feet, and almost fell before Will caught him. Once he was steady, Will walked him between the sleeping bodies to the bank of the river where the horses waited. Braxton had to be helped up in the saddle, and fell forward to lay on the roan's neck as Will led him down into the water. "Hold on good," Will said, "we ain't got time for you to fall off." Once he was across, he held the roan's reins and nudged Spades into a slow gallop. He had considered taking the time to scatter the rest of the horses, but decided it better to steal quietly away and hope for a sizable head start before anyone there knew what had happened.

They had not gotten out of sight of the camp when Braxton lost consciousness and slid off his horse. Will pulled up sharply and leaped off his horse to help him. The impact with the ground caused the wound in Braxton's shoulder to bleed, oozing shiny red as the moonlight reflected from it. "Damn," Will swore. In his haste to escape the camp, he had not realized Braxton had been shot. He had dismissed the crusty shirt as the result of many beatings. This put a different light on his plans for flight. Braxton was obviously in serious condition, no doubt from a great loss of blood. He was in no shape to run. "Damn," Will swore solemnly again, while he decided what to do. He had planned to simply make a run for Fort Dodge, figuring that if they were chased, the hostiles would not risk riding past the Smoky Hill for fear of encountering army troops again. And since they had been successful in stealing away from the Cheyenne camp, their lead would be insurmountable. Now all that had changed. Maybe the Cheyenne would not chase after them, but Will had to assume they would, if only to recover the horse. He was tempted to tie Bradley across the saddle and make a run for it, anyway, but knew it would probably kill him. "Damn," he swore for the third time while he thought of his options. Finally, he decided on what he believed to be his best chance.

"Come on, Bradley," he said as he pulled the confused lieutenant to his feet. "I'm gonna put you on this horse again, and you hang on good and tight. If you can stay on for just an hour or so, I'll let you rest, and we'll see what we can do about that wound and maybe get you somethin' to eat. All right?"

"I'll try," Bradley mumbled. "I don't know if I can."

"Try, hell," Will responded, "stay on that horse. Think about Sarah. By God, if I had somebody like Sarah Lawton waitin' for me, I'd damn sure make it back if I had to crawl all the way."

Braxton was too weary to recognize the honest envy in Will's statement. "How far back are the troops?" he asked.

"Troops?" Will replied brusquely. "I'm all the troops you've got. I'm your whole damn cavalry, so you'd better hope I know what I'm doin'."

Braxton was clearly shocked, but too weak to question why the regiment had not seen fit to come to his rescue. Later, after regaining some of his strength, he would express his indignation at having been abandoned. But for now his mind was in too much of a fog.

After getting Braxton settled securely in the saddle, Will turned the horses away from the initial course south, and headed back toward the Saline River, angling to strike the river at a point downstream from the camp from which they had just escaped. Once they reached the river, he guided the horses into water up to the stirrups and walked them slowly downriver, hoping Bradley didn't fall off and that the horses didn't churn up too much sand and pebbles from the river bottom. After about three quarters of a mile they left the river and climbed up in the bluffs. The bluffs were not more than ten feet high at this point, but the climb almost caused Bradley to fall out of the saddle again. Will caught him with a hand on his shoulder and encouraged him to gut it out for just a little longer while he looked for a place to hide.

When they came across a deep ravine that dropped from the prairie, through a stand of cottonwoods, to the river, Will declared it to be as good as they were likely to find. Looking at the lieutenant hugging his horse's neck, he figured Braxton wasn't going to make it much farther, anyway. "Lemme get you settled," he said as he helped Braxton down. "Then I'll see to the horses. After that, I'll see if there's anything I can do for that bullet wound." Braxton didn't reply, but looked as if he didn't care what happened anymore. Will stood glaring down at him for a moment before warning, "Don't you go checkin' out on me, dammit. I ain't haulin' no damn corpse back to Sarah Lawton."

Gambling on the probability that no one in the Cheyenne camp was likely to check on their prisoner in the middle of the night, Will unsaddled the horses and prepared to stay the night. He built a small fire in a crevice of the ravine, but he didn't want to risk frying some of the bacon in his saddlebag for fear some sharp-nosed hostile might smell it on the wind. But he provided coffee and deer jerky to help his patient regain some of his strength. He had made his camp a hell of a lot closer to the party of Cheyenne than he would have cared to, but that simple fact might be reason to believe they wouldn't think to look for him that close. Plans to head straight back to Fort Dodge had been abandoned due to Bradley's condition. Fort Hays was a good bit closer than Dodge and it was the reason he had brought them back to the river. The task now was to see if Bradley was strong enough to make the two-day trip. If he could rest enough for the balance of that night, they would follow the Saline east in the morning. *If he can't ride in the morning . . .* He didn't finish the thought, because the alternative held little hope.

CHAPTER 11

Bloody Hand was furious. How could the soldier have cut his bonds and slipped out of the camp, even then stealing a horse? The lieutenant looked too weak to walk, so someone came into their camp to free him. Who then? It was not the soldiers. This much was certain. And without any evidence to support his suspicions, he somehow knew it was the one white man who always seemed to appear to plague him — *Okohome,* the coyote. Impatient to prove his suspicions, he carefully inspected the ground where the soldier had been bound, searching for tracks that did not belong. It proved to be a hopeless endeavor, for there were too many tracks, and none that left the imprint of a boot. How could the coyote walk through the camp without leaving a footprint? Was his medicine that strong? Had Bloody Hand been more observant upon the few times he had seen Will, he might have noticed that the white coyote wore moccasins and not boots.

Determined to find him, he told Brave Elk that he would not go with them as they continued their journey to the Arapaho village. "Why do you care?" Brave Elk responded. "All that has happened is that the wounded soldier is gone and we lost one of the soldier horses. No one in our camp was hurt. Get this annoying white man out of your mind. It is making you crazy."

The look in Bloody Hand's eyes told his friend that such talk was useless. "His medicine is strong, but I will find him and I will kill him. Then I will take his medicine."

"If his medicine is strong enough to let him walk without leaving footprints, how will you track him?"

"The soldier must leave tracks," Bloody Hand answered impatiently. "Maybe the coyote's horse is a medicine horse, too. But the soldier horse is not. I will follow *his* tracks."

Brave Elk shook his head in frustration, but understood Bloody Hand's obsession with this white man who seemed to appear almost everywhere unexpectedly. "I will tell the others to go on without us," he finally said. "I will go with you to help you find this ghost."

"I need no help," Bloody Hand replied. "You must go with the others."

Brave Elk shrugged off the comment. "I am your friend. We have always fought side by side. I will go with you."

Although the two warriors began their search as soon as the rest of the camp started north toward the Solomon River, it was late in the afternoon before Bloody Hand found the tracks that he decided were the right ones. It was an almost impossible task to sort out any pattern from the faint prints barely discernible in the tall grass where the horses had grazed. But as the sun sank lower in the western sky, Bloody Hand found a series of prints that, upon closer inspection, proved to be the tracks of two horses moving toward the river. They had evidently walked together, straight toward the bank, as if being led.

"He must have led his own horse into the herd, so he could hide behind it and not frighten the other ponies," Bloody Hand said, excited now and eager to follow.

"Here!" Brave Elk exclaimed and pointed to a set of distinct tracks leading into the water. "This is where he crossed." He stood waiting for his friend to come inspect the tracks. When Bloody Hand hurried to the spot, a patient smile spread across Brave

Elk's face. "Maybe the coyote's pony is not a magic pony," he said, pointing to the two sets of hoofprints. "And maybe the coyote's medicine is not as strong as we thought," he added, pointing to a clear moccasin print at the edge of the water. It was obvious then why Will's tracks were lost amid the many moccasin tracks surrounding the place where the soldier had been tied.

Eager to start after the coyote and the soldier, the two Cheyenne crossed over the river and found the tracks on the other side. They led back to a point directly opposite their camp. "He left the horses here while he walked into the village and freed the soldier," Bloody Hand said. Then, turning to follow the trail with his eyes, he pointed to the south. "Come, we will overtake them before they reach the Smoky Hill." Brave Elk harbored some doubt regarding that possibility, since their quarry had such a head start, but he did not voice his thoughts, knowing that his friend was feverish with the sickness of revenge. Both warriors were astonished, however, when after only a distance of about one hundred yards, the trail stopped and turned back toward the river.

"Maybe it is not his trail," Brave Elk said, but Bloody Hand insisted that it was and that it was just another of the confounding things the coyote did.

Carefully following the trail, they found themselves at the riverbank, some distance downstream from their camp. "He wanted us to think he had gone back to the Smoky Hill," Brave Elk said. When there were no tracks to be found on the other side of the river, it was obvious to them that Will had kept the horses in the water to lose anyone trying to follow. By now it was already getting dark under the trees that flanked the river. And although difficult for him to admit, Bloody Hand reluctantly agreed to give up the chase until morning. They would need sharp eyes to see where the coyote had left the water.

They had not gotten far since starting out that morning. Will assigned some of the blame for it on his insistence to get Braxton up on his horse early in order to put some distance between them and the Cheyenne camp. Braxton obviously needed more time to regain some strength, but Will assured him that time was the one thing they didn't have, depending on how good those warriors were at discovering their trail. "Maybe they won't see that we turned back, but we didn't take a helluva lot of time tryin' to cover our trail in the dark last night."

So now, a little past noon, they had only covered about ten miles, a point where Will decided it time to leave the Saline and head more to the southeast if they were to strike Fort Hays. Instead of going on, however, Will realized he was going to have to stop there to let Braxton rest, so he picked a spot near a plum thicket on the riverbank. A hole had been formed by the water when it was high in the spring that provided a natural redoubt, and he figured if he had to, he could hold off a good-sized war party with his rifle.

After hobbling Braxton's horse, he built a small fire and broke out his battered old coffeepot again. While it was boiling, he took a look at Braxton's wound. He had bandaged it with a piece of cloth from what was left of an old shirt that had seen its day and was retained for this purpose. "How do you feel?" he asked.

"Like hell," Braxton replied weakly.

Will had no notion as to what he should do for the wounded man. Braxton seemed to have a fever, for he was sweating profusely and was barely able to hold his head up. Maybe the bullet was causing his fever. Will had known more than one person who was still carrying a lead slug in their arm or leg, but maybe there was something about the one in Braxton's shoulder that was causing the problem. "Maybe I oughta try to dig that slug outta your shoulder," he suggested.

His suggestion got an immediate response from the patient. "Hell, no," he responded. "I need a doctor. If you go digging around in there, you'll probably make it worse."

His forceful response surprised Will. "Well, you ain't as near dead as I thought you were," he replied. "But we're gonna have to do somethin' to cover more distance than we did today." He paused for a moment to think about their situation. "I'll see if I can't find somethin' to give you a little nourishment. I can't take a chance on shootin' anythin', but I saw a couple of good-sized turtles on that far bank. Maybe I can catch one of 'em for supper." He got up to leave, then paused and looked back at Braxton. "If some food and another night's rest don't fix you up, I'm gonna dig that bullet outta you. And if that doesn't work, I reckon I'll have to shoot you and pack you back to Fort Hays." The lieutenant didn't appreciate the humor, but he refrained from responding.

True to his word, Will managed to catch a couple of turtles, and soon had them rotating over the fire on a green plum branch for a spit. He pulled Braxton up to a sitting position and handed him a chunk of the roasted meat. The lieutenant eyed it suspiciously, but his hunger got the best of him and he took a small bite. "Ain't bad eatin', is it?" Will asked with a smile, amused by the officer's fastidiousness. "Eat it; turtle's the best thing you can eat for a bullet wound," he stated with no idea whether it was good or harmful.

"It could use a little salt," Braxton replied, and took another bite.

Will laughed. "If I'd known you were gonna be so picky about your food, I'da come after you in a chuck wagon."

Braxton studied the rangy scout who had risked his life to rescue him when his own company and regiment had deemed it unwise to remain in the area. To be honest, he could not understand Will's motive for coming after him. It was an unstated fact that the two men did not like each other, and Braxton was clearly irritated by the scout's apparent friendship with his intended. He would have thought that Will would have been the last person to try to rescue him. The fact that Emma obviously adored Will was another burr under Braxton's saddle. Although there was some reluctance involved, he knew that he was remiss in not having at least acknowledged Will's heroic efforts to save him. "I guess I'm overdue in expressing my thanks for getting me out of that camp," he managed.

His declaration of thanks was met with a knowing smile from Will, and he offered another chunk of the roasting meat, which the lieutenant accepted a little more eagerly this time. "Not at all," Will said. He had a pretty good idea how painful it was for Braxton to thank him. He felt it unnecessary to tell him that he had done it for Sarah and certainly not for him, for he was sure the lieutenant knew it. *Yes, sir,* he thought, *if it wasn't for the fact that Sarah wants you, I'd be back in Fort Dodge with the rest of the regiment and probably getting ready to head back to Camp Supply.* To Braxton, he said, "If our luck holds out, maybe those Injuns won't figure out we're headin' for Fort Hays, and I'll get you to the doctor by tomorrow night."

The two Cheyenne warriors worked their way along the river, one on each side, searching for the place where the white men had left the water. They had ridden less than a mile from the place where the horses entered the water when they found tracks climbing up the north bank. A short ride brought them to the deep gully where the remains of a fire were discovered. Realizing that the coyote had made his camp so close to the Cheyenne camp only served to intensify Bloody Hand's anger. Brave Elk suggested that maybe the reason they had made camp so close was due to the condition of the soldier. "I think that maybe this coyote had to stop to rest the soldier," he said. "If he is too weak to travel, then maybe they are not a full day ahead of us as we thought." Brave Elk's reasoning made sense to Bloody Hand and served to increase his fever to waste no more time. "I think," Brave Elk continued, "that the coyote changed his mind and is now heading to the soldier fort at Big Creek."

"I agree," Bloody Hand said, but even guessing where Will was heading, they were still forced to follow his tracks. There was no established trail to Fort Hays from where they now stood, so they had to find the place where the coyote left the Saline and turned south to strike Big Creek. They could move faster, however, galloping over long stretches along the river, then slowing to confirm that they were still on the trail before another sprint. The sun was directly overhead when they came to the place where the tracks crossed over to the other side of the Saline, then angled to the south-east. Coming upon some horse droppings on the opposite bank, they dismounted to examine them. They were fresh, still warm, and Bloody Hand knew that they had caught them. "We must be careful now," he said, respectful of the coyote's rifle.

No more than two or three miles ahead of the two Cheyenne warriors, Will Cason stood beside a shallow stream that fed into the river he had just recently left behind. Walking back to the edge of the willow trees, he looked behind him at the open expanse of grass between the stream and a line of rolling hills. There was no sign of anyone following their trail, but that fact was not sufficient to give him peace of mind. He went back then and studied the prone figure of Braxton Bradley and tried to decide what to do. The lieutenant was feverish again and seemed to be getting worse. This past leg of the journey, from the river to this point, had lasted only a couple of miles before Braxton slid off his horse again. Will had little choice but to let him rest. He supposed this was as good a place as any to stop for a while. The stream was thick with willows, chokecherries, and gooseberry bushes, of-fering ample seclusion.

He was frankly mystified that Braxton was

suffering so badly from a single bullet wound in his shoulder. He had lost a great deal of blood and the wound was still seeping enough to soak the bandage Will had applied. But it was not at all uncommon to see men with shoulder, arm, or leg wounds able to continue fighting. He had to assume that the beatings Bradley had suffered, along with his hunger and thirst for a couple of days, must have somehow contributed to his poor condition. The question facing him now was what to do for him. It might be that the rifle slug was causing infection and needed to come out right away. Will had no idea, but he couldn't think of anything else to do, and he was beginning to worry that Braxton was going to die on him before he could get him to the doctor. He knelt down beside him to give him the bad news.

Thinking Will was about to badger him to climb back on his horse, Braxton gazed up at him with heavy eyelids. "I can't do it," he mumbled. "I've got to rest."

"I know you wanna get to the doctor to take care of that shoulder," Will said. "But I don't think we're gonna make it if you can't stay on a horse, and I don't see anythin' big enough here to make a travois to carry you." He paused to make sure Braxton was hearing him. "So, I think I'm gonna have to cut that bullet outta you, 'cause you sure as hell ain't gettin' any better with it in you."

Feeble at best, Braxton immediately protested. "No," he gasped. "You'll kill me, you crazy savage."

"As appealin' as that sounds, I don't reckon so," Will replied, unable to suppress a grin. "I can't see how it could make it any worse, and it might help. Anyway, I'm gonna dig it outta there, but I ain't got no whiskey or anythin' to make it easier on you. I doubt if you could hold any whiskey if I had it, anyway, sick as you are."

"I said no, damn you," Braxton insisted, his anger serving to strengthen his tone a little.

His patience in short supply at this point, Will replied, "I'm gonna take that bullet out or I'm gonna leave your ass out here to take care of yourself." A trace of a smile returned to his face as he suggested, "Besides, this'll give you a chance to show how much man you are." He drew his knife and tested the edge. "Those damn turtles didn't do my knife any good. I'd best sharpen it a bit."

While Will went to his saddlebags to find his whetstone, Braxton tried to get to his feet, but sank back when he found himself too weak. Will shook his head, astonished by the lieutenant's great dread of an operation Will would have performed on himself if the situation were reversed. While Braxton laid back in dreadful anticipation, Will gathered some dead branches to build a fire. When he had a steady flame going, he propped his knife in it for a while to rid the blade of anything he thought the turtles might have left on it. While his knife was heating, he pulled Braxton's shirt aside and removed the bandage. "Damn if that ain't a pretty sight," he remarked when he saw the puffy flesh around the wound.

After removing the knife from the flame, he waited for the blade to cool down a little before he committed it to Braxton's shoulder. "It's gonna hurt like hell," he said, "but I'll try to make it quick." He picked up a willow limb from the edge of the fire and pressed it against his patient's lips. "Here, bite down on this."

"Oh, Mother of God," Braxton wailed, knowing he was helpless to stop the attack on his shoulder, and clamped his teeth down on the stick.

"Damn," Will uttered as he cut the center of the wound and jerked his head back, recoiling from the putrid odor that accompanied the release of yellow pus. Braxton's body, which had tensed rigidly, suddenly went limp and the stick dropped from his mouth. He had fainted dead away. "Good," Will said, and went to work with his knife. The operation didn't take long. It was a messy surgery, but he found the rifle slug and removed it while the lieutenant was still out cold. Once the bullet was out, he put the knife back in the fire, this time letting it stay there until the blade began to glow. Noticing that Braxton's eyelids were beginning to quiver, he hurried to take the red-hot knife and apply it to the bleeding wound in an effort to cauterize it. Braxton screamed in pain before fainting again.

After rinsing his knife in the stream, he took a handful of sand from the bank to thoroughly clean the blade. Then he stood up and looked at his patient, still lying motionless on the low bank. "Well, I either killed him or cured him. I reckon I'll carry what's left of him back to Sarah." As he started up the bank, he was startled by a sudden spray of dirt in front of him. He reacted immediately, dropping to the ground even before hearing the sound of the rifle that fired the bullet. The first shot was followed at once by several, all kicking up dirt around him. With no time to be gentle, he grabbed Braxton's ankles and yanked him roughly down below the bank. "Stay down!" he commanded to his confused patient when Braxton tried to struggle to a sitting position. He pulled out his revolver and stuck it in Braxton's hand. "Take this in case I get shot." He snatched his rifle from the willow he had leaned it against and crawled as fast as he could up the streambed.

He had been lucky and he knew it. He had gotten a little careless while his mind was occupied with the surgery he had performed. Now he had to get to a position where he could see where and how many they were. When he got to a spot where the willows were thickest, he crawled up the short bank into the middle of the trees and worked his way back toward Braxton until he could scan the open prairie between the stream and the hills to the north. There was no one to be seen. Knowing then they had to have circled around to approach from downstream, he moved farther toward the edge of the willows until he had a better angle to watch the bushes below the spot where Braxton lay. *Just don't stick your head up,* he thought, hoping Braxton would remain below the bank. As he concentrated his gaze on the bushes and the stand of trees beyond, he waited until he saw something move near the edge of a thicket of berry bushes. He continued to fix his gaze on the spot, his rifle aimed and ready to fire at the next sign of movement. In a few seconds it came and he responded with six rounds rapid fire, filling the thicket with lead.

Caught in the sudden barrage, Bloody Hand and Brave Elk beat a hasty retreat with only luck to account for neither of them being hit. They scrambled back to a grassy mound by the water's edge and took cover. "It is my fault," Bloody Hand said, admitting something they both knew. "I should have waited until we got closer before I shot the first time." His burning desire to kill the white man had grown to such proportions that he had raised his rifle and fired at the first glimpse of the one he called Coyote. His premature shot surprised Brave Elk, who was left no choice but to fire as well. Now the white scout had fled somewhere farther up the stream and had come close to hitting them.

"We should split up and see if we can get on both sides of him," Brave Elk suggested, and Bloody Hand agreed. "The soldier is still hiding under the bank," Brave Elk continued. "I will cross over the stream and kill him. Then we will trap the coyote between us."

Bloody Hand nodded and crawled toward a clump of berry bushes close by the bank as his friend leaped across the stream to make his way up behind Braxton. Bloody Hand, obsessed with the belief that anyone who killed the coyote would take his medicine for his own, was convinced that it was he who Man Above had chosen to slay him. It would be even stronger medicine if he could kill him in hand-to-hand combat, but he would not hesitate if he got a clear shot.

Lying helpless beneath the low bank, Braxton struggled to try to pull himself up closer to it, feeling he had no protection from the opposite bank, and he didn't know where Will was. Even with the adrenaline increase caused by his desperate situation, he didn't have the strength to move himself very far. Finally he gave up and lay there flat on his back, groping behind him for Will's revolver, which had fallen from his stomach as he had tried to wiggle backward. On his back, he couldn't see much on either side of him, and only straight behind toward the opposite bank of the stream. He wondered where the scout was, thinking he'd feel a lot less concerned if Will was with him. He had heard the shots fired by the Henry rifle a few moments ago and they sounded to be some distance away. It occurred to him then that Will had nothing to lose and possibly something to gain if he just concerned himself with his own safety.

Overtaken by a moment of anger, it was almost immediately replaced by one of terror as a Cheyenne warrior suddenly appeared at the edge of the stream, a fearsome-looking savage Braxton recognized at once as Bloody Hand's friend. Brave Elk grinned triumphantly as he saw the soldier frantically fumbling for the pistol. Seeing it was a little out of Braxton's reach, Brave Elk sneered contemptuously and took his time to aim his carbine at the helpless man, enjoying the fear on the soldier's face. Braxton could only stare wide-eyed at his executioner, too terrified to even move. A moment before closing his eyes in anticipation of meeting his Maker, he was shocked to see the Indian stagger backward as two slugs impacted on the middle of his chest. Startled by the two hammerlike blows to his breastbone, Brave Elk looked down at the bullet holes in disbelief as he felt his legs grow suddenly weary beneath him. Defiant to the end, he attempted to raise his carbine again, but a third shot dropped him facedown in the stream.

Moving catlike through the thick bushes, Bloody Hand heard the series of shots to his left and quickly made his way toward the stream. None of the shots sounded like they had come from Brave Elk's carbine, so it worried him that he had not heard answering shots. After crawling around a clump of larger plum trees, he parted the brush to see Brave Elk lying in the water. He almost cried out at the sight, but had to delay his thoughts of revenge when a rifle bullet snapped a plum branch close to his head. Reacting instantly, he rolled over behind the small tree and returned fire toward a spot from where he guessed the shot had come.

A duel ensued, in which neither opponent knew exactly where his adversary was, with both men firing at the last muzzle flash and quickly moving before there was time for return fire. It continued for almost a quarter of an hour before Bloody Hand's frustration caused him to issue a challenge. Confident in his destiny to gain the coyote's power, he called out to him. "Okohome!" he yelled. "I have seen your medicine and it is strong. I say we are wasting good bullets while we hide in the bushes. Let us lay down our guns, and I will meet you with only our knives to fight with. I am Bloody Hand and I give my word that I will let the soldier go. It is only you that I fight. You have killed Brave Elk, so it is only the two of us now. What say you? Lay your gun aside and come out to fight me and we'll see whose medicine is stronger."

Will didn't respond at once while he tried to decide if there was a trick up the Indian's sleeve just to get him in the open. *Why did he call me coyote?* he wondered. The thought left his mind as swiftly as it had occurred, for he assumed it just an insult to further taunt him. "All right," he yelled, "I'll meet you by the stream. Lay your weapons down and I'll come out."

Bloody Hand smiled. He could not have hoped for more. No man could best him in a knife fight and he had waited for this day for quite some time. He would take the coyote's scalp and absorb his medicine. There would be many songs sung about this day. Propping his carbine against a tree trunk, he removed his cartridge belt and his shirt, ready for battle. Then he stepped out in the open a dozen yards from the spot where Braxton lay, his scalping knife in hand. The white scout was not there yet.

Watching from beside a clump of bushes, Will waited as the powerfully built warrior stepped out into the open. A formidable opponent by any means, and more muscular than the average Indian — *No wonder he wants to knife fight,* Will thought. *Well, best not keep him waiting.* He stepped away from the bushes, exposing himself to Bloody Hand's look of shock when he saw the rifle in Will's hand.

"Put your gun aside," Bloody Hand implored. "I trusted your word. Have you no honor?"

"Shit, no," Will replied, "not when it comes to savin' my neck. Besides, who'd be fool enough to trust a coyote?" He raised his rifle and placed two shots neatly in the center of Bloody Hand's chest, just as he had done with Brave Elk. "Well, that takes care of that," he said, and turned to look at Braxton. "You all right?"

Weak, but indignant enough to protest vigorously, the lieutenant retorted. "You left me lying helpless here like so much bait," he fumed.

"Well, hell, I figured you weren't doin' anythin'," Will replied with a grin. "And it worked real good, although I thought you mighta used that pistol I left you." Actually, it *had* worked pretty well. Will figured the warrior that jumped across the creek would most likely come out in the open when he saw the helpless man lying there. It was the other one he couldn't pinpoint. He found it hard to believe the man had challenged him to hand-to-hand fighting with knives and then presented himself to be shot. *Sometimes you eat the bear, sometimes the bear eats you,* he thought.

Although his feathers were still ruffled over the way Will handled the situation, there was little Braxton could legitimately complain about. Will had once again saved his life. Still, he had to find something to criticize. "The savage was right in saying that you agreed to his challenge and then took unfair advantage."

Will was forced to laugh at the lieutenant's comment. "Did you get a good look at that son of a bitch?" he retorted. "I'da been a damn fool to knife fight him. Hell, he mighta been better at it than me. Matter of fact, I'm sure he woulda been. The only thing I use a knife for is to skin a deer." He walked over to look at the body, and couldn't help thinking what a shame it was to have to shoot such a fine physical specimen. *I wonder what in the world possessed him to think I'd want to fight him with a knife when I had a rifle,* he thought, with no way of knowing that he was somewhat of a legend, thanks to Bloody Hand's obsession with him. *Coyote . . . huh.* Looking back at Braxton, he asked, "What do you reckon woulda happened to you if I lost to this buck? He mighta kept his word about not killin' you, but he didn't say anything about whether or not he was just gonna leave you here to die, did he?" There was not much

Braxton could say to refute the question, so he chose to ignore it.

Will felt fairly sure there had been only the two Indians following them, but he was not willing to count on it until he had scouted the trail behind them. Leaving Braxton where he lay, he rode a few hundred yards upstream, then did the same in the other direction before riding out to the hills behind to look over their back trail. Satisfied then, he returned to make camp right where he was for the night. He got Braxton as comfortable as possible, using saddle blankets to fashion a bed for him. Then he rounded up the two horses the Indians had ridden and hobbled them with Braxton's horse. "I've got some coffee left and a little bit of bacon," he told his patient. "I think you need some fresh meat. I don't know if I can find anything to shoot around here, especially since all the shootin' that just happened most likely scared any game away. But I'll see what I can find. If I can't find some meat, I might slaughter one of those horses." He was only halfway serious, but it was enough to trigger a fastidious response from the lieutenant.

"What kind of savage are you?" Braxton demanded. "I'll not eat any horse meat."

"If you get hungry enough, you will," Will

replied. "Course, it's up to you how long you're gonna lay there on your back. We ain't but a day's ride from Fort Hays. When you get done actin' like a woman in childbirth, we can get the hell outta here."

Whether Will's stinging remarks had anything to do with it was questionable, but Braxton's fever broke later that night. And by early the next morning he was able to eat the rabbit Will had flushed out of the brush a hundred yards up the stream. "That mighta been the only rabbit within fifty miles of here," he jokingly speculated. "I swear, I thought there'd be somethin' fit to eat with all these berries to feed on." Seeing the lieutenant obviously feeling better, he couldn't resist teasing a little. "I reckon it depends on how fast you get ready to ride, but if we stay here much longer I expect I'll have to carve a haunch offa one of those horses." Knowing by now that Will had no intention of killing one of the horses, Braxton did not see fit to grace the threat with a comment. His expression was response enough. Will continued. "Course we've got a couple of perfectly good Injuns we ain't thought about yet. That big one looks like he might be a little bit tough, but the other one might do to turn over the fire."

In truth, Will was a good deal more particular about what he would eat, almost as much as Braxton. But he would not have hesitated to butcher a horse if the situation had been dire enough. In this case, it did not even approach it. There was always game to find if a man looked hard enough, and they weren't but a day's ride from Fort Hays. He just couldn't resist picking at Braxton a little. The bodies of the two hostiles had been dragged away — far enough so that the buzzards could feast on them — right after he had hobbled the horses.

On the second morning at the stream, Braxton climbed into the saddle — with Will's help — and assured him that he was ready to make the ride. The two unlikely companions left the little stream to boast three less members of the rabbit population, leading the two extra horses behind them. True to his word, Braxton remained upright and asked for no stops along the way. Will watched for signs of wilting on the lieutenant's part, but other than a stop to rest the horses, there appeared to be no need for further delay.

They reached Fort Hays by early evening and Will took Braxton directly to the post hospital, where he received the direct attention of the surgeon. Will stood by while the doctor examined his handiwork, the surgeon's face a constant frown as he uncovered the several layers of bandage Will had fashioned. "It's a mess," the doctor said, "but it oughta heal up just fine. The best thing you did was cauterize it."

Will was glad to hear him tell Braxton that he was going to keep him in the hospital for a couple of days before releasing him to return to Fort Dodge. That would give Sarah two more days to change her mind. It was an encouraging thought, but one without much hope. *I should have left him in that Cheyenne camp,* he thought as he left to check in at the orderly room in hopes of getting resupplied with some ammunition and maybe a credit slip for the sutler's store.

Since he was going to hang around for a couple of days, he decided to take advantage of it and give Spades a chance to rest up and feed on some army grain. He was afraid the horse was showing some effects of a lot of hard riding over the past weeks. He decided to rid himself of the two horses the Cheyenne warriors had ridden. They were cavalry mounts, anyway, and Will was just as well rid of them. He hadn't been at Fort Hays long before he encountered Captain Daniel Forrest of the Tenth Cavalry. The captain insisted that Will join him in the officers' mess for supper. Will couldn't help but smile when he thought how Braxton Bradley would disapprove.

Eager to return to Fort Dodge as soon as humanly possible, Braxton was out of his hospital bed and dressed in new issue uniform on the morning of the second day. The doctor shook his head and said, "I think you'd do well to give it another day's rest, but if you think you're able to make the trip, hell, I don't care."

"I've got a wedding to get to," Braxton replied, affecting as solid a facade as he could for the benefit of the doctor. "And I need to get back to my regiment." He would have preferred to part company with Will, but he knew he wasn't really recovered enough to venture forth on his own. It was a three-day ride to Fort Dodge and there were no troops scheduled to make the trip anytime soon. As much as it galled him to admit it, even to himself, he was afraid he might need the rangy scout if he ran into any trouble. Even more difficult to admit was the fact that he wasn't sure he knew the way. It was a long ride and he wasn't willing to risk losing even more time if he wandered too far off track. His pride couldn't stand the possibility that Will might be sent to find him again. So he sent a hospital orderly to find Will with orders that he was to escort him to Fort Dodge.

"I thought you mighta been thinkin' about goin' to Fort Dodge by yourself," Will commented upon joining the lieutenant at the hospital. "You sure didn't take much time healin' that wound."

"We both have to report back to Fort Dodge," Braxton replied coolly. "It just makes sense to travel together."

"You mean *you* have to report back to Fort Dodge. If I'm obliged to report back anywhere, it'd have to be Camp Supply. Ben Clarke, chief scout, that's who I work for. You just want me to go with you because you're afraid you'd miss me too much," Will kidded. He had a pretty good idea that Braxton was reluctant to try the trip on his own. Safe now from the constant threat of death at the hands of hostiles, the lieutenant was rapidly regaining his air of hostility and superiority. Ignoring Will's attempt at joking, Braxton advised the civilian scout that he wanted him ready to ride after breakfast in the morning. "Yes, sir, Lieutenant," Will said, taking on an exaggerated tone of respect. "I'll sure be ready to ride. Any other orders?"

"If there are, I'll let you know," Braxton replied icily.

So bright and early the next morning the two unlikely traveling companions left Fort Hays soon after Braxton had breakfast, a late hour to start on a three-day trip according to Will's way of thinking. He supposed he shouldn't be judgmental, what with Braxton's weakened condition. He really didn't care when he thought about it, however. He just figured they'd go as far as the Smoky Hill and camp. Then, instead of striking out straight for Fort Dodge, they could alter their course a little and ride on in to Fort Larned on the second day. And if it turned out they had started back too soon for Braxton to hold up, he could lay over there until he regained his strength. As far as Will was concerned, he wasn't in any particular hurry to get back to Dodge or Supply. There was nothing waiting for him at either place that mattered a great deal. His natural inclination was to bid Braxton Bradley good-bye as soon as he had safely delivered him to any army post. But he had kind of promised Sarah that he would see that her husband-to-be was returned safely to Fort Dodge. *As soon as I deliver his pompous ass to his lady love,* he told himself, *I'm heading back to Camp Supply. I might even do what Ben Clarke has been trying to get me to do for a while now — ride with the Seventh Cavalry.*

Chapter 12

They made good time after leaving Fort Hays. Braxton, eager to return to Dodge, seemed to be up to the ride, so they didn't stop to rest the horses until striking the Smoky Hill River directly south of Hays. Without making it obvious, Will watched the lieutenant carefully as he climbed down from the saddle. Braxton moved very deliberately and Will decided his wound was paining him some. "The horses need a good rest," Will commented, thinking the lieutenant needed it more than the horses. "We'd best wait up here for a while. Hell, long as we've got time, we might as well have a little coffee to go with this hardtack we brought with us."

"I suppose you're right," Braxton said. "We'd better rest the horses." He sat down with his back against a cottonwood trunk while Will rustled up some wood for a small fire. When he thought Will wasn't watching, he reached over to check the bandage on his shoulder and grimaced with the pain. The Smoky Hill was only about fifteen miles from Fort Hays, but Braxton felt like he had been in the saddle for a full day. Will had suggested that they could try to make Walnut Creek before dark, so Braxton asked, "How much farther is it to Walnut Creek?"

"I expect it's a good twenty miles," Will answered. He got his fire going good before suggesting, "We don't have to make Walnut Creek today, if you think that's pushin' it. It's up to you. I don't care one way or the other."

"No," Braxton immediately insisted. "We'll go on. I don't want to waste any more time than we have to."

"Whatever you say," Will replied. There was little wonder why Braxton was so eager to continue — the same reason Will would be if he was in his shoes. "As soon as the horses are rested and we've had a cup of coffee, we'll be on our way."

After resting for an hour, they continued on toward Walnut Creek, Will leading with Braxton following silently behind. The lieutenant was as good as his word. He was still upright in the saddle when Will pointed to the trees in the distance that framed

Walnut Creek, but there was a definite slump in his shoulders. Will selected a spot for their camp and pulled the saddles off the horses while Braxton slumped to the ground. There was little effort this time to hide his fatigue. In spite of his dislike for the man, Will couldn't help but feel empathy for him. "You rest up that shoulder," Will said. "I'll take care of everythin' else." He busied himself then with setting up their camp.

Feeling spent and in a pitiful condition, Braxton sat there silently while Will broke out his coffeepot and a slab of bacon to cook. Feeling a hint of remorse for his disdain for the rangy scout, he forced himself to remark, "I expect I've been somewhat remiss in expressing my appreciation for everything you've done for me, Cason. I wouldn't have been surprised if you had left me on my own after pulling me out of that Cheyenne camp. So I thank you." He paused after satisfying himself that he had atoned for any actions unbecoming of an officer and a gentleman. "I have to be honest, however," he continued. "I don't like you and I don't think I ever will. So I'll have to stand by what I told you about staying away from Sarah and Emma. I hope you understand my position on this."

This was the second time Braxton had forced himself to thank Will for his rescue, and as before, he was amazed by the lieutenant's capacity to express his appreciation and total disdain almost in the same sentence. Will had to laugh. "You know, Bradley, I've run into a lot of stuck-up officers in my time scoutin' for the army. But damned if you ain't the biggest horse's ass I've ever seen. I've a mind to let you find your own way back to Fort Dodge." He handed the lieutenant a cup of fresh coffee.

"What makes you think I couldn't find my way back?" Braxton responded indignantly. "It's your job to act as a scout. I'm just telling you to do your job. Whether we get along or not has nothing to do with you carrying out your duty."

Too astounded to reply with anything of a civil nature for a few seconds, Will just shook his head, thinking of what a dictatorial father Braxton would likely be for Emma. Controlling his temper, and remembering his silent promise to Sarah to take care of her fiancé, he responded, "I reckon this means you ain't gonna ask me to be your best man at the weddin'." When Braxton chose not to dignify the remark with an answer, Will continued. "Just so's we get things perfectly straight, I'll cart your worthless ass back to Fort Dodge, although I would be doin' Sarah a helluva favor if I didn't. I'll nurse you along, get you some food, take care of your horse till I get you back. After that, I don't wanna hear or see you again. So drink your damn coffee and this meat'll be done in a minute." No two rivals for a woman's attention ever had a clearer understanding without physical violence occurring.

In spite of Braxton's resolve to persevere, the twenty-five mile ride had almost been too much for him. Seeing the lieutenant's weakened condition, Will decided not to start out again the next morning over Braxton's protests. "Hell," he responded, "you wouldn't make it five miles. We'll rest you up here for another day; then I'm takin' you to Fort Larned to let the doctor there take a look at you." Although he continued to object, Braxton could not honestly disagree.

Will decided that the lieutenant needed some red meat to encourage the healing of his wound, so after a breakfast of coffee and bacon, he left Braxton to rest while he followed the creek downstream on the chance of finding game. Considering himself fortunate if he was to happen upon a varmint of some kind, he was pleasantly surprised to

301

run up on a small group of antelope drinking from a pool in the creek about a mile from his camp. Moving as quietly as possible, he managed to get a little closer, to a point where he had a clear shot. It was only then that he realized there was no cartridge in the chamber, so he readied himself to shoot quickly. As he expected, the antelope bolted upon hearing the metallic clank of the lever when he cocked his rifle and were off through the cottonwoods immediately — all except one that limped noticeably in trying to keep up with its family, giving Will time to take a careful shot.

The antelope was not a big one, so Will decided to carry the whole carcass back to his camp to butcher it. Hefting it up on his shoulders, he walked back upstream. "You're in luck today, Bradley," he commented cheerfully when he returned. "This little feller was just waitin' around for me to come along. He had a broken leg. I reckon if we hadn't got him, a coyote probably would have." Then a thought occurred to him that caused him to smile. *I reckon a coyote got him after all,* he thought, thinking of the name Bloody Hand had called him. He dropped the carcass on the creek bank and started skinning it. Cutting off a piece of haunch, he set it over the fire to roast while he continued with the butchering.

"I heard the rifle shot," was the only thing Braxton said. But the gleam in his eye told Will that he eagerly awaited the meat.

Ned Spikes inched his way forward a little closer to a small cottonwood on the crown of the bank. Lying on his belly, he took a good long look at the camp by the creek before whispering back to French and Boley, "There's two of 'em. One of 'em looks like a soldier, and he acts kinda puny, like he's been shot or somethin'. They got a couple horses we could use. One of 'em's a fine-lookin' bay." He slid back down below the bank then to join his friends. "Don't look like but one of them fellers could give us any trouble, and he won't be none if we're careful not to let him know we're here."

"I could use some of that meat they're cookin'," French said, and tilted his head back again to sniff the breeze.

"Amen to that, partner," Boley said. They had not had much luck in finding game during the past few days. Like Braxton, they had heard the rifle shot and had been on their way to investigate when they saw the antelope bolting from the creek and bounding off across the prairie. French had im-

303

mediately raised his rifle, prepared to take a shot at the fleet animals, but Ned had stayed his aim and stopped him from firing.

"Use your brains, man. We need to see who fired that shot first," Ned had cautioned. "Might be a Injun war party, or a bunch of soldiers, and we don't need that comin' down on our behinds. There was only one shot, so they musta got one. If they didn't, there'da been more shots. If we're lucky, it was just one man — might be we can get us an antelope and a horse to boot."

Now, after finding the camp, their prospects had increased to an antelope and two horses plus whatever weapons, ammunition, and possessions the two men might be carrying. Prone to act upon instinct alone, the half-breed, French, was eager to charge into the camp at once, but Ned, more prone to take precautions, calmed him down. "Just hold your horses," he said. "That one feller looks familiar. I mighta seen him around Fort Dodge or Hays. If it's the man I think it is, we gotta be careful how we do our business. He don't miss with that Henry he carries."

Boley, a more cautious man by nature, and always so in any situation that wasn't slanted to his advantage, was content to let Spikes take the initiative. "Whaddaya thinkin' on doin', Ned?" he asked.

"There ain't no sense in takin' no chances," Spikes replied, taking a moment to look around him for a vantage point. His gaze lingered on a small hill about fifty yards from the edge of the creek and directly opposite their victims' camp. "French is a better shot than you, so me and him'll crawl up behind that little hill where we can get a chance for a clear shot. You stay back and hold the horses till I call you to bring 'em up."

"Hell, French ain't no better shot than me," Boley growled, but protested no further since he was just as happy to remain safely back with the horses. He flipped the black eye patch up to rest on his forehead while he dabbed the empty eye socket with his bandana to dry up the thin seepage that seemed constant to his companions. "Maybe we oughta wait till dark before we go chargin' into that camp," he suggested, " 'specially if that jasper's as good with a rifle as you say."

"Nah," Spikes said. "I'd rather be able to see what I'm shootin' at. Hell, all we need is one clear shot, and then we can stroll right in." He cocked his head in French's direction, looking for the half-breed's endorsement, and grinned confidently when

French responded with a wide grin of his own. Ned was more concerned with reining in the simple-minded French's inclination to charge blindly in without looking a situation over thoroughly. Lady Luck had turned a cold shoulder to the three outlaws during the past three weeks, limiting their opportunities for victims. Now that they had stumbled upon this chance for a clean bushwhack, he didn't want to mess it up with a wild Indian charging in to get them all shot. "You keep the horses where we can get 'em if we need 'em in a hurry," he said to Boley. "Me and French'll take care of the rest."

Busy carving up more of the carcass, Will paused for a moment and listened. He felt a need for caution for no particular reason — just a nagging feeling that something was amiss. He glanced at Braxton, who seemed comfortable and unconcerned. Then he looked beyond the lieutenant to the horses grazing beside the creek. Spades was busy pulling up grass, showing no signs of anything out of the ordinary. The other horse was calm as well. There had been no reports of hostile Indian activity in this part of the territory, but still he had an uncomfortable feeling. Had he heeded his instincts and what they were trying to tell him, he might have sought cover and avoided the rifle slug that suddenly tore into his side, spinning him around to fall on the ground. With no idea how badly he was wounded, he rolled over and over to get to his rifle, which he had left propped against a tree, at the same time yelling to Braxton to take cover in the streambed.

With lead zipping through the air all around, spitting up plumes of sand as they struck the bank on either side of him, he searched desperately to see where they were coming from. Spotting a muzzle flash from a low hill about fifty yards away, he cranked out four quick rounds. It was enough to silence the firing from the hill long enough for him to scramble down into the creek bed with Braxton. "You're hit!" Braxton exclaimed when he saw the blood already soaking Will's side.

"Hell, I know it!" Will reported frantically. "Get the horses over here! We don't wanna lose them." The shots from the hill resumed almost at once, cutting chunks from the bank and ricocheting off the water behind them. Ignoring Will's instructions, Braxton hugged the creek bank even closer. Disgusted with the lieutenant's reluctance to act, Will managed to grab the reins of

Braxton's horse, but Spades came obediently to stand at the top of the bank over his master. "Spades, get down here!" Will shouted. He handed Braxton the reins for his horse and reached up to take Spades' reins. When he did, he placed himself neatly in Ned Spikes' sights. Hit in the shoulder, he fell back in the creek bed as two more shots rang out, striking the excited horse, one low in the withers, the other a lethal shot beside the faithful horse's head. Spades stumbled over the bank, his last conscious thought an effort to avoid trampling his master. "Spades!" Will cried out, but it was too late for the big bay gelding. He took a half dozen drunken steps before collapsing at the water's edge.

Up on the hill, Ned swore, "Damn the luck. I didn't go to hit that bay. I got that son of a bitch with the rifle, though. What about the other'n?"

"Don't know," French replied, reloading. "He ain't stuck his head up."

Ned called back behind him. "Boley, work around to the creek now. See if you can come up behind 'em." Boley nodded his understanding and left to work his way through the trees downstream from the camp.

Holding his only weapon, a revolver, in

one hand — the other desperately clutching his horse's reins — Braxton crouched under the bank, fearful and completely bewildered. He stared at Will with eyes wide and panic-stricken. The scout was soaked in blood from two wounds and Braxton was certain that he was staring at a dead man, for his stare was met with a vacant gaze that focused somewhere beyond him. Seemingly in great pain, Will raised his rifle and struggling to hold it steady, aimed in Braxton's direction. At once alarmed, Braxton squeezed tighter to the creek bank in an effort to shield his body from the bullet he anticipated. He cried out involuntarily when the rifle barked, thinking he must surely be hit. Twenty yards behind him, Boley slid down the creek bank, killed instantly by the bullet in his chest.

On the hilltop, Ned cursed angrily. "They shot Boley. The damn fool let hisself get spotted. Dammit! I warned him to watch out for that bastard with the Henry rifle." Certain now that the man he had just shot was Will Cason, he immediately sent more lead flying to churn up the sandy creek bank in hopes of a lucky shot. "Why don't the son of a bitch die? He's been hit twice. Why don't he die?" he exclaimed when he was forced to duck when an answering shot snapped the air as it passed over his head.

"Well, as long as we're up here," French said, "they can't go nowhere without us seein' 'em. He can't hold on much longer. We can just wait him out."

"Maybe so," Spikes said, "but there's that other'n down there, too."

"I don't know. He don't seem to be able to do nothin'. He ain't fired a shot that I could tell. I don't think he'll be no trouble."

Ned nodded. "I reckon you're right. We'll wait him out. The stubborn bastard can't make it much longer. Why don't you go down and round up all the horses and bring 'em to the bottom of the hill behind us? I'll stay here and make sure they keep their heads down."

Propping himself against the roots of a cottonwood that protruded from the bank, Will was able to remain sitting upright. He wanted desperately to lie down, but he feared that if he did, he would never be able to sit up again. He blinked repeatedly in an effort to keep his vision from blurring as he strained to keep a constant eye on the hilltop. Feeling as if the life was slowly draining from his body, he knew it was up to him to hang on long enough to hold his attackers at bay until dark. Then maybe they might have a chance to steal away in the night. Braxton was of little use, but he had not expected him to be. Their antagonists were two. He was certain of that now, and they evidently had decided to wait them out. Every now and then, when he glanced at Braxton, he could read a pronouncement of death in the lieutenant's eyes as he stared back, desperately clutching the still cold pistol in his hand. *It ain't his fault, I reckon,* the thought struck him. *They don't teach this kind of stuff at West Point. He could be a little bit of help, though, instead of sittin' over there shittin' his pants.*

The creek bank grew quiet as the afternoon wore slowly on, each party awaiting the coming darkness. Fighting the almost overpowering urge to simply close his eyes and slide into unconsciousness, Will could not prevent his heavy lids from closing for a few seconds every now and then, the frequency increasing as the day finally approached darkness. It was during one of those moments when he was jerked awake by the sound of his name.

"Cason!" Braxton exclaimed. "They're coming!"

Will immediately forced himself to awaken. In spite of the pain caused by even a slight movement, he raised his rifle to train on the open prairie beyond the creek. The light had faded the outline of the hill and he was not sure if it was caused by approaching nightfall, or simply the fading of his life. In that sobering moment, he knew that he would not live to see another morning. Suddenly, everything seemed to become a little clearer, and he determined to make those who would take his life pay dearly for their efforts. Looking toward the hill, he now saw more clearly the two men working their way cautiously down the slope to the broad floor of the prairie. *Come on, dammit,* he thought, *we'll take the train to hell together.* Then he glanced at Braxton again, huddled there wide-eyed and shaking. In the moment just passed, he had almost forgotten the lieutenant was there. "Get up from there," Will commanded. "Get on that horse and get the hell outta here while you've got the chance."

Reluctant to move from the protection of the bank, Braxton still hesitated, not certain what he should do. But one thing struck him abundantly clear, Will was fading rapidly. "What about you?" he managed to ask.

"I'm done for," Will replied. "You've got a chance. Get on that horse and ride like hell." He pointed toward the southeast. "That way — about twenty miles you'll hit the Pawnee, follow it east to Fort Larned. I'll hold these bastards off as long as I can to give you a head start."

Still Braxton hesitated, uncertain about his chances of escaping and finding Fort Larned. But looking at Will, he saw the possibility of being left to face the two bushwhackers alone, and that was not a prospect he cared for. "I'm sorry it ended this way, Cason," he said quickly. Then, without taking the time to saddle the horse, he led it into the water and jumped on its back. *Yeah, I am, too,* Will thought, suddenly growing weary again as Braxton galloped out onto the open prairie, accompanied with a new round of shots from Spikes and French. Will did not return their fire.

"There goes one of 'em!" Ned shouted to French as the two crept closer to the cottonwoods by the creek. Certain then that the rifleman had finally gone under, since the soldier was fleeing the scene and there were no answering shots from the Henry, they both started to run, shooting at the fleeing rider. None of their shots found the target on the galloping horse. "We'll get him. Let's make sure about the other'n, then we'll get the horses."

In the dim light of dusk, they almost landed on Spades when they charged over the bank and jumped to the creek bed. French saw him first — huddled over against the roots of the cottonwood. He started immediately toward him only to suddenly be cut down by a rifle slug in his belly. With French between him and Will, Ned could not see to shoot until his partner dropped to the ground. Seeing that it was too late then, he dived back up on the bank, but not before he took a rifle slug in his thigh. His one thought in that moment of panic was to escape with his life. Limping as fast as he could, he fled toward the hill and the horses as Will strained to push himself up so he could shoot. He had only a few seconds to get a good look at his antagonist, but he was able to identify Ned Spikes, Sarah's treacherous guide to Santa Fe. Spikes managed to lose himself in the gathering darkness before Will could do more than throw a few wild shots in his general direction.

A coward by trade, Ned was not willing to chance another encounter with the wounded man at the creek. Pained by a wound of his own, he had to get to someplace where he could tend to it. Grimacing as he stepped up in the saddle, he gathered up the reins of the other horses and fled. *I know the spot,* he thought as he rode away. *After I take care of my leg, I might come back when that bastard has had a chance to die.* On the other side of the river, heading in the opposite direction, Braxton held on to his horse's neck, terrified by the sound of the gunshots behind him. The one thought in his mind was to save himself.

Behind the two panicked cowards, Will fell back against the tree roots, exhausted from the loss of blood and his efforts to kill Ned Spikes. He made no effort to keep his eyes open, closing them against the burning pain in his side and shoulder. Many thoughts streamed through his brain as he attempted to make sense of what had just happened. He knew that he was dying, but he did not fear it. He just hoped that death would go ahead and take him and not drag it out painfully. He tried to think if there were any debts that he left unpaid, and the only one he could think of was a promise to Sarah that he would look after Braxton. *If he's got the brain of a sand flea,* he thought, *he oughta be able to find Fort Larned. So I reckon I did the best I could.* He slowly nodded his head to confirm it, took a deep breath, and lay back to wait for death to come for him. A last thought before sliding into sleep was wondering if Spades would be waiting for him.

■ ■ ■ ■

His father was there, as big and robust as when he had last seen him when Will was just eleven years old, and he was leading Spades as he walked toward him. Familiar sights of his boyhood home surrounded him and he knew he was back in Missouri. "Hello, Pa," he heard himself say. "I reckon I've come home."

"You ain't done a helluva lot with your life up to now, have you, son?" His father smiled then — the little half smile that Will had forgotten about. "I reckon you are a pretty good scout, but what the hell are you gonna do when the Injuns are all on the reservation?"

Will paused to look all around him and discovered he was no longer in Missouri, but back in Kansas again. "I don't know, Pa," he replied, "but it don't look like it matters much since I'm up here with you now."

"We ain't ready for you yet, son. You've got a lot more to do before you're through down there. Don't worry about Spades — I'll take care of him for you."

He was aware of a deep feeling of disappointment as his father's image faded away with the light that had shone for a moment, but was now gone.

Not sure whether he was in heaven or hell, Will slowly opened his eyes to see the light again, realizing then that the light was the sun peeking over the eastern horizon. A stinging pain in his side told him that he was still alive, and upon blinking away the veil of sleep from his eyes, he saw that he was still lying against some tree roots a helluva long way from heaven or hell. The dream he had did not come to mind until much later, lost in the urgency of his present condition.

Forcing himself to shift his body slightly in order to look behind him in the creek bed, he at once felt a stab of grief when he saw Spades' carcass. He silently apologized, then looked beyond the horse to the body of one of the men who had attacked him. He remembered then, Ned Spikes, although wounded, had escaped. *A good thing,* he thought, *for if he hadn't he could have easily finished me off while I was asleep.* He spent a brief thought on Braxton, wondering if the bewildered lieutenant had been able to find Fort Larned. Then his concerns were captured by the painful spasms in his side. Looking down at the bloody mess that had crusted his shirt, he started to reach for it, but was stopped abruptly by a sharp pain in his shoulder. He had forgotten that he was wounded there as well. Only then aware that he was still holding his rifle, he laid it aside and used that hand to examine the wound in his side.

After a great deal of effort, he managed to pull his shirt away from the ugly hole left by the bullet. The blood had plastered the fabric of his shirt to the wound, causing him considerable pain to separate the two, and starting the flow of blood anew. Realizing for the first time that the pain he experienced ran through him all the way to his back, he felt behind him and found an exit wound. Maybe this was a good sign, he thought. The bullet had gone all the way through. He then promptly felt the back of his shoulder to see if the same had happened there. It had not and he told himself he should have known that because of a feeling like a five-pound ball of iron in his shoulder. He had been so sure that he was going to die before he passed out last night, but now it seemed that death was not ready for him. One of the things that convinced him was his desire for food.

Although still reluctant to move, he told himself that he had to force his body to obey him. With his good hand, he took hold of a tree root and strained to pull himself up on his feet. Gasping with the pain, his head swimming, he immediately dropped down on his knees, and remained there while he readied himself to attempt it again. This time he remained on his feet in spite of the feeling that he was tearing his insides apart. After he steadied himself, he reached down and picked up his rifle. Using it as a walking stick, he slowly made his way over to Spades' carcass, where he sat down on the dead horse's quarters and took his canteen from the saddle. Suddenly realizing how thirsty he was, he downed a good portion of the contents, then paused to wait a few minutes as if expecting the water to stream out through the holes in his body. When that failed to happen, he decided that it was all right to eat something. Evidently the bullet had not punctured any internal organs.

With each step producing a stab of pain, he moved slowly to the remains of the campfire, where he found a large slab of antelope hump lying in the ashes. He brushed it off and ate as much as he could hold. The major portion of the antelope had not yet been cooked, and was most likely too far spoiled to salvage. The small quantity of roasted meat would soon turn, as well, so food, in spite of being in great supply, would not be fit to eat.

Feeling tired from the simple motions of taking food and water, he sat down and leaned back, using Spades' croup as a backrest, to think over his situation and evaluate his chances of getting out of his predicament. He decided there was nothing he could do about his wounds other than trying to contain the bleeding. There was no treatment that he knew to render unto himself, so it was just going to have to be in the hands of fate as to whether he survived. Then there was concern about the third member of the bushwhackers. He was sure he had wounded Spikes in the leg, but the question he could not answer was would he return to see if Will was alive? There was a lot for a murderer to come back for — saddles, weapons, ammunition. Would he return with others? At any rate, Will decided that he could not remain there, waiting to heal on his own. *Come hook or crook,* he thought, *I'm gonna have to walk to Fort Larned.* It was not a promising decision, but he felt he had little choice but to try. *Die here, or die on the way to Fort Larned,* he thought, *not a helluva lot of difference.*

Forcing his every move as he struggled to prepare for the trek to Fort Larned, he filled his canteen with water, then removed one saddlebag to carry what food he decided was all right to eat. There was a small quantity of hardtack left that would do in a pinch, so he put that in the bag as well. He took his extra revolver from his saddlebag and stuffed it in his belt, draped a cartridge belt over his injured shoulder and the saddlebag over the other one, and still using his rifle as a cane, he took a few steps toward the creek to test his steadiness. The weakness in his legs almost caused him to sit back down immediately, but he fought the urge, fearing that if he sat down, he might not be able to get back up. Running on willpower alone, he forced himself to concentrate on one step at a time as he entered the cool water of the creek. Fighting against a current that he would not even have noticed before, he managed to make it to the other side and up the bank, ignoring the fresh bleeding from both wounds. Once he had gained the other side, he stood for a moment, soaking wet from the waist down, and stared out at the prairie before him. "It ain't but twenty-five miles," he announced and took the first unsteady step.

CHAPTER 13

It was early morning, before reveille, when Braxton reached Fort Larned. The private on guard duty did not know what to make of the sudden appearance of a greatly disheveled lieutenant riding bareback on an exhausted horse. But he directed him to post headquarters, where Braxton explained his unlikely arrival to the officer of the day, Lieutenant Chad Williams. After hearing Braxton's tale of his escape from a Cheyenne camp, his wound treatment at Fort Hays, and his narrow escape from an attack on Walnut Creek, Williams insisted that the surgeon should look at his wound.

"Lieutenant Williams," Braxton implored, "it is extremely important that I return to Fort Dodge as soon as possible. My wound is healing fine and I don't want to waste any more time before reporting back."

"I'm sure Colonel Thompson would advise a visit to the doctor after what you've been through," Williams said. "You should take the opportunity to rest here before you think about heading back to Fort Dodge."

Braxton released a heavy sigh and shook his head. "Look, Williams. . . . Chad, is it?" When Williams nodded, Braxton continued. "Look, Chad, you seem to be someone I can confide in. I was supposed to be married right after that mission to attack the Cheyenne village. My fiancée doesn't even know if I'm alive or not. I need to get back right away. Surely you can understand my anxiety to return to her."

Williams' face relaxed into a wide smile. "Well, I certainly can understand your hurry. I guess I would be, too." He chuckled, delighted in Braxton's situation. "I'm sure the colonel will understand as well. I'm gonna be relieved here in about fifteen minutes. Why don't you and I go have some breakfast? You look like you could use some, and by the time we're through, the colonel should be here."

The lieutenant was accurate in his anticipation of the colonel's reaction to Braxton's ordeal. "My God, man," he said after hearing the story, "it's a miracle you've made it back." A man of understanding and compassion for the gentle pleasures of life, he understood Braxton's urgency to return to

Dodge and the grieving lady who prayed for his safe return. "If you're sure your wound has healed enough to make the trip, I'll send a detail to escort you back right away — today if that is your wish."

"It is, sir," Braxton replied at once.

"But you've ridden all night," Lieutenant Williams interjected. "Are you sure you don't want to wait until you've had time to rest?"

"I'm ready to go today," Braxton replied emphatically.

The colonel had to chuckle. "Oh, to be a young man again . . . I'll tell you what, we'll detail an ambulance to take you back. You can rest on the trip."

"Thank you, sir," Braxton replied, blushing slightly. "I guess I am thinking with my heart instead of my head."

"Hell, nothing wrong with that," the colonel said, then remembering part of the lieutenant's story, he asked, "What became of the civilian scout that was with you?"

"He was killed at Walnut Creek," Braxton replied.

Ned Spikes rode about five or six miles before stopping to determine how badly he was wounded. His first thought when fleeing the half-dead man with the rifle was to ride to the little settlement at the great bend of the Arkansas River. There was no doctor there, but there was an old Indian woman who could remove a bullet or sew up a knife wound. Although his thigh was paining him some, he was still able to walk on it, and the bleeding had not been extensive, so he decided to make camp there on the riverbank and see how bad it was in the morning before making up his mind. When he thought about the scene he had just fled, he had to wonder why his first reaction was to escape. After all, he allowed in defense of his decision to run, the crazy bastard killed Boley and French. But the man was more dead than alive from the looks of him, so there was no need to worry that he might be coming after him. "Hell, he ain't got no horse." That thought, although late, just came to him.

After examining his leg the next morning, he decided that the wound was not as bad as he had first thought. The bullet was lodged in muscle and the stiffness caused him to limp, but it didn't appear to be too deep. His focus returned to the man he had left beside the river and the potential possessions to be taken. He told himself that he didn't care if the man was Will Cason, he was most likely dead by now, or so close to death that he couldn't do much to defend himself. There were two saddles to be gained, and there was bound to be ammunition and weapons, maybe some food. It was too much to leave for some stray Indian hunting party to stumble over. "I need to settle up with that son of a bitch for puttin' this hole in my leg," he stated emphatically. With that, he decided to forget about the doctor for the time being, and go back to claim what he felt he had rightfully earned.

He took his time looking over the spot on the riverbank where the camp had been before riding straight in. There was no sign of Will Cason, but Ned was still not eager to ride into a possible ambush, especially when he remembered the last time he thought it safe to rush the camp — he damn near lost his life. So he waited and watched for a long time, but there was still no movement of any kind in the camp. *He musta crawled off someplace to die,* he thought. *Or he's still backed against the roots of that tree, deader'n hell.* Finally, after more than an hour hanging back and watching the camp, he decided that Will was dead. Even then he walked his horse slowly at an angle to the camp, with the purpose of using the cover of the trees downstream of the camp.

Dismounting a couple dozen yards away, he limped through the cottonwoods that lined the banks, his rifle ready to fire, pausing for only a moment when he came upon Boley's body. Picking up his late partner's rifle, he continued upstream until he came to French's corpse and the carcass of Cason's horse. Here was the spot where he had barely escaped with his life. The memory of that caused him to lay Boley's weapon down beside French in order to have both hands to use his own rifle. Looking now to the place in the bank where Will had leaned against the tree roots, he was alarmed to find no body. He was gone! But where? And what kind of shape was he in? Recalling the glimpse he had gotten of Will just prior to the shot that had sent him running, he was convinced that the man was nearly dead at the time.

Kneeling on his good leg, he paused to look all around him, trying to stay low behind the protection of the bank. He inched over to the tree roots. There was a great deal of blood that had seeped into the ground there. *That son of a bitch has got to be dead,* he thought. He looked back at the dead horse, noticing for the first time the tracks that led into the water. "Well, I'll be . . . ," he muttered and went at once to examine them. They were no doubt the tracks of a man on foot, and looking across the creek, he could plainly see where they had come out on the opposite bank. "The bastard just won't go ahead and die, but lookin' at them tracks, it ain't gonna be long before he does." The thought brought a smile to Ned's face when he pictured the wounded man trying to walk for help. "Don't you worry, Mr. Will Cason, ol' Ned'll be along pretty soon to help you." *But first,* he thought, *I'll see what kind of plunder you left for me here.*

Of the two saddles that he found on the ground, one was an army cavalry model, the other, he fancied for himself. Deciding it better not to have to explain the possession of an army saddle, he left it where it was and went back to admire the other saddle. With the assurance that Will was wandering around out on the prairie somewhere, he felt no panic to hurry, so he let the saddle rest for a few minutes while he continued searching the camp. Chewing on a piece of charred meat that he found in the ashes of the fire, he searched through the bags of cooking utensils and cups. Giving Will's battered old coffeepot a brief glance, he tossed it into the bushes along with his cup. When he had plundered everything he could find, he returned to the task of swapping Will's saddle for the one he owned. After putting his old saddle on French's horse and discarding French's, he took a moment to admire his new saddle — it was not fancy, but well made, and an improvement on the one he used.

After saddling the horses, he collected the weapons and ammunition left behind on the bodies of his partners and packed them on the horses. Next, he searched the two bodies for anything he fancied. There was not much he wanted other than a pocket-knife and Boley's boots. "I always admired them boots of your'n, Boley. They oughta fit my feet just fine." Satisfied that he had everything he could use, he stood up then and gazed at his ex-partners. "Well, boys, I reckon I'll be goin' along now. I wanna get upwind before you start smellin'." He chuckled, amused by his sentiment. "Hell, Boley, you didn't smell real sweet when you was alive." He climbed in the saddle and hesitated there before moving on, trying to decide whether to head for Great Bend or track Will Cason down. He subconsciously reached down and laid his hand lightly on the bullet wound in his thigh. *I would like to see the buzzards carving up that son of a bitch's body,* he thought. *Besides, I don't see that Henry rifle around here nowhere and that's worth going after.* His mind made up then, he turned his horse toward the creek, and leading his other two horses, he crossed over and climbed up the opposite bank.

It was not a hard trail to follow. The footprints, labored and unsteady, scuffed the grass and dragged through the bare spots, causing a chuckle from Ned as he pictured the walking dead man, trying to make it all the way to Fort Larned on foot, knowing that he would overtake him before another night came. "He's mighty damn considerate," Ned allowed. "When he don't drag his feet, he leaves a little trail of blood on the grass."

As he predicted, it was late in the afternoon when he spotted a circle of three buzzards hovering over the prairie beyond a low rise several hundred yards away. *Didn't get very far, did you?* he thought, and smiled to himself. Coming to the rise, he noticed a change in the trail he followed. The blades of grass still bent over indicated that a saddlebag Will had carried was now being dragged behind him. *Won't be long now,* Ned thought. Before crossing over the rise, he paused to survey the range ahead. He could see where the buzzards were circling, but was unable to spot the object of their attention. Prodding his horse, he rode to the top of the rise and paused to look again, and then he saw what he was looking for, a body lying still in a shallow gully just a few dozen yards short of a little stream. He shook his head and smiled. *You almost made it to water, didn't you? Too damn bad.*

Still unwilling to abandon all caution, he held his rifle up, ready to fire, as he walked his horse slowly toward the body. There was a saddlebag lying on the ground a few yards short of the gully, further evidence that the man was finished. Ned took his eye off of the body for only an instant to take notice of it. He stopped his horse beside the gully and sat there with his rifle aimed at Will's back as he lay facedown, his rifle under him. After a few minutes ticked slowly by with no response from the body, Ned lowered his rifle and dismounted. "Will Cason," he pronounced, thinking how much he was going to enjoy bragging about this moment. "Did you think I was gonna let you get away with killin' my partners and shootin' me in the leg? I swear, though, I am disappointed to see you died before I had a chance to put a bullet in your head." His attention drawn then to the Henry rifle lying beneath the body, he reached down, grabbed Will's arm, and rolled him over. The wicked grin on Ned's face was suddenly replaced by a look of startled horror, caused by the .44 revolver in Will's hand, the muzzle of which was pointed directly at his face. Too stunned to react rapidly, he wore the expression through eternity as the gun exploded in his face.

Will had been nearly as surprised as Ned, for he had no notion the confrontation was going to occur. Weak and near exhaustion, he had stumbled toward the stream, but as Ned had observed, his body gave out before he reached it. With his brain spinning uncontrollably, he had not even noticed the gully before him until he tripped on the edge of it and fell heavily, facedown. Disoriented, and too tired to move, he made no effort to get up right away. He figured he must have passed out for a few minutes, because the next thing he remembered was the sound of horses' hooves padding toward him in the grass. *Indians? White men?* It was too late to react. So with no way of knowing if it was help or trouble on the way, he had chosen to play dead, wondering if he was about to feel the impact of an arrow in his back. His questions were answered when he heard Ned Spikes speak and he tightened his grip on the handle of the Colt .44 stuck in his waistband.

Although free of further worry about Ned Spikes, the incident brought a new and immediate, although temporary, problem. With a bullet in his brain, Ned's body landed on top of Will to lay across his stomach and hips. Weary to the point of exhaustion only a few short minutes before, Will's disgust for having the body of the vile bushwhacker draped upon him was incentive enough to summon the energy necessary to shove the loathsome corpse from him. Calling upon all the reserve determination he possessed, he sat up and took a fresh look at his circumstances. There was new bleeding from his wounds, but it was not excessive. Ned's horses had spooked when Will's pistol went off, but they had not scattered far. This helped to bolster his determination now with the possibility of riding instead of walking. He was in no shape to chase after the horses, but hopefully one or more of them would wander back toward him.

Two of the horses were linked together by a lead rope that Spikes had held, and they were standing twenty yards or so from the gully. The other, the one Spikes had been riding, was a speckled gray horse, and it was standing between Will and the others. Will tried to call it several times, clucking his lips, but the gray did not come, seemingly curious as he looked at the man seated on the side of the gully. After a few more attempts to call the horse, he decided he had to try something else. With painful effort, but new resolve, he got to his feet and walked back a few yards to recover the saddlebag he had dropped. Then he turned and began slowly walking toward the stream some fifty yards away. The horses remained still, watching him. After a moment, the gray turned and ambled casually after him as he had hoped. A moment later, the others followed the gray. All three horses passed him, walking slowly, and were peacefully drinking from the stream when he caught up with them.

As soon as he got to the water, he took hold of the gray's reins before dropping to his belly and drinking beside the horse. The gray didn't seem to mind. When he had his fill, Will struggled to his feet again and stroked the horse's neck while it continued to drink. Again, the gray seemed gentle enough. "I believe you're gonna be all right, boy," Will said, looking the horse over. "It ain't none of your fault that your last owner was a sorry son of a bitch." His next concern was climbing into the saddle. He wasn't sure he had the strength to do it, but he told himself he was determined to die trying. Moving back to the stirrup, he put a hand on the saddle horn and reached over the saddle to slip his rifle in the empty saddle sling. "Damn," he uttered, realizing only then that it was his saddle on the gray. It was time to climb on. He took a deep breath because he knew it was going to feel like he was tearing his side apart. Then, before giving himself time to think about it, he put his foot in the stirrup and pulled himself up. As he had anticipated, he felt a stinging fire rip through his side, so severe that he didn't notice the pain in his shoulder caused by his pulling on the saddle horn.

Once he was seated in the saddle, he decided that he was there to stay. He was not planning to dismount until he reached Fort Larned, for he figured it wasn't worth the pain to go through it again. It felt good to be seated in his saddle again, but something didn't feel right, and he realized that Spikes had shortened the stirrups a little. *It'll have to do,* he thought, *because I sure to God ain't gonna change them now.* He let the gray drink until satisfied; then he pulled over next to the other horses and was able to take hold of the lead rope and looped it around the saddle horn. There was no sense in leaving two good horses to run around in

335

the prairie, all tied together. Ned Spikes' rifle was another matter. A seven-shot carbine like the cavalry issue, the rifle was lying on the ground where Ned had dropped it. Will paused to look at it, but decided it was not worth the pain and trouble to dismount and mount again. His wounds were already bleeding anew from the effort the first time. He took a last look at the body of Ned Spikes. "There oughta be a big party in hell tonight," he said. "One of the devil's boys is comin' home." After taking a look at where the sun was in the afternoon sky, he turned the gray gelding toward a line of distant hills to the southeast and let the horse settle into a comfortable pace.

He had traveled through this part of the territory a few times before, but not enough to recognize landmarks. In the weakened state he had been in, he could not accurately estimate how far he had walked before dropping in that gully. But he could well guess that it had not been very far, so he prepared himself for a ride of more than fifteen miles.

His sense of reckoning, even in these dire circumstances, was dead on as usual. He struck the Pawnee fork of the Arkansas after dark and followed it into Fort Larned, barely able to remain upright in the saddle. One look at the blood-covered rider was enough to prompt the sentry to call out, "Sergeant of the Guard, post number three!" As the call was passed on by the guard at the next post and relayed back to the orderly room, the sentry tried to help Will down from his horse.

"Hold on, soldier," Will said weakly. "You'd best leave me be till I can get to the doctor. If I get down, I ain't sure I can get back on."

The private stepped back away from his stirrup, not sure what he should do and wondering if he should lead the wounded man's horse to the hospital while knowing that he was not supposed to leave his post. He was saved from making the decision, however, for the Sergeant of the Guard came running on the double. While the sergeant was assessing the situation, the officer of the day arrived to assume command of the situation. "He's a scout outta Fort Dodge, sir," the sergeant reported. "He's the scout that lieutenant who showed up was talkin' about."

"Well, I'll be damned," the lieutenant exclaimed. "He said you were dead."

"Might be I am," Will replied. "I ain't

sure, to tell you the truth."

"Let's get you over to the surgeon's," the lieutenant said. He took hold of the gray's bridle and started leading him toward the hospital. "Sergeant," he ordered, "get somebody to take care of the man's horses."

Will was not in a state to remember much about what happened after that, except that he found himself on a hospital bed with the doctor probing about on his side and shoulder. He would be told that he had passed out when they got him off the horse and he was trying to pull his rifle from the saddle scabbard. Although dead to the world, he had still made a feeble effort to keep them from taking his rifle from him. Uncertain later if he had dreamed it or had actually heard someone say, "He oughta be dead," he knew now that he had evidently survived. Blinking his eyes rapidly against the sunlight shining through the open window, he winced when the doctor probed a little too deep.

"Well, I see you're awake," the doctor, Major Devlin, remarked upon witnessing his patient's recoil. "All I can say is you must have one helluva strong constitution. I suspect you haven't got a canteen cup full of blood left in you."

"How long have I been here?" Will asked,

not really sure.

"Just since last night." He studied Will intensely for a few moments. "You feel like eating anything?"

"I usually do," Will replied, suddenly feeling hungry.

Devlin smiled. "I'll order some breakfast for you." He shook his head, amazed. "Tell you the truth, I thought last night that I'd be ordering a burial for you this morning."

"I reckon they ain't ready for me yet in heaven or hell," Will said with a wide grin. Then the thought struck him that he had dreamed something about that, but he couldn't recall the details of it. "There was a lieutenant ahead of me. Did he make it back here?"

"That he did," the surgeon replied, "and he's already gone — on his way to Fort Dodge to get married. I looked at him briefly, but he wasn't gonna stay no matter what I said." He prepared to apply a fresh bandage, then paused to give Will a stern look. "I hope you're not thinking about going after him, because you're not in any condition to go anywhere for a good while yet."

Will shook his head, satisfied that his obligation for Braxton's well-being had now been discharged. *Go on back to your wed-*

ding, he thought, *even though Sarah and Emma deserve better.* To the doctor, he said, "Hell, no, I ain't in no hurry to go anywhere." He meant what he said, and his body was telling him that he had pushed it too far. He was content now to let it recover.

Later in the evening, Lieutenant Chad Williams stopped by the hospital to see him. "I was officer of the day when Lieutenant Bradley rode in. From what he told me, you two had quite a battle on your hands. I know you must have been glad to hear that he made it here all right."

"Yep," Will replied, "I'm plum tickled."

"He thought you were dead," Williams said. "I don't expect he would have left you if he'd known you weren't. He'll really be surprised to find out you made it — probably would have waited here for you." He chuckled then at the image of Braxton. "Maybe not, though, he was mighty anxious to get back, and I expect his fiancée will be really happy to see him safely back in her arms."

"I expect," Will replied, although the picture of that tended to give him a sour stomach. "To tell you the truth, Lieutenant, I was pretty sure I was dead back on that creek bank, myself." He was glad when the colonel came in, effectively changing the subject.

The colonel's visit was no more than a courtesy call, but he questioned Will on the location and strength of the Cheyenne camps before getting around to asking about the men who had attacked him and Bradley at Walnut Creek. When he learned the identity of the three bushwhackers, he was not surprised. "We've been looking for those three for quite a while," he said. "Several ranchers have been hit by them, and we always seemed to be just a day or two behind them." He smiled then and stood up to leave. Extending his hand, he said, "So I guess you've taken care of the army's business as far as Ned Spikes and his henchmen are concerned."

"Always tickled to help the army," Will replied with a grin.

With no particular desire to return to Fort Dodge, Will was an ideal patient for a few days, content to sleep and eat and do little more. Always a fast healer, he began to recover rapidly near the end of the week, so he started thinking about making plans to report back to Camp Supply. He had still not fully regained his strength, but he was strong enough to take an interest in the three horses he now owned. When he first went to the stables to check on them, he was immediately able to recognize the gray gelding that had once belonged to Ned Spikes, and he was reasonably sure of the little paint mare that one of Spikes' partners rode. But he had to admit that he would not have been able to pick out the other one without help. He wasn't seeing anything too clearly on that ride from Walnut Creek.

Making idle conversation with one of the soldiers on stable duty one afternoon while watching his horses feed, he suddenly remembered a promise he had casually made to Emma. "I need to work with that little paint," he said to the private. "I just remembered I owe a little lady a horse of her own, and that little horse might just fit the bill." The thought brought a smile of pleasure to his face until it occurred to him that he would have to go back to Fort Dodge to deliver the gift. He had already decided to bypass Dodge on his way back to Camp Supply. The idea of seeing the newlyweds this soon after the wedding was not something he cared to experience. *I don't know, Whiskers,* he thought, *it might not be the right time.* He was afraid he couldn't hide his feelings if he saw Sarah, and he had no reason to want to see Braxton

Bradley ever again — and he was certain the feeling was mutual. He knew it was unrealistic to think about avoiding Bradley and Fort Dodge if he continued working as a scout. But he hoped to delay the encounters until a little time had passed, so maybe he wouldn't feel like a damn fool if he ran into Bradley or Sarah. All those thoughts made him feel restless and he decided that he had laid around Fort Larned long enough. There was too much time for thinking. He needed to get back on a horse and head to the open country. He turned then to find the private studying him.

"You're the feller that came back from the dead, ain't you?" When Will was too astonished to answer right away, the soldier continued. "That's what they're sayin' about you. At least that's what Major Devlin said. He said you were just hangin' on to this world by a thread — said he didn't expect you to make it through the night, but you woke up bright-eyed and bushy tailed the next mornin'."

"Ha," Will exclaimed. "Is that what they're sayin'?" He wasn't sure how to respond. "Well, I hope I didn't disappoint the grave-diggin' crew."

CHAPTER 14

The morning was too pretty to waste sitting around an army post, so Will decided it was time to take his leave. The fact that the chaplain had left that morning on his way to Fort Dodge to hold his monthly service there had not improved Will's mood — especially when one of the hospital orderlies had remarked that the chaplain had said that he had a wedding to conduct. So with the briefest of good-byes to the staff at the hospital, he collected his belongings and made his way over to the stables. Another private was on stable duty, one he had not met before. "I'm gonna pick up my horses," Will said, "and get 'em outta your way."

"You the scout from Fort Dodge?" the private asked as he walked to the tack room with Will to help him with his gear. When Will allowed that he was, the soldier smiled and recited, "That'll be that gray yonder, the paint, and the chestnut. Right?"

"That's right," Will replied. With the private helping, they cut the three horses out and got a bridle on each one.

As Will threw his saddle on the gray, the soldier saddled the chestnut. "What's his name?" he asked, nodding toward the gray.

"I don't know," Will replied. "The feller I got him from didn't tell me." He paused to think about it for a few moments before continuing. "I think I'll call him Ned," he said, then hesitated. "No, that would be too much of an insult to the horse. I reckon I'll just call him Coyote. He kinda reminds me of one."

"This little mare is about as gentle as a lamb," the private said as he led the paint over to Will, who was checking over the saddle.

Will paused to study the horse. "Yeah, she is, ain't she? She belongs to a friend of mine. Maybe I'll get around to givin' her to her one of these days."

He set out directly south, taking his time, letting the gray set his own pace for much of the distance between Fort Larned and the point where he would strike the Arkansas. Once he struck the river, he would follow it until he was directly east of Fort Dodge. When he reached that point he would have to make a decision. Although the fort was on the river, the Arkansas took a wide turn before curving back to the west, where the fort was located. It was a site shorter to take a shortcut across the bend in the river, but if he was going to Camp Supply, he would leave the river and continue due south.

He tried to tell himself that he was in no hurry simply because he wanted to take it easy on his horses and let the gray and himself get to know each other. The fact of the matter, however, was he still had not made up his mind whether to stop by Fort Dodge or bypass it and go directly to Camp Supply. The little mare that he had in mind to present to Emma seemed to be gentle enough without a lot of work on his part. It made sense to go ahead and give it to her now when he was going to be so close to the fort. He had to ask himself if the real motivation to stop now was really simply to get the horse off his hands. Or was it just a morbid desire to witness the woman he thought he loved happily married to a man he despised? He would not reach the point directly east of Fort Dodge until nightfall, so he still had time to worry over it and decide which way to go in the morning.

Lieutenant Braxton Bradley had returned

to Fort Dodge to a hero's welcome. The entire post had turned out to welcome him back and hear the report of his fight to escape his Cheyenne captors and the heroic battle on Walnut Creek that took army scout Will Cason's life. He described the treacherous attack by the three murderers and the gallant defense the two of them waged, fighting side by side, until Cason went down with a bullet in his side and another in his shoulder. When he was certain that Will was dead, and after killing one of the three assailants, he took the opportunity to escape and made his way to Fort Larned.

Hardly knowing what to think after so many days of uncertainty, Sarah Lawton greeted her fiancé with a fond embrace that drew a hardy round of applause from the crowd that had gathered around the ambulance Braxton arrived in. Emma's response to the lieutenant's verification that Will was dead was to turn away.

"Now we can get back to planning a wedding," Edna Boyle sang out, prompting another round of applause.

"We can get married tomorrow," Braxton had suggested.

Before Sarah could comment, Edna Boyle had interrupted. "Oh, no, you don't, Lieutenant Bradley. You're not going to ruin our chance to have a big wedding. We don't get many opportunities like this — a wedding at this dreary post — and Sarah deserves a wedding she can remember." Her comments were met with a chorus of cheers from the wives gathered around. "Besides, we're gonna have a real wedding with a real preacher to tie the knot," she had continued, "and the chaplain's regular visit isn't until next Sunday." Captain Tuttle, the chaplain at Fort Larned, made regular monthly visits to Fort Dodge since Dodge had none at the present time. It just made sense to wait and let him perform the ceremony.

"I guess we'll have to wait until Edna says we're ready," Sarah had responded to Braxton's suggestion. Although she fashioned a pleasant smile for his benefit, inside she found that she was relieved to put the wedding off for now, even if for only a week. Deeply troubled by the news of Will's death, it was difficult to feel elation over the prospect of her coming nuptials. While others were in a celebratory mood over the prospects of a wedding, she could not escape the black cloud that Will's death had cast over her. Somehow she had felt that Will would always survive — he was nothing if not a survivor. How could he be dead? If she had chosen to examine her feelings more closely, she might have realized that she had been able to accept the news of Braxton's probable death when he had been reported missing more calmly than this tragic news about Will. Aware then that everyone was beaming in her direction, she said, "I guess I had better go after my daughter. She was very fond of Will, and I think the news has upset her."

Emma had joined her mother when the ambulance arrived on the post, escorted by a patrol of six troopers, and minutes later they heard the people shouting her mother's name. The soldiers had told her mother several days before that Lieutenant Bradley was missing, so everyone was happy to see that he was all right. Emma was glad that he was safe, but she had not been prepared for the news that Will was dead. Colonel Arnold and Captain Evans had come to see them one night with the news about Braxton, but they said that Will had volunteered to look for him on his own. So Emma had known in her heart that Will would find him and everything would be all right. Today, when Braxton had reported that Will was dead, she turned and ran back to the wagon so no one would see her tears.

Braxton had come to the wagon that night just as soon as he had finished his reports to his superiors. Sarah greeted him with a kiss on the cheek, even though it was obvious that he expected more. But he assumed that her less than passionate embrace was due to the presence of her six-year-old daughter. He could not help but notice the lack of the usual enthusiasm in the child. She was quiet, hardly speaking a word, which was noticeably uncharacteristic. In an effort to elicit a response from her, Braxton had said, "Looks like about another week before you'll be my little girl. What do you think about that, Emma?"

Emma had responded by instructing the lieutenant, "Don't call me Emma — my real name is Whiskers."

Unaware of the origin of the nickname, Braxton had replied, "Oh, well, I didn't know that, but I think I like Emma better for a pretty little girl like you. So I'll call you Emma."

"My name's Whiskers," she muttered under her breath and promptly left their presence to find seclusion in her bed in the wagon.

"Are we going to have trouble with that child?" Braxton asked when she had gone.

"No," Sarah answered. "She's just fond of Will and misses him. She'll get over it before long." The thought occurred to her then that Emma had gotten over her father's death in a shorter time — a little more than a day, in fact.

"Where did she get that name . . . ? What was it — Whiskers? Kind of an odd name for a little girl."

"It's nothing," Sarah replied, hesitating to tell him, since he was already showing signs of irritation with Emma. When he continued to gaze inquisitively, she told him, "It's just a little nickname Will called her."

"Will again," Braxton had fumed, clearly irritated then. "The man was an issue when he was alive. Am I going to have to put up with his ghost now with Emma?"

Sarah had tried to reassure him that Emma would come around, but inside, she knew that Braxton was going to have to make a major effort to replace Will in Emma's heart. Now, almost a week later, there had not been much progress along those lines, and the wedding was scheduled to take place the next day.

The wedding day broke bright and clear with the promise of a perfect day for Braxton and Sarah. Emma lay awake in her bed beside her mother, staring up at the canvas top of the wagon. The night just past would be her last in the wagon. After the wedding, she and her mother would move into the small quarters prepared for them and her new father by the carpenters. Emma found that she was reluctant to leave the wagon, and she had been awake since before sunup thinking about her new life with her stepfather. Young as she was, she had a level head on her shoulders, and she resolved not to make the union difficult for her mother, in spite of her personal preferences.

She paused to listen — there it was again, a slight kind of snuffling noise outside the wagon. This was the second time she had heard it since waking, and this time she decided to investigate. Moving as slowly and as quietly as she could so as not to disturb her mother, she left the wagon and sneaked through the tent attached, hoping to surprise the varmint that was no doubt sniffing around their camp. Pushing the tent flap aside very carefully, she was at once astounded to find the gentle noises had emanated from a brown and white paint pony.

The horse was tied to the back wheel of the wagon, patiently standing, saddled and bridled. Emma, still in her gown, went out and looked for the rider. There was none that she could see. She walked all around the wagon and tent, still finding no one, so she went back to look at the paint again. It was then that she noticed a piece of paper tied with a length of rawhide cord to the saddle horn. Concentrating on each word carefully, she managed to read the message. *This horse is for Whiskers. She's saddle broke and gentle.* It was not signed.

Emma's screams of joy brought Sarah out in a panic, thinking her daughter was in danger. "Mama!" Emma fairly screamed. "It's Will! It's Will!"

Confused and frightened that Emma's imagination had run rampant, she sought first to calm her hysterical daughter before spying the strange horse tied to the wagon wheel. When she saw it, she, like Emma had, looked around thinking to find the rider. When there was no one to be seen, she turned again to the excited child, who was even then trying to climb up in the saddle. "Emma, get down from there. You'll get hurt. We don't know who that horse belongs to." The mysterious appearance of the horse was now beginning to worry her.

"It's my horse, Mama!" Emma insisted. "Will promised he would get me a horse of my own, and he kept his promise."

Sarah was about to tell her that she had let her imagination run away with her when Emma suddenly thrust the note in her hand. Sarah felt as if her heart stopped temporarily as she read the words scrawled upon the back of a duty roster, evidently ripped off the bulletin board outside the orderly room. Feeling suddenly chilled inside, she tried to force her mind to make sense out of the appearance of the horse and the note, which defied reason. Will Cason was dead. Braxton had confirmed it, so where did the horse come from? Sarah was not a firm believer in things spiritual, but she could not dispel the eerie feeling visited upon her. At this point, Emma was her only source of information, so she questioned her daughter about the promise she claimed Will had made to her.

"I told him I wanted my own horse," Emma insisted. "And he said he would get me one, but he told me not to tell you because you might not want me to have one. It was our secret, and he kept his promise!"

Sarah was beside herself. She had no reason to disbelieve her daughter. Emma had never shown a tendency to make up stories, but the incident was too bizarre to explain. She believed Emma when she said no one but she and Will had known of the secret promise they shared. For a moment, she considered that Braxton had made the gesture as a bridge between him and her daughter. Just as rapidly, however, she discarded the idea simply because the note had said *Whiskers* and not *Emma.* With her mind in a quandary, she didn't know what to do about the horse. However it arrived at her wagon, someone had obviously meant it as a present for Emma, so she could do nothing to solve the mystery until she talked to Braxton or maybe Edna Boyle — someone must know something about it. She wasn't ready to believe a ghost had left it there.

Knowing she must make some effort to return normalcy to the morning, she told Emma to leave the horse where it was until Braxton came over later. "Come on," she said. "Get dressed and we'll start some breakfast." *And this is supposed to be my wedding day,* she thought, wondering how she could possibly be less excited over the prospect.

A little while after breakfast, Edna Boyle came over to inform Sarah that the preacher had arrived late the night before from Fort Larned and the ceremony could proceed as planned, with the actual vows scheduled to be exchanged at two o'clock that afternoon. She was taken aback when Sarah told her of the mystery pinto. Like Sarah, she could think of no reasonable explanation for its appearance at her wagon. "We oughta unsaddle it, though, and maybe let Emma lead it down to the water to drink," she suggested. "The horse seems gentle enough, and we can watch them from here."

It was while Emma was down beside the river with the mare that Braxton joined the two ladies. When told of the gift for Emma, his reaction was stony and his ire was immediately turned upon the little girl watering the horse, as if it were her doing. "I'm sick of hearing about that damn ghost," he railed, "and I think you're going to have to do something about your daughter's infatuation with that saddle tramp."

Thinking Braxton's attitude a bit overboard, Sarah felt obligated to defend her friend. "I think it's a little harsh to call Will a saddle tramp. He means a lot to Emma, and certainly to me, too. You must give Emma a little time to get over this."

Her comments were not well received by the annoyed lieutenant. "I want that man out of our lives," he complained. "If you're going to defend him every time his name's brought up, I don't see how that's going to happen. The man's dead. It's time for Emma and you to accept it."

"I'm sorry, Braxton," Sarah replied softly. "Let's just give it a little time, and I think you'll understand Emma's attitude."

"The hell I will," Braxton replied, fully steamed up by now. "I intend to find out who left this horse here and why." He was convinced that it was a ploy by someone opposed to the wedding to upset the ceremony, and his mind was already racing to come up with likely suspects. Principal among these were possibly Lieutenant Bordeaux and Corporal Kincaid of C Company. They were big friends of the civilian scout.

A silent witness to the discussion to this point, Edna Boyle was beginning to have concerns about the chemistry between the bride and groom. She was seeing a side of Braxton Bradley that had not surfaced before. A more pragmatic woman had never lived, so the thought that the ghost of Will Cason had delivered on a spiritual promise to the six-year-old never gained a foothold in her mind. "If I can interrupt this lovers' spat for a moment," she commented, "maybe we should talk to Captain Tuttle. He just came from Fort Larned. Maybe he knows something about the horse."

"Begging your pardon, Mrs. Boyle," Braxton stated coolly, "but this really doesn't concern you."

"Oh, I think that it does," Sarah said, her own hackles rising a bit by then. "Edna's my friend and is the one person most responsible for the whole wedding."

Even though indignant over the rebuke by Sarah, Braxton realized that he was not exhibiting himself in a favorable light by continuing his opposition. "Very well," he said, "we'll go talk to Captain Tuttle."

Sarah called Emma up from the river, and the docile mare followed the tiny child back to be tied again by the wagon wheel. "We have to go see the preacher for a little while," Sarah told her. "You stay here and watch the horse, and I'll be right back." Emma, content to stay with her present from Will, raised no objection. Sarah turned to follow Braxton and Edna, then paused to issue instructions. "Do not try to ride that horse under any circumstances."

Captain Leonard Tuttle was enjoying a leisurely cup of coffee with Lieutenant Bordeaux when Lieutenant Bradley and the two women walked in. Surprised to see the women in the officers' mess, the two immediately got to their feet while Edna introduced the reverend to the wedding couple. Edna quickly explained that their impromptu visit had nothing to do with the wedding plans, but was merely an effort to solve a minor mystery about a horse. After hearing the question, Tuttle replied that he had no knowledge of the horse, and that it had not come from Fort Larned with him.

An interested bystander to the unusual circumstances that delivered the horse and note to Sarah Lawton's wagon, Lieutenant Bordeaux said nothing until Braxton made it a point to ask him directly whether he had anything to do with it. As a friend and admirer of the capable scout, Bordeaux had found it difficult to believe the news when he had heard that Will Cason was dead. "No, Bradley," he replied. "I didn't have anything to do with it. Why in the world would you think I did?"

"You and Cason were always pretty thick," Braxton answered, for want of anything better in the way of a reason.

"He was a damn good man," Bordeaux countered. "Begging your pardon, ladies," he quickly added. The whole story didn't add up to him, and the more he thought about it, the more he came to agree with the little girl's contention that Will gave it to her. "Tell me somethin', Bradley. You're the last person to see Will alive, right?" Braxton nodded and Bordeaux continued. "Shot twice, you said, and you are absolutely sure he was dead before you left him on that creek bank."

"Of course," Braxton answered in a huff. "Do you doubt my word?"

"I got a feeling Will Cason was still alive when you left him."

"I'm not sure I like what you're insinuating," Braxton charged, his handsome face now flushed red.

Astonished by the storm brewing between the two officers, Captain Tuttle offered a piece of information that just then occurred to him. "There was a badly wounded civilian scout that arrived at the fort about a week ago," he said. "I heard that he had been in some kind of ambush, now that I recall. Could this possibly be the man you speak of?"

"He's alive!" Bordeaux exclaimed. "I knew damn well he wasn't dead — pardon me again, ladies." He cast an accusing glance in Braxton's direction. "You left him on that creek bank to die."

Taken aback by Bordeaux's damning accusation, Braxton reacted before thinking. "There was only one horse! He told me to escape while I had the chance! He knew he was dying. I wouldn't have left him otherwise." He turned to plead his case to Sarah. "It made no sense for both of us to die, and I had you to think of." His outburst was followed by a shocked silence that left him gazing beseechingly at Sarah. "I had a responsibility to get back to you."

The confusion of emotions racing through Sarah's mind was almost too much for her to cope with. Contrasted with the elation over the sudden prospect that Will was alive was the sobering confession of the man she was intending to wed. Still able to keep a clear head, Edna Boyle was quick to grasp the turmoil going through the younger woman's mind. She took Sarah by the arm and pulled her toward the door. "Come on, darlin'," she said. "You need to get outta here and go someplace where you can think." She wasn't sure exactly what Sarah's feelings might have been regarding Will Cason, but she was certain beyond doubt that most of Braxton Bradley's shine had rubbed off him.

"Wait, Sarah!" Braxton called after them. "We have to talk to the captain about the wedding."

Sarah stopped and looked back at him. "I'm not sure there's going to be a wedding," she said. She was surprised to feel that the statement seemed to lift a great weight from her mind, and suddenly she felt that she had been saved from making a grave mistake — for her and Emma. She had been so fearful of failing to provide for her daughter that she had let it overshadow her personal feelings. She had convinced herself that she would learn to love Braxton as she had loved Edward. But now she was not sure she could love a man who would desert another — especially when that other had risked his life to rescue him.

Bordeaux favored Braxton with a brief glance and a shake of his head before following the women outside. Left in a state of confusion over whether there was to be a wedding or not, Captain Tuttle called after them, "I'll be holding regular church services at noon. I hope you will all attend."

Outside the officers' mess, Lieutenant Bordeaux had taken his leave of the two women and gone at once to find Captain Fischer, his company commander. It took a few minutes' time to explain the whole affair to Fischer, but the captain readily understood the lieutenant's intent. With Fischer's blessing, Bordeaux went in search of Corporal Kincaid. He found him in the process of instructing a group of new recruits in the care and feeding of their horses. After hearing what Bordeaux wanted him to do, Kincaid let go a little yelp of elation and immediately went to saddle his horse. In a matter of minutes, he was dismounting beside the brown and white paint pony at the rear of Sarah's wagon.

Kincaid was not the tracker Will Cason was, but he was a far sight better than most. It could also be said that he was not a deep thinker, but he was smart enough to put two and two together and come up with an appropriate answer. He had suspected that Will's recent comments about quitting the scouting business and settling down to a more steady life had something to do with a particular woman. After hearing Bordeaux's report on the discussion at the officers' mess, he was eager to get the news to Will, just in case he had been accurate in his speculations. Evidently Bordeaux was of the same opinion, else why would he have sent him to find Will? He couldn't imagine his superiors going to this much trouble over finding the person who left a horse tied to a civilian's wagon. But Will Cason was not the average person.

He took a moment to look the pinto over just to satisfy a natural curiosity to see what kind of horse she was. Nodding his approval, he then examined the horse's hooves in case there might be some irregular marks that would make tracking easier. There were none, although the horse would probably need new shoes before very long. Kincaid had a pretty good notion that Will was heading to Camp Supply. All he was looking for now was verification of that, and an indication of the trail he took. In spite of the difficulty of tracking in the grassy river plain, he found the tracks leading into camp but none going back out. That indicated to him that Will had walked into the camp leading the mare, so as not to make any noise. Then he walked out again to some point where his horses were waiting. He back-tracked the mare's hoofprints to that point and verified his belief that Will had headed south toward Camp Supply.

"Looks like we got company, Coyote," Will commented to the gray gelding as he walked over to the saddle on the ground and pulled his rifle from the scabbard. He had stopped to make camp early in the afternoon, figuring that his horses needed a good long rest. "Maybe we shoulda gone on to Bluff Creek," he said after a quick glance at his campsite.

The stream he had stopped beside offered scant protection other than a screen of berry bushes and brush, so he moved a few yards away from the horses and knelt behind a gooseberry thicket to wait for his visitor. Though still several hundred yards distant, he soon was able to identify the rider as a soldier and riding hard. After a few minutes, he smiled and softly uttered, "Corporal Kincaid." He lowered his rifle and remained kneeling where he was, watching his friend as he pulled up short to take a closer look at the camp before riding in. When it appeared that Kincaid was a little cautious about proceeding, Will yelled, "It sure would be easy to pick you off, Kincaid. You're lucky I ain't a Cheyenne warrior."

Startled but recovering immediately, Kincaid yelled back, "Hell, a Cheyenne wouldn'ta pitched his camp on that little crick where everybody could see it." He rode on in and dismounted. "I did take a second or two before I made up my mind when I didn't see that big bay of yours — thought I mighta rode up on somebody else's camp." His face lit up then with a great big grin. "You're lookin' pretty spry for a dead man."

Walking forward to greet him, Will said, "Spades didn't make it from Walnut Creek. Where the hell are you goin' in such a big hurry? I thought somebody was chasin' you."

"Hell," Kincaid replied as he dismounted, "I was lookin' for you. Sorry to hear about your horse. What happened to him? Any coffee left in that pot?"

Will chuckled before answering. "What were you lookin' for me for? Ned Spikes shot him. And there's a little left, enough for a cup."

Kincaid emptied the remains of the coffee into his cup and found a place to sit down near the stream. "Lieutenant Bordeaux sent me to find you," he began. "You set off a real storm when you left that little paint by Sarah Lawton's wagon."

"How so?" Will asked.

"It'da been a whole lot simpler if you'da told somebody you were leavin' it. Hell, man, we thought you were dead. There was people thinkin' a ghost brought that horse and tied it there." When Will's expression clearly revealed that he didn't understand, Kincaid laughed. "Nobody knew you survived that mess at Walnut Creek. The most anybody knew was what Lieutenant Bradley told 'em, and he said you were dead."

"He did, did he?" Will replied. "Well, he was pretty nigh right, but I don't see why that stirred up all the fuss about the horse."

"You don't see what I'm gettin' at, do you?" Kincaid asked. He went on then to paint the picture for him, relating the scene when Captain Tuttle told them Will was still alive, and Bordeaux's accusation that Braxton had deserted a wounded man. "Here's the icing on your cake," he said. "Sarah called off the weddin'."

The news was sobering to him, and he had to hesitate before responding. "What's that got to do with me? It ain't no icing on my cake."

"The hell it ain't," Kincaid exclaimed. "I ain't got but two stripes on my sleeve, but I ain't stupid. I know you been thinkin' about that woman ever since you brought her into Fort Dodge. You better decide what you're gonna do and make your move before somebody beats you to it. That's what I think!"

"I thought you weren't paid to think," Will said with a slight smile. He hesitated then, thinking about what Kincaid had just told him. There was a long pause while he tried to sort things out in his mind. Just because Sarah had decided she couldn't marry Braxton, there was no reason to assume she wanted to marry him or anybody else. Most likely she would simply choose to return to the east as she had originally planned. It didn't occur to him that Bordeaux must have sent Kincaid to find him for some reason, when there was no official purpose as far as his scouting duties were concerned. In the end, he decided that Sarah was more than likely in a state of devastation caused by the sudden turn of events. And since it seemed he was a major party in the cause of her destroyed plans, she might not be receptive to seeing him at all. *Hell,* he thought, *I can't support a wife and child right now, anyway.* The more he thought about it, the more he came to believe that any attraction Sarah might have had for him was wholly created in his mind. She had never said anything or given any real indication that she regarded him as more than a friend, and the rest was wishful thinking. He decided that it would be best to wait a spell before seeing Sarah again, and give her a chance to decide what she wanted to do. "I appreciate you ridin' all the way out here to tell me," he finally said to Kincaid. "But I expect Sarah will do what she wants to do, and I've got to report back to Camp Supply right now. I expect Ben Clarke mighta already fired me by now."

Kincaid was not one to give up easily on a cause he believed in, so the discussion continued on into the evening. But he finally gave up when Will steadfastly insisted that the right thing for him to do was to report back to his boss at Camp Supply. Of course, he said, he would plan to stop in to visit Sarah and Emma if they were still there on his next trip to Dodge, but now was not the right time. He expressed a desire to see how Emma and her horse got along. However, he had no way of knowing whether he would be sent to Dodge for any reason anytime soon. Kincaid respected his feelings, although remaining perplexed over Will's stubborn attitude, and the next morning he returned to Fort Dodge alone.

CHAPTER 15

The following week was a troublesome one for Will Cason. Ben Clarke noticed the difference in attitude from that of the usually unperturbed scout. There was certainly no slackening of his work ethic. In fact, he seemed to volunteer for every patrol that left the post. He even stepped up to muster for Lieutenant Bridges' patrol, although Bridges rejected him. The first week back from Fort Dodge turned into two, and then three weeks, with still no change in the scout's stoic, moody disposition. Sensing a discontent in Will's demeanor, Clarke decided to give him a change of scene. Ordinarily, the chief scout could care less what personal demons might be bothering one of his men as long as it didn't interfere with the job. But Clarke had always held a special interest in Will ever since he signed on as a scout. So on a Saturday afternoon Clarke went in search of him, with a fair idea where he might find him.

Will tossed down his third shot of rye whiskey, and waved Mickey's hand off when the bartender lifted the bottle to refill his glass. "I expect that's all the whiskey I need right now," he said.

Ben Clarke was not the only person at Camp Supply to notice the somber change in the rangy scout's attitude. Lula McGraw, standing at his elbow, had sensed it as well. Still it had not impeded her constant campaign to bed the indifferent young man. "Yeah, Mickey," she echoed Will's remark, "he's had all the whiskey he needs. And now he needs somethin' else. Don't you, darlin'?"

Will didn't answer at once. He turned to gaze at Lula for a long moment. The woman had been trying to lure him into the back room for more than a year, and he had always resisted her advances. Why? he wondered. Lula was nothing to look at, but underneath her painted exterior there could be a compassionate heart. Why he had never seen fit to answer his more primal needs was something he had never given much thought when it came to Lula. After thinking about it for a moment, he decided he might as well donate three dollars since she had pressed so long for his business. "All right," he said.

It came so sudden and so succinct that she was not sure she had heard him right. She met his eyes for a moment, waiting to see if he was toying with her again. When his gaze remained steady and unblinking, she asked, "You mean it?"

"I reckon," he replied.

She looked at Mickey briefly, then back at Will, waiting for the joke. "You ain't foolin' with me, are you?"

He fished in his pocket for three dollars. "You want the money, or not?" he asked.

With no further hesitation, she swept the money from the bar with one hand and grabbed his hand with the other. "Come on, darlin', before you change your mind."

He let himself be led toward the door to the back room where Lula conducted her business. There was no desire on his part to complete the transaction, and he wondered now why he had agreed to it. The fact of the matter was that he just didn't care one way or the other. It was obvious to the point where Lula picked up on it, causing her to pause in the process of removing her frock. When he showed no enthusiasm for the generous amount of skin visible so far, she was inspired to comment, "Well, you ain't exactly chompin' at the bit, are you?" She laid her dress across the foot of the bed and stood there studying him for a moment, still in her petticoat. "Somethin's eatin' at you," she said, accustomed as she was to the frantic, puppy-dog impatience of her usual customer.

"Nothin'," he said, and made a half-hearted attempt to unbutton his shirt.

She reached up and stopped him with her hand on his, realizing at that moment what the problem was. "It's a woman, ain't it? You've done gone and fell in love with somebody!" It was not a question and she could tell by his reaction that she had hit the nail on the head. "And it ain't goin' the way you want it to, is it?"

He was at a loss for words, surprised that she had seen through the haze in his mind right to the root of the problem. "Nah," he drawled, trying to deny the message his face conveyed, "it's no such thing."

He wasn't very convincing. "The hell it ain't," she insisted, convinced now that he was trying to cover the pain in his heart. She sat him down on the bed and seated herself beside him, and for a moment simply sat there gazing at his face, studying the boyish longing that had remained hidden beneath the rugged profile. "What are you gonna do about it?" she asked softly.

"I don't know," he answered in a voice equally soft. He was reluctant to talk about it, but under pressure from a compassionate Lula that he would never have guessed existed, he finally told her the reason for his melancholy.

"Well, much as I hate to admit it," she said, "this ain't gonna help it none." She got up from the bed and took the three dollars from a chest by the bed. Handing it to him, she said, "Go on back up to Fort Dodge and tell her how you feel. That's the only way you're gonna find out how she feels about it. You owe her that."

He pushed her hand away. "You keep the money," he said. "You earned it . . . and more, I reckon."

"Get on outta here before I remember who the hell I am," she ordered and put the money back on the chest. She remained there a while after he left the room, taking enough time to dry a tear that had gathered in the corner of her eye. She had been young once, a thousand years ago, when it wasn't necessary to paint her face to hide the miles. She heard him saying good-bye to Mickey as he left the saloon, and she thought about the time when she and a young man stood facing a fork in the road, only to make the wrong decision when she sent him away. "Well, that's enough of this horse shit," she suddenly declared and grabbed her hand mirror to survey the damage to her face. "Damned if I ain't gettin' soft in my old age."

It's probably too damn late, he told himself as he held the spotted gray gelding to a businesslike gait, heading north. He had decided to take Lula's advice with or without Ben Clarke's permission, but the chief scout had met him minutes after leaving Mickey's saloon with word that he was sending him to Fort Dodge. Ben told him that Colonel Arnold had requested his services for quite some time and he decided that he would let him go for a while. "It's temporary," Clarke stressed, "and I expect you back here in a couple of months or so." So at least he hadn't lost his job over his personal problems. His chief worry now was whether he was too late to let Sarah know his mind.

His first reaction was one of elation when he rode into Fort Dodge late in the afternoon and saw the wagon still parked by the river. Then the thought wormed into his mind that maybe the wedding was back on. It was enough to cause him to hesitate before approaching the wagon, wondering if he should report in to the orderly room first. That notion was immediately discarded and he nudged Coyote forward again. Although it was surely suppertime, he saw no one about the tent or wagon. Sarah's two horses and Emma's paint were grazing nearby, all three hobbled — Whiskers' doing, he figured.

Inside the tent, Sarah realized that she was late in starting supper. She started to call Emma to put some wood on the fire, but decided to leave her where she was, playing in the wagon with her dolls. Stepping outside, she paused to breathe in the evening air for a moment. Glancing toward the river, she was startled to see what she thought at first was her mind playing tricks on her. But as the illusion became real, she suddenly felt a feeling of calm flow over her body. "Will," she whispered softly.

As he pulled the gray up before the wagon, their eyes met in silent greeting. But the spell lasted for only a brief moment before Emma, suddenly aware, burst from the tent in a bubble of excitement. "Will!" she exclaimed. "Mama, it's Will!"

"I know," her mother said, smiling as she stood and watched Emma clamoring to be picked up, almost before he had time to dismount.

After Emma had settled down enough to give the grown-ups time to talk, Will said, "I thought you mighta been gone before I could get back. I reckon there haven't been any trains goin' back east."

"There was one last week," Sarah replied, "but Emma and I decided to stay here a while longer." He nodded solemnly, thinking that over. "You're just in time for supper. I was just getting ready to start it." She smiled at Emma. "Put some more water in the coffeepot, honey. You know how Will loves coffee."

Emma started to do her bidding, then paused to ask Will, "Where's Spades?"

"I'll tell you about him later. We got a lot of time to talk."

Once again embracing the peace that his presence always brought her, she silently agreed. There was time to talk, time to let things happen the way fate intended.

ABOUT THE AUTHOR

Charles G. West lives in Ocala, Florida. His fascination with and respect for the pioneers who braved the wild frontier of the Great American West inspire him to devote his full time to writing historical novels. Visit his Web site at www.CharlesGWest.com.

The employees of Thorndike Press hope you have enjoyed this Large Print book. All our Thorndike, Wheeler, and Kennebec Large Print titles are designed for easy reading, and all our books are made to last. Other Thorndike Press Large Print books are available at your library, through selected bookstores, or directly from us.

For information about titles, please call:
  (800) 223-1244

or visit our Web site at:
  http://gale.cengage.com/thorndike

To share your comments, please write:
  Publisher
  Thorndike Press
  295 Kennedy Memorial Drive
  Waterville, ME 04901